DAN TURNER

HOLLYWOOD DETECTIVE

NO. 10

DAN TURNER

HOLLYWOOD DETECTIVE
NO. 10

BY

ROBERT LESLIE BELLEM

"Dead Man's Head", *Spicy Detective Stories*, August 1936; "Falling Star", *Spicy Detective Stories*, September 1936; "Silver-screen Spectre", *Spicy Detective* Stories, October 1936; "Veiled Lady", *Spicy Detective Stories*, October 1937; "Death's Passport", *Spicy Detective Stories*, December 1940; "Drunk, Disorderly, and Dead", *Dan Turner Hollywood Detective*, April 1942; "Star Chamber", *Dan Turner Hollywood Detective*, April 1942; "Riddle in the Rain", *Speed Detective*, January 1943; "Sleeping Dogs" *Dan Turner Hollywood Detective*, January 1943; "Sing a Song of Murder", *Dan Turner Hollywood Detective*, March 1943.

Published November 2018

ISBN 978-1947964778

Copyright 2018 by Fiction House Press
www.FictionHousePress.com

TABLE OF CONTENTS

	Page
Dead Man's Head	1
Falling Star	31
Silverscreen Spectre	57
Veiled Lady	85
Death's Passport	113
Drunk, Disorderly, and Dead	137
Star Chamber	187
Riddle in the Rain	213
Sleeping Dogs	241
Sing a Song of Murder	269

DEAD MAN'S HEAD

Some one sends Dan Turner a gruesome package of murder, and his opening it plunges him into new depths of deadly Hollywood intrigue

I OPENED the package and a human head rolled out into my lap. A man's head—with a bullet-hole between the eyes.

It was late at night, in my apartment. I'd been to see Chaplin's latest picture at the Chinese, and when I got home I found a bundle wrapped in brown paper outside the door of my flat. I picked it up and carried it in.

There weren't any postage stamps on it; no express-tags, either. Evidently someone had delivered it personally. Printed across the front was: "For Dan Turner, private detective." That was all. No sender's name; no return address.

I cut the strings and unwrapped the bundle. And that's when the severed head rolled spang into my lap.

It startled hell out of me. I said: "What the hell!" and jumped to my feet. The head hit the floor with a gruesome bounce. It rolled half-way across my living-room rug. Then it came to rest, face upward. A damned nasty sight.

For a minute I was shaky as hell. I reached for a bottle of Vat 69 and tilted it down my throat. That

1

made me feel a little better, but not much. I walked over and picked up the severed head.

There wasn't any blood around the bullet-wound in its forehead. None at the neck, either. That had all

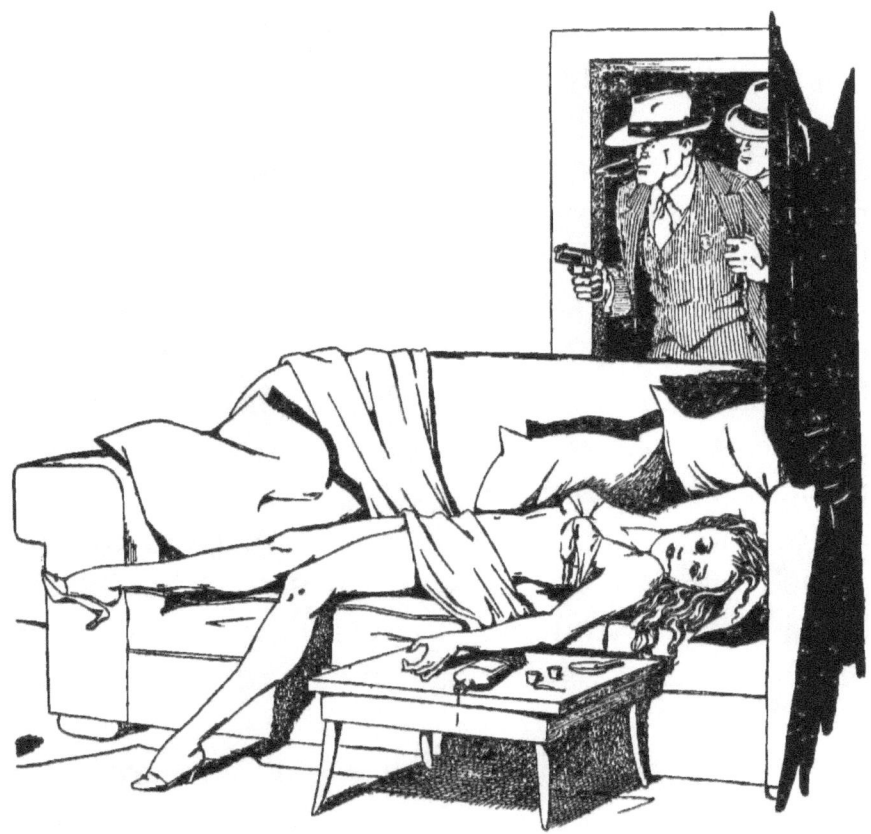

been washed away, nice and clean. I took one good gander at the white, cold features; and I recognized the face right away.

IT WAS the head of Skinny Arkle. Maybe you remember him. He was a big-shot screen comedian back in the silent days. Skinny Arkle had been even funnier than his name. He'd been tops in the old pie-throwing class, and the way he used to pop his false teeth out of his mouth and fold up his face kept the whole country in stitches. But at the height of his popularity, Skinny Arkle had got himself in a hell of a jam.

He'd gone on a binge down in San Diego with an obscure extra dame named Nancy Norward. He and the Norward girl had got plastered together—and the dame had kicked the bucket. They'd tried to pin her death on Skinny Arkle, but a jury finally decided she'd cashed in from acute alcoholism coupled with gizzard-trouble or something. Anyhow, they'd turned Skinny loose.

Just the same, the scandal had cooked Skinny Arkle's goose in the movies. All the studios black-listed him; the stink had given Hollywood too much of black eye, so Skinny had to take the rap—be the goat.

He'd faded out of pictures; hadn't appeared in a single film since the mess. For a while he went back to his native Jugo-Slavia; then he returned to Holly-wood and married a cute kid named Kitty Calvert— a wren with red hair and a shape like seven million bucks. She was an Altamount semi-star, and she dragged down enough cookies in her weekly pay-envelope to keep herself and Skinny well fixed. For that matter, it was rumored that Skinny himself had salted away a nice stack of geetus from the days when he was in the big dough.

Well, that was Skinny Arkle's history as I remember it. And now, here was his decapitated head grinning at me from my living-room floor—with a bullet-hole in its brain.

I picked up the head and put it on my library table. Then I grabbed for my phone. I dialed the home number of my friend Dave Donaldson of the homicide squad. When he answered I said: "This is Dan Turner. Listen, Dave—something screwy has happened." I told him what.

Dave said: "For God's sake! Say—you're not drunk, are you? You haven't got pink elephants, have you?"

"Hell, no. This is on the level," I told him.

He said: "Cripes! Meet me down at headquarters in fifteen minutes. Bring that head with you!"

I said: "Okay," and hung up. Then all of a sudden I thought I heard a sound outside my door.

I was nervous anyhow. I had the jitters. I dragged out the .32 automatic I always carry in a shoulder-holster, and I dived for the door.

THERE was a tall, statuesque blonde standing there. I couldn't tell whether she'd just arrived or whether she'd been standing outside my door for some while. She looked scared as hell when I popped out at her. She said. "Oh-h-h—!" in a sort of muffled gasp.

I said: "Who the hell are you? What do you want?"

"I—I'm looking for Dan Turner," she answered me.

I looked her over. She seemed worried, all right. But she was gorgeous, too—in a flashy sort of way. Her blonde head came above my shoulder, and I'm over six-feet-two. At a guess I'd say she was close to

thirty—but she wore a damned good make-up that made her look younger. And her figure was something to remember.

She wasn't skinny, like a lot of tall dames. She wasn't too hefty, either. Just well-proportioned for her size. Sleek hips and slinky thighs. Breasts that would have been mammoth on a smaller cutie, but exactly right for this dame. Nice, firm mounds of breasts.

I said: "Well, kiddo, I'm sorry you're worried, but I haven't got time to talk to you now. See me at my office tomorrow."

She said: "No! You've got to listen to me right now, Mr. Turner! You must!"

I thought of my date with Donaldson at headquarters in fifteen minutes. I said: "Sorry, sister. You'll have to excuse me."

"You—you mean you won't listen to me?"

"Sure I'll listen to you. Tomorrow."

Her eyes got sort of wild-looking. She said: "I'll make you listen!" And before I could stop her she rumpled her yellow hair and ripped at the front of her dress. She said: "I'll scream and tell people you attacked me!"

"Hell!" I said. "If it's that important, go ahead and spill your story. But cover yourself up or maybe I'll begin to get ideas—and then you'll have something to scream about." I reached over and pulled her frock together, covering her breasts. My fingers

7

were tingling at the near contact.

The girl said: "I—I'm Constance Calvert. I'm Kitty Calvert's sister. Kitty Calvert, the Altamount star. She's Skinny Arkle's wife."

I stiffened. "Yeah?"

"Yes. And I'm worried for Kitty. Afraid for her. Skinny Arkle and she have had a terrible row. Skinny left after the fight. That was three days ago. He left, threatening to come back and m-murder Kitty. We haven't seen him since, but I'm frightened. I want you to find him—"

I grabbed her by the arm and said: "Come on in my apartment. I want to show you something. You won't have to worry about Skinny Arkle any more."

I PULLED her into my living-room. She saw Skinny Arkle's severed head on my table. She went white. "Oh, my God!" she choked. And then damned if she didn't faint!

She fell sprawling on the floor, and the torn front of her dress gaped open. Her breasts bulged half out of the ripped frock.

I said: "What the hell—!" and leaned over her, lifted her up. I carried her into the next room, put her on the divan. She was dead to the world. I didn't know how long it would take me to bring her around—but I didn't have time, just then. I had to scram down to headquarters to keep my date with Donaldson.

On the other hand it struck me that this blonde baby, Constance Calvert, might be a key to the whole business. It was stretching the long leg of co-incidence to think she had just accidentally come to me the same night I'd received Arkle's decapitated noggin. She was mixed up in the deal some way. Maybe she was the one who'd brought that package and left it at my door!

Well, I couldn't take her down to headquarters with me. Not when she was unconscious. But I didn't want her to get away. So I used a trick I'd pulled many a time before.

I stripped the dress off her limp form, and took her shoes and chiffon stockings off while I was at it. Fumbling around with her silk garters made my fingers itch. But I stuck to my job without any monkey-business, and pretty soon I had her down to her black lace panties, and brassiere.

She was a hell of a sweet number, there on my divan with practically nothing on. Her skin was as smooth and warm as new cream, and she had what it takes to drive a man utsnay. But I didn't have time to be driven utsnay, so I covered her with a blanket and left her.

I carried her duds out with me. I picked up Skinny's head, wrapped it in the brown paper, and went down to my jalopy. Then I drove to beat hell.

DAVE DONALDSON was waiting for me outside

headquarters. We went into his office and I showed him the head. He said: "For Cripes' sake! It's Arkle, all right. Now, who in hell—?"

I said: "Wait a minute. Don't pop off with a lot of screwy questions. Don't ask me why this damned thing was delivered to my apartment That's one goofy thing I don't pretend to understand. But I've got a theory about Skinny Arkle's death."

Donaldson said: "A theory?'

"Yes. Now listen. Arkle was married to a girl named Kitty Calvert. Kitty has a sister, Constance Calvert. Well, just as I was starting downtown to meet you, Constance came to my door. She's a tall, blonde bimbo with plenty of sex-appeal."

"The hell with that," Donaldson grunted. "What did she want?"

"She claimed she was scared for her sister," I said. "She said Kitty and Skinny Arkle had a hell of a row three days ago. Skinny threatened Kitty's life. Then he took it on the lam and hasn't been seen since."

"So what?" Donaldson rasped.

"So this. Maybe Constance Calvert's story was a frame-up. Maybe her sister did have a fight with Skinny; and maybe Kitty shot the poor devil. Then maybe Kitty sent her sister to see me."

"What for?"

I said: "To cover the murder. To make it look as if they didn't know where Skinny had gone to."

Donaldson said: "Yeah. Sounds reasonable,

maybe. Except I still don't see why they'd send Arkle's head to you."

I said: "I don't think Kitty or her sister knew the head was being sent to me. Maybe it was brought by somebody who knew of the murder and wanted to tip it off."

Donaldson said: "Where is Kitty Calvert's sister now?"

"In my apartment. She won't get away."

He said: "Wait till I turn this head over to the medical examiner. Then we'll go see Kitty."

He was gone about two minutes. Then we went out and piled into my jalopy. I drove—and I didn't spare the speedometer. Pretty soon we parked outside the Arkle home in Westwood.

I NOTICED another machine standing at the curb a couple of doors away. It was a big, shiny maroon Cad, and somehow I thought I recognized it. But I couldn't be sure, and there was no point in checking it up just then. Donaldson and I went up to the porch of the Arkle house and rang the bell.

A cute little Chink maid opened up. I said: "We want to see Mrs. Arkle, please."

The Chink maid spoke perfect English. American-born, probably. She said: "Miss Kitty Calvert has retired, sir. You'll have to come in the morning."

Dave Donaldson shoved me aside and flashed his badge. "We'll see her now!" he growled.

The maid widened her slanted eyes. "But—there's someone with—" she started to say. Then she stopped and blushed a little.

I said: "Somebody with her, eh? A man?"

"I—I don't know anything about it, sir," the Chink dame said. I could tell she was lying. Her left hand sort of fluttered toward her heart, covering the tiny mound of her breast through her uniform.

Donaldson didn't waste any more time. He pushed the Oriental girl aside and said: "Come on, Turner." He ran up the stairs. I followed him. And then, just as we reached the second floor, I heard a shot.

I said: "What the hell—!" and made a dive for a closed door. The shot had sounded from within the room beyond that door. I jammed into it with my shoulder, burst it open. I had my .32 automatic in my fist. I leaped into the room, with Donaldson at my heels.

The room was all done in pink, with a pink-shaded lamp glowing in one corner. I sniffed the scent of expensive perfume. But I smelled something else, too. It was the acrid odor of powders-moke.

IN one second I caught the whole scene. There on the bed lay a nude woman a girl. A girl with red hair and the prettiest breast I ever saw. The prettiest legs, too. An absolute knockout. It was Kitty Calvert— Skinny Arkle's wife.

She was as dead as a smoked fish,

There was a bullet-hole in her breast, right over the heart. She'd been shot plumb center, And where she was shot there was a round red hole, with blood seeping out of it.

Directly beyond the bed I saw a man standing. He had his coat and vest off, and he was in his stocking feet. He looked white as hell. And he had a roscoe in his mitt.

I recognized him. He was Billy Sanston—a big-shot director for Altamount Studios. In fact, he directed all Kitty Calvert's productions. And now 1 knew where I'd seen that maroon Cad before—the one that was parked downstairs. It was Sanston's

own Cad. I'd seen him driving it many a time.

Donaldson said: "You murdering son of a—" and took aim at Sanston. "Drop that gun, you louse!"

Sanston dropped the gun. It hit the floor. He said; "Good God—you don't think I—?"

Donaldson said: "I don't think anything. If you've got anything to say, save it for your lawyers. Stick out your fins for the nippers."

The movie director staggered a little. "But—but you can't arrest me for something I didn't do! My God, I'll be ruined! My wife will divorce me—I'll lose my job—"

"You should have thought of that before. You been playing around with Kitty Calvert, haven't you?"

Sanston flushed. "Y-yes. But—but didn't kill her; I swear I didn't! I was here with her tonight. I admit that. I—I got up and went into the next room for a minute. Then I heard a shot. I ran in here and saw Kitty on the bed. She was dead; the gun was beside her. I—I picked it up, and then you men broke in. She—she must have shot herself—"

"Nuts!" Donaldson growled. "Come on—or shall 1 sock you on the dome with the soft end of my ros- coe?"

Sanston swayed toward us, holding out his hands for the bracelets. Then he pulled an unexpected stunt. With his left he smashed Dave Donaldson's service .38 aside. Then he planted a haymaker on

Donaldson's jaw. Dave went down.

I leaped at Sanston, but he got away from me. He scooped up the gat he had dropped. I drew a bead on him, pulled my trigger. But like a damn' fool I'd forgotten to unlatch the safety on my automatic. When I squeezed the trigger, nothing happened.

And by that time, Billy Sanston was out of the room and pelting hell-for-leather down the stairs.

I HURLED myself after him. Behind me I heard Donaldson getting on his feet. Dave was cursing and staggering along in my trail. I hit the stairs, started down. But Sanston had a good start. Before I was half-way down I heard the front door slam shut. It slammed so hard that the glass shattered. I knew damned well that Sanston was out of the house.

I yelled: "You lousy rat!" and took the last five steps in one flying jump. I jerked open the front door, raced outside. I saw Sanston in his maroon Cad—at the wheel. Then two shots roared in the night.

I ducked, thinking Sanston was firing at me. But I didn't hear any slugs whistling past my ears. Then I noticed something queer. Sanston wasn't trying to thing step on his starter, get his car under way. He was sort of slumped over his wheel.

Dave Donaldson caught up with me. We both jumped for the maroon Cad, yanked its front door open. I said: "What the hell!"

Sanston was bleeding at the mouth—great, crimson gushes of blood spewing out of him. He coughed once. A nasty sound, the bloody cough of a dying man. Then he shuddered, stiffened and went limp.

Donaldson looked at the gun in Sanston's relaxed hand where it rested on the upholstered seat. The gun which Sanston had carried with him out of Kitty Calvert's boudoir. A trickle of smoke curled up from the gat's muzzle. Donaldson said: "Jeeze! He shot himself!"

I said: "Yeah. Maybe."

"What do you mean, maybe?"

I said: "Well, maybe he didn't commit suicide. Maybe he was murdered."

Donaldson looked at me. "Are you bughouse?"

"No. I don't think so. I'm just trying to figure a couple of things out. Listen—suppose Sanston told us the truth a minute ago. Suppose he was in Kitty's house, making whoopee. And suppose he left her for a minute to get a drink of water or see a dog about a man. And suppose while he was gone, Kitty was shot?"

"You mean maybe she really killed herself and he walked in and picked up the roscoe where she'd dropped it?"

I said: "Don't be dense, Dave. You didn't see any powder-burns on Kitty Calvert, did you?"

"No. Come to think of it, I didn't."

"Well, then, she didn't shoot herself."

Donaldson said: "Well, hell! It was Sanston that killed her. Now he's bumped himself off because he realized he was out on a limb."

I said: "Not so fast. You heard Sanston say something about his wife? He didn't want to he arrested because his wife would divorce him and the scandal would make him lose his movie job?"

Dave narrowed his eyes. "By God! You think it was Sanston's wife—?"

I POINTED toward the side of Kitty Calvert's house. I said: "Take a look. There's a ladder up against the house. It's right up against Kitty's boudoir window."

Donaldson said: "I get it! Mrs. Sanston followed her hubby here, saw him making love to Kitty Calvert, and shot Kitty. But she didn't have a chance to shoot her husband too, because he was out of the room a minute, and when he came back we busted in. So she laid for him out here by his car. Huh?"

"At least that's a theory," I said. "It matches with the ladder against the window."

Dave said: "Then we've got to get Mrs. Sanston, by God! Maybe she's still around here somewhere, Come on—let's start searching!"

Even as he spoke, I heard the sound of a motor roaring from somewhere around the next corner. I said: "If it was Mrs. Sanston she's making her getaway right now. She'll probably go home to establish an alibi for herself."

"Alibi, hell!" Dave Donaldson roared. "I'll catch her! I'll put the collar on her and sweat the truth out of her!"

I said: "Go ahead. Use my jalopy. I'll go back in the house and phone headquarters to come and take the two corpses away."

So Dave got into my coupe and got going. I went back into the house. I picked up the phone, notified headquarters what had happened. When I hung up, I thought I heard somebody tiptoeing in the back of the place. Funny thing about people trying to sneak around without making any noise. You'll notice it quicker than you'll notice ordinary footsteps.

I made a flying dive for the dining-room where I'd heard the sound. Then I saw the Chink maid. She was trying to get out through a French window.

I jumped for her, grabbed her. She was trying to stuff something down the neck of her dress. I got my fingers into the vee of her uniform and yanked. The material tore. I ripped at the dress until something fluttered to the floor from between her tiny breasts. I grabbed it. It was an oblong of yellow paper.

The Chink girl tried to grab it from me. I slapped her across the face, pinioned her slim wrists with one hand. Then I looked at the slip of yellow paper. It was a check. It was made out to Miss Violet Chang, and it was signed: "Rodney Arkle." That had been

Skinny Arkle's real name. The check was for five hundred smacks.

I said: "Where the hell did you get this?"

"Mr. Arkle g-gave it to me two or three d-days ago," she whimpered. She looked scared as hell.

I said: "What for?"

SHE closed up like a clam. Her red lips got tight. I knew I'd have to pull the cave-man stuff on her to find out anything. So I grabbed her shoulders, shook her until her teeth rattled and her tiny breasts jiggled around like cups of jello.

I said: "Now look, Miss Violet Chang. If you don't want to get mauled groggy, you'll talk. How would you like a good punch in the jaw?"

"No—no—! Don't hit me!"

"Okay, then. Answer me. Why were you trying to sneak out that window?"

She said: "Be-because I'm afraid! I don't want to get mixed up in this case!"

I ran my fingers over her shoulder, pretended I was about to pinch hell out of her. I'll admit I got something of a kick out of touching her. But I didn't let on. I said: "Why are you afraid to get mixed up in the case?"

All of a sudden the slant-eyed cutie pressed herself up against me, put her arms around my neck. She said: "Please, Mr. Detective—I'll do anything you ask if you'll keep me out of this! I-1 have a brother who was smuggled into this country illegally. If I'm dragged into this shooting, the police will question me, look into my family. They might find out about my brother and deport him—"

She fitted against me like tissue paper. Her breasts against my chest, felt like little apples, and yet they were nice and pliant. She was offering me her lips.

Well, after all, I'm human. So I leaned down and kissed her . . . felt her lips part against my mouth. My blood was racing, way out of control. I remembered seeing a divan in the front room, so I lifted the Chink cutie in my arms and carried her . . .

IT was some time later when I said: "Okay, baby. Now you know I'm your friend. Maybe you'll answer a couple of questions, huh?"

"Such as what?" she asked me.

I said: "Well, for one thing, how long had Billy Sanston been intimate with your mistress, Kitty Calvert? How long had he been coming to visit her?"

"A—a long time. Almost a year. N-now let me go, please—!"

"Not yet. Tell me something else. Did Kitty know Billy's wife?"

"Y-yes. Just slightly. They weren't good friends. Sometimes I got the impression that Mrs. Sanston suspected her husband of being in love with Miss Calvert. Of course I wasn't sure. Now please let me get away—before the police come!"

Outside, in the distance, I heard sirens moaning. I said: "Sure, kiddo. Put on a coat to cover yourself. Then scram out the window."

She got a coat and I held it for her. I fumbled the job, killing time. Then finally I helped her out through the French window in the dining-room, just as the headquarters men rang the front door-bell.

I raced for the hall, yelled through the broken glass in the door. I said: "Quick—around the side! A Chink dame on the lam! Grab her!"

Those coppers moved fast. I heard them running around the side of the house. That was what I wanted.

For a minute I was alone. I set fire to a gasper and went upstairs. I didn't know what I was going to look for, but I figured maybe I might find something. I had three murders on my mind: Skinny Arkle's, his wife's and Billy Sanston's. I was convinced they were all murders; and I had a hunch they were linked together some way or other.

FIRST I squinted around the boudoir where Kitty Calvert's corpse was. Then I walked into the next bedroom. It had been Skinny Arkle's room. I saw a desk-drawer open.

I saw an old book of faded press-clippings from the days when Skinny had been a big-shot comedian. There were pictures of him in costume and in everyday dress. There was even a picture of Skinny as a kid with his family, back in Jugo-Slavia. It showed his mother, father, grandparents, a brother exactly the same age, two older sisters, and a couple of uncles and aunts. But I didn't take the scrap-book. It was too big, too bulky.

Then I found an empty book of check-stubs. I looked at the last three stubs. One showed that check for five yards drawn to the Chink maid, Violet Chang. The second said: "Pasadena Hospital, $250.00, in full." The third was to cash—for fifty grand!

Before I could look around any further, I heard a hell of a rumpus down below. The headquarters men had the nab on the Chinese girl. I didn't want them to catch me going through Skinny Arkle's things, so I went downstairs on the run. I said: 'You guys better take that girl to the jug. I think she knows something. And how about lending me a car for a while? Dave Donaldson took my hack."

One of the dicks said: "All right. Use the red road-ster, Mr. Turner. Run it back to headquarters when you get through with it."

I went out, got into the red roadster. I drove back to my apartment. Just as I parked outside my building, I saw somebody in the entrance. Somebody in a suit that looked familiar.

It was one of my own suits!

I said: "What the hell!" and jumped for the guy. I

grabbed him. Only it wasn't a him; it was a her. It was the blonde bimbo, Constance Calvert.

She fought at me. She said: "Damn you! Let me go!"

"Like hell!" I told her. "How long have you been out of my place?"

"I—I just got out. I found a suit of yours and put it on. Why did you take my clothes?"

BEFORE I could answer her, I heard brakes squeaking. I turned. There was Dave Donaldson driving up in my jalopy. He jumped out, saw me holding the blonde dame. He said: "What—?"

"Put the nippers on this girl, Dave," I told him. "She's hard to hold."

Dave slipped the cuffs on her. Then he said: "Turner, I've got news!"

I said: "What kind of news?"

"Well, in the first place," Donaldson growled disgustedly, "Mrs. Sanston had a perfect alibi. She's been playing bridge with friends all evening. Hasn't been outdoors. That eliminates her as a suspect. But down at headquarters I found out something damned interesting. Billy Sanston had been married before. His first wife's name was Nancy Norward. Ever hear of her?"

I said: "Good God! Nancy Norward was the girl who died down in San Diego on a party with Skinny Arkle!"

Dave said: "Yeah. Now do you see the set-up? Sanston must have nursed a grudge against Arkle all these years. To get even he played around with Kitty Calvert, Arkle's wife. Then, finally, he bumped Arkle off and decapitated the body. Maybe Kitty found out about it, so he had to kill her too. Then when we busted in on him in Kitty's boudoir he committed suicide. There was no other way out."

I said: "Dave, maybe you're right. It all checks up pretty well. Except one thing. Why was Arkle's severed head sent to me?"

"I don't know that," Donaldson grunted. "And there's one other goofy point, too. The medical examiner's report says that the bullet was fired into Arkle's noggin *after he was dead!* The condition of the tissues, or something. Look—here's the report."

He handed me a sheet of paper. I let him hang onto Constance while I took the paper to a streetlight. It was the usual formal report of the medical examiner—the description of the bullet wound, condition of the flesh, color of the hair and eyes, so many fillings in the teeth, and the way the head had evidently been sliced from the body itself. I read it over once. And then, suddenly, had the answer.

I jumped back toward Donaldson. I said: "Quick! Get in my hack! We'll take this dame with us. And we've got to move fast!"

Dave said: "Where the hell are we headed?"

"Pasadena!" I told him. "The Pasadena Hospital!"

IT took us just thirty minutes to make the trip, and I thumbed my nose at a dozen stop-signs on the way. I jerked all the tread off my tires skidding to a stop outside the Pasadena Hospital, and I grabbed Donaldson's arm. "Come on!" I yelled.

"What about this dame?" He pointed to Constance Calvert,

"Leave her here in my hack. She's handcuffed." I shoved Donaldson into the hospital and we went up to the desk.

There was an eldery woman on duty. I said: "I want to see a record of the deaths in this place during the past three days." Dave Donaldson flashed his badge for authority.

The woman dug into her records, handed me four or five cards. I found the one I wanted. It said: "Rodney Arkellmeister. Age 48. Male. White. Entered hospital in dying condition. Pneumonia. Unable to talk. Died two days later . . ." Then it gave the date of death and all that stuff.

I whirled on Donaldson. "Get it?" I said. "Rodney Arkellmeister! That was Skinny Arkle's real name before he came to America from Jugo-Slavia."

Dave said: "You mean Skinny died a natural death? Then who the hell cut off his head and put a bullet in it? Who sent the head to you?"

Before I could answer him, I heard a scream from outside. A woman's scream. I said: "What the hell—!" and jumped for the door. I saw a car parked behind my coupe. There was a guy leaning in my hack. He was choking Constance Calvert.

I said: "Damn! He must have been lurking around my apartment-house. He heard me saying we were coming here! He followed us!" And I hurled myself at the guy.

He heard me. He turned. I saw a roscoe in his fist. It vomited flame. A slug zinged past my skull. I whipped out my own automatic, thumbed the safety, squeezed the trigger. I sent three slugs into the guy's guts.

Even before he fell I yelled out to Donaldson. I said: "There's your killer. It's Skinny Arkle!"

Dave said: "You're crazy! How can a headless corpse get up and walk around—?"

By that time I was kneeling over the fallen man. I turned him over. It was Skinny Arkle, all right. I'd have known his face anywhere. Especially after seeing the decapitated head drop in my lap earlier that night, in my apartment.

Donaldson stared. He said: "Good God!"

I reached down, shoved my fingers in Skinny Arkle's mouth. I twisted—and pulled out his false teeth. I said: "Well, that proves it, Skinny."

Arkle glared up at me. His eyes were beginning to glaze. He said: "Damn you—!"

I said: "I see the whole thing now. You were the murderer, Arkle. You knew your wife, Kitty Calvert, was intimate with her director, Billy Sanston. You got proof of your suspicions from your wife's Chink maid, Violet Chang. You gave her your check for five hundred clams for telling you the lowdown."

Skinny Arkle gurgled in his throat and vomited a little blood.

I said: "By sheer luck, your brother had just come to visit you from Jugo-slavia. *Your twin brother!* You and he were identical twins; looked exactly alike. I saw a picture of you two in your scrap-book a while ago. It showed you and your twin as kids back in the old country. You looked alike even in those days."

Dave Donaldson said: "I'll be damned!"

I WENT on talking to Skinny Arkle.

"When your brother got to Hollywood, he was already stricken with pneumonia. You knew he was going to die. You saw a swell chance to murder your chiseling wife and her lover without being suspected of the crime. So you had your brother brought here to Pasadena—to a hospital. He died here. You arranged his burial somewhere—then you exhumed his corpse and cut its head off, put a bullet in it as a blind. That was the head you sent to me!"

Arkle said: "Ar-r-r-gh—!"

"You sent your twin brother's severed head to me, knowing I'd call the cops and notify them you'd been murdered. Then, tonight, you put a ladder outside your wife's boudoir and climbed up. You shot her and threw the gun on the bed alongside her, to

28

make it look like suicide. Maybe you'd have shot Billy Sanston at the same time but he'd gone into the next room. Then when Donaldson and I broke in, you saw that Sanston would be accused of murdering Kitty Calvert—and probably convicted. So you sneaked down the ladder, satisfied. But a moment later, Billy Sanston escaped. So you shot him with a second gun you had on you. You shot him as he got into his Cad. That made it look as if Sanston, too, was a suicide."

Donaldson stared at me. "How the hell did you guess?"

I said: "I knew, the minute you showed me the medical examiner's report of that severed head. It mentioned several fillings in the teeth. And I knew that the real Skinny Arkle *had false teeth!* He used to take them out and fold up his face, in the movies! Then I remembered that check-stub I'd seen in Arkle's book—a check made out to the Pasadena Hospital. I realized the truth. Arkle had done the killings, and now he'd probably try to escape by going back to Jugo-Slavia on his dead brother's passport."

Dave Donaldson leaned over Skinny Arkle, felt in his pockets. He brought out a passport and a steamship ticket. That cinched the thing.

Skinny Arkle's eyes fluttered. He mumbled: "Well . . . Turner . . . they won't . . . hang me . . . you took . . . care of that . . . damn you . . ."

A spew of crimson gushed out of his kisser, and he folded up. And that was the end of Skinny Arkle.

THEN I remembered Constance Calvert. She was slumped over in my jalopy. Arkle must have followed us and maybe she'd spotted him. Anyhow he'd tried to murder her quietly, probably figured on bumping Donaldson and me, too, when we came out of the hospital. He must have known the jig was up. But I wasn't thinking about Skinny Arkle any more. I was thinking of the blonde Calvert wren.

She'd been choked unconscious; but she wasn't seriously hurt. I turned to Dave Donaldson. I said: "Dave, you stay here and notify the Pasadena police have them take Skinny's carcass away."

Dave said: "Where are you going?"

I said: "Well, I took this girl's clothes off in my apartment earlier tonight. So now I'm going to take her back to my joint and put 'em back on her."

"Hell!" Donaldson growled. "I'll bet you won't hurry about it."

I said: "You flatter me, Dave." But it turned out that he was right, at that.

FALLING STAR

It was the dizziest looking diamond ring Dan Turner had ever seen—and a girl was giving it to him to keep . . . handing him plenty of Hollywood trouble on a platter

IT WAS sundown when Sid Grainger let me out of his swanky Rolls in front of my office-building in downtown Hollywood. Sid was president of Cosmotone Pictures. I'd been golfing with him all afternoon.

He waved to me and drove off. I went upstairs to my office to look over the mail and close up shop for the night. I'd just sat down at my desk when the door opened and a girl walked in.

She was a Filipino cutie, and plenty neat. Her clothes were good, she had nice legs, and her shape was easy on the eyes. But I could tell she was scared of something—or somebody. It showed in her face.

When she spoke, her English was as good as mine. She said: "Are you Mr. Dan Turner, the private detective?"

I said: "Yes. What can I do for you?"

She handed me a small, sealed package about the size of a match box. She said: "Will you please open this, Mr. Turner? It is very important."

I said: "Sure," and started to break the sealing-wax. While I was doing it, the Filipino wren went to my office door and closed it. Then she stood there with her hand on the knob. She seemed to be listening for something.

I finally got the little package untied. I threw the string and wrappings in my waste-basket, and held a white plush-covered jeweler's box in my hand. I thumbed the catch and the lid opened. Stuck into

the slotted purple satin lining of the box was a woman's finger-ring.

It was a screwy-looking ring. I'd never seen anything quite like it before. It was set with diamonds; but the stones were cut in a funny way. They stood up from their platinum prongs like thinly-whittled slivers of congealed fire. They were arranged in some sort of irregular design.

It struck me as a hell of a queer way to spoil a lot of good blue-white sparklers. I looked at the girl and said: "What's this all about!"

She said: "You are to keep it and guard it with your life, Mr. Turner. My mistress will pay you a thousand dollars if you will hold it until—"

THAT was as far as she got. All of a sudden I heard hard-heeled footsteps in the corridor outside my office. Through the door's frosted glass panel I saw the silhouette of a man's head and shoulders. The door-knob started to turn.

Quick as a flash, the girl twisted the key in the lock. She whirled to face me. Her tiny breasts heaved up and down under her frock. She whispered: "Quick, Mr. Turner—hide the ring—"

I made one move with my hand. At the same instant there came a hell of a crash. Somebody smashed the door-glass with the butt end of a roscoe.

I made a dive for the .32 automatic I carry in a shoulder-holster; but I froze before my fingers could get half-way under my coat. A masked hombre poked his face through the door's busted glass and covered me with his rod.

He said: "Listen, snoop. This cannon ain't stuffed with feathers, and I'll feed you a lead supper."

I said: "Okay, brother. It's your play. Call the signals."

He reached in with his free hand, turned the key on the inside of the door. Then he twisted the knob and walked in.

I took a quick gander at my wrist-wateh. It was a little past six. That made it tough, because all the other offices on my floor close at five sharp. There probably wasn't anybody around to hear my glass door being knocked in.

The masked bozo walked toward me. He shoved

the Filipino wren ahead of him, toward my desk. I studied the situation and wondered what might happen if I jumped up and started swinging my dukes. I decided it wouldn't pan out very well.

The masked man wasn't such a Hercules; I could have mopped up the floor with him in ten seconds. But he had a gat, and I'm not bullet-proof. So I sat still and waited for a better chance.

The guy with the gun grabbed the girl with his free hand. He kept one eye and his roscoe aimed at me. To the girl he said: "Where's that ring?" in a voice that sounded plenty surly and ugly.

"I—I don't know what you m-mean," she said.

"The hell you don't know what I mean!" he rasped at her. He put his left hand on her throat and squeezed with his fingers. He said: "Tell me where the ring is or I'll pinch a cancer on you!"

She let out a yip of pain'

I wanted to leap up and give him a taste of my knuckles. But be still had me covered. He spoke to the Filipino chicken again. "I'll put you under the daisies if you don't kick in with that ring, you damned Gugu slut!"

She whimpered. "N-no—"

HE started frisking her with his free hand. First he caught hold of the neck of her dress and yanked downward. The silk ripped. She wasn't wearing much of a brassiere. Coffee-colored skin peeped through lace. She moaned and tried to cover herself with her hands.

He biffed her wrists with the heel of his fist and said: "Keep still." Then he finished tearing her dress away.

She shivered there in the middle of my office with nothing on except her step-in, that band of lace, her stockings, and her high-heeled shoes. In spite of her light brown color she was plenty cute. She was built like a little bisque doll. Her whole body was miniature, her curves tiny and rounded. Her skin honey smooth, and her legs were tapered, shapely gams. I'd have got a boot out of looking at her if it hadn't been for the masked bozo's automatic pointing toward me.

He started searching her. He didn't miss a trick. He stuck his finger in her month and felt under her tongue. He went through her black hair. When he got through, stepped back and said: "You ain't got the ring. You musta slipped it to Turner before I got here."

She said: "No—no—" in a himporing whisper.

He gave her a shove and turned to me. He said: "Come on, snoop. Cough up that sparkler. Make it snappy—I ain't got all day."

I said: "You're damned right you haven't got all day, wise guy. While you've been wasting time I've had my foot on a buzzer under my desk. If you look around, you'll see a cop standing at the door, ready

to ventilate your spine."

I was lying like hell, of course. But the trick worked. The masked hombre wheeled around. I grabbed a paperweight from my desk and heaved it.

But my aim was bad. The paper weight sailed past his shoulder, missed him clean. He spun back to face me. I was on my feet by that time. I made a a flying dive over my desk and bashed into him full force. He went down on his back. I straddled him and made a dig for his cannon. Somehow, he managed to squeeze the trigger. The roscoe said: *"Chow!"* and spat a stre of flame past my ear.

Behind me, I heard a muffled, gasping moan and a slumping sound on the floor. I twisted my head around; saw the Filipino doll stretched out on the rug. There was a bluish-red hole in the firm flesh of her breast, on the under side. It was right over her heart. Blood was beginning to seep out of the hole. Her bare arms and legs were quivering.

I said: "You murderous rat!" and smashed my fist down at the masked guy's kisser. But he jerked his head aside and my knuckles hit the floor. It almost paralyzed my arm. The guy lifted his knee and socked it into the pit of my belly. I got sick. I lost my hold on his gun-hand.

He twisted out from under me, squeezed his trigger again. He pumped a slug at me and missed. Then his rod jammed. He said: "Damn you to hell!" and reversed the roscoe, slammed the butt toward my cranium. I tried to duck, but I was a split-instant too slow. I heard the swish of the gun, and then it felt as if Mount Wilson had hit me. A blast of pain shot through my noggin. After that, everything got dark for a while.

WHEN I came to, somebody had me by the shoulders shaking hell out of me. I opened my eyes and saw my friend, Dave Donaldson of the homicide squad, leaning over me. There were a couple of harness coppers with him.

The Filipino cutie was lying where I'd last seen her. She was as dead as a smoked herring. My office was just about turned upside down. Desk-drawers and filing cabinets had been opened; the contents were strewn to hellangone all over the place. There was no trace of the masked bozo.

I swayed to my feet and grabbed Donaldson's arm to steady myself. I said: "How the hell did you get wind of this, Dave?"

"The cop on the beat heard some shots and came up to investigate," he clipped back. "It took him a while to find out which office the sound had come from. When he reached this room, he took one gander and then phoned headquarters. I came on the double-quick. What happened, Turner? Did you bump this Filipino frill?"

I said: "Hell, no!" I yanked my automatic from its shoulder-holster and handed it over. "You can see my rod hasn't been fired."

He sniffed the muzzle, examined the full clip. He

said: "Yeah. I can see the slug didn't come from this gun. Besides, yours is a .32 and the girl was killed by a .44 bullet. But you've got some tall explaining to do."

I told him as much as I knew; gave him the whole screwy story. When I got through I said: "That's the works as far as I'm concerned, Dave."

He looked at me. "What became of the ring the Filipino wren handed you?"

I went to my desk, picked up a pen, fished in the inkwell. I snagged out that funny-looking diamond ring from the black ink where I'd dropped it when my glass door was first smashed open. I said: "This is it. The girl said something about her mistress paying me a grand to guard it. Before she could tell me anything else, hell broke loose."

Donaldson took the ring, held it under the faucet of my washbasin. When the ink was rinsed off he said: "Queerest-looking ring I ever saw. What do you make of it?"

"I don't know," I told him. "But let me have it back. Sooner or later the ring's owner will come to me for it. That might give me a lead on the killing."

Donaldson hesitated a moment. Then he handed the ring over to me. He said: "Okay. Turner. But the minute anything turns up, you phone me. Understand?"

IT was dark when I got down to where my jalopy

was parked. I started to get under the wheel, when somebody came up to me and touched my arm.

I looked around. I recognized the guy who was standing there. He was Carson Block, a big-shot banker from the east who'd been in Hollywood several months trying to get control of a string of minor movie studios. I didn't like him. He had a crooked look.

He said: "Are you Dan Turner?"

"Yes," I told him. "Why?"

He reached into his pocket, pulled out a fistful of banknotes. "There's five grand in this stack, Turner. It's yours if you hand me a certain ring. You know what I'm talking about."

I shook my head. "I don't get you."

He scowled. "Yes you do. Quit stalling. A girl delivered a certain diamond ring to you. I'm offering you five thousand dollars for it, and no questions asked—or answered."

I stared at him. He seemed to know a hell of a lot about that ring. Maybe he was the guy who'd worn the mask and bumped the girl. I said: "Okay, Mr. Block. I'll give you the ring. Here it is." And I reached under my coat for my automatic.

It wasn't there.

Then I remembered how I'd handed it to Donaldson and hadn't got it back. I cursed under my breath; and then I pivoted on my heel, balled my fist, swung on Block's paw. I caught him on the but-

ton. He nagged.

I left him on the pavement, went racing back to my office-building. The night elevator-man didn't answer my signal. I hit the staircase, took the steps three at a time. I reached the third floor and yelled: "Donaldson—hey, Donaldson!"

Dave came out of my office. He said: "What—"

I grabbed him. "Downstairs—quick!" I said. "I think I've got the guy you're looking for!"

We went pelting downstairs to the street; reached

my coupe. I started to point; and then I said: "What the hell—!"

Block wasn't there.

I said: "The louse must have a cast-iron jaw!"

"What louse?" Donaldson grated.

"Carson Block, the banker. He stopped me just now; offered me five grand for that damned ring. I popped him and left him here while I went after you."

Dave said: "Carson Block, huh! I'll put out a dragnet for him." He went back into my building to phone headquarters.

I GOT into my coupe and stepped on the starter. Driving toward my apartment, I thought things over; tried to fit the pieces of the puzzle together.

There was no way of finding out the answer just then. It all depended on whether Donaldson's dragnet succeeded in picking up Block. I parked my jalopy in the basement garage under my apartment-house and went upstairs to my flat.

The minute I started to stick my key in the lock, I sensed something wrong. The door was unlatched. There was a light burning in my living room. I heard somebody moving around inside.

I didn't have my roscoe, and I didn't know what I might be up against. But I decided to take a chance. I shoved my hand into the side pocket of my coat and stuck my finger through the cloth to look like the barrel of a gun. Then I kicked the door open and went bouncing inside. I said: "Stick 'em high, damn you!" Then I widened my eyes.

There was a woman in my room. A girl. She was a knock-out. She had honey-yellow hair and the face of an angel. Her blue silk dress stuck to her as if she'd been poured into it; and the way her slinky curves moved under the silk was enough to make a wooden Indian come to life. Her hips had a sleek, rippling smoothness, and her chiffon ankles looked like a Petty drawing. She certainly had what it takes, and I don't mean perhaps.

She said: "Mr. Turner—!"

"Yeah," I said. "And who the devil are you?"

"I—I bribed the janitor to let me in," she faltered. "I had to see you alone. I didn't want anyone to see me waiting for you in the downstairs lobby. I—I'm Chloe Cabot."

I suppose I should have tabbed her from the start. Chloe Cabot had been a hell of a big screen star. Recently she'd started hitting the skids as a box-office attraction. For some reason she was losing her hold on the public; her films were turning out to be flops. She was under contract to Cosmotone Pictures, and I'd seen her plenty of times on the screen. But this was the first occasion I'd ever met her face to face, and somehow she looked different. She looked younger, fresher.

I said: "What did you want to see me about, Miss

Cabot?"

"I came to pay you the thousand dollars I promised you. I want my diamond ring back. The one I sent to you through my maid."

I STEPPED toward her. "Listen," I said. "There are a few questions I'd like to ask you. In the first place, did you know that your maid was bumped off in my office a while ago?"

She got pale. "You mean—k-killed?"

I said: "Yeah. A masked bozo rubbed her out and slugged me on the dome. He was after the ring. Then, later, a man named Carson Block offered me five grand cash if I'd turn the ring over to him. It looks to me as if you'd better spill what you know about that ring, Miss Cabot. What's so damned important about it?"

She was trembling. "C-Carson Block tried to . . . buy the ring from you!"

I said: "Yeah. Why did he want it so bad?"

"—I'll tell you everything," she whispered. "Carson Block is trying to gain control of Cosmotone Pictures—the company that has me under contract. I own some stock in Cosmotone; took it in lien of salary on my last production. Carson Block is after that stock. It would give him the controlling vote in the company's management. I refused to sell it to him; and since then he's made several attempts to steal the stock from me.

"He even h-had me k-kidnaped last week; kept me under narcotics in a private sanitarium in Hollywood Hills—the Sunaire Hospital. I—I just managed to escape from there today. That's when I sent my maid to you with the ring. . . ."

I said: "What's the ring got to do with all this, Miss Cabot?"

She touched my arm. Her fingers were trembling. "That ring is really the key to my private strongbox at home, where I keep the stock. The diamonds fit into slots in the lock, so that the box unlatches when the ring is twisted."

There was something hurried, nervous, furtive, in the way she was talking. I got the impression she wasn't telling the whole truth. I decided to test her out. I said: "Can you describe the way you sent me the ring, Miss Cabot?"

She hesitated. Her face flushed. "It—it was in a little plush box. A purple box with white lining."

That was the wrong answer. The ring had actually been in a white plush box with purple satin lining—just the reverse of what this dame said. Of course, in her excitement she might have got mixed up a little; but she sounded as if she was guessing in the dark. I couldn't be sure.

As a matter of fact, I wasn't even sure that this honey-haired cutie really was Chloe Cabot. She certainly looked a lot younger than she did on the screen. An idea came to me. I seemed to remember some sort of tiny mole that always showed in the upper cleft of Chloe Cabot's bosom in her films, when she wore deep decolletage. It was just a vague recollection in my mind; I wasn't positive. But I knew a way to make sure.

I said: "I'm sorry, Miss Cabot. I'm afraid I can't give you back your ring. After all, it's linked up with a murder now. The oolice will want it as evidence against Block when they arrest him."

" Oh-h—!" she gasped. "But I've *got* to have it!"

I shook my head. "Sorry."

She grabbed me. "Listen Mr.Turner. I promised you a thousand dollars to keep the ring for me. Now I'll pay you two thousand if you'll return it to me!"

"No soap."

She looked at me. "Is—is there anything else that might . . . interest you. . .?"

I said: "Such as what, kiddo!"

SHE whipped her hands up to the shoulder-straps of her dress; unsnapped the catches, hesitated with drooping eyelashes. She said: "Such as . . . this . . . Mr. Dan Turner!"

I looked at her; felt my blood pump faster in spite of myself. She was an eye-full of sweetness and her half-naked body was a challenge hard to resist. But I held out long enough to get a good gander at the scented, blossom-smooth skin above her breasts. I didn't see any mole there. Her skin was milk-white and completely flawless.

She must have misunderstood my hesitation; for she came up to me. She pressed herself against me, grabbed my hands, pulled my arms around her waist. "I—I'm yours, Dan Turner, if . . . if you'll give me back my ring!" she whispered.

That was more than I'd bargained for. I could feel her clinging to me, and her lips were close to mine. My hands were on her back, and the touch of her flesh sent tingles racing through me. After all, I'm human. I did what most guys would have done under the circumstances. I kissed her. What the hell? The minute our mouths met, I forgot everything. I felt her breath, hot, sultry, moist. I picked her up in my arms with a sweep. . . .

AFTER a while, I calmed down a little. I got my brain to working again. I went over to my cellarette; dragged out a fifth of V69 and two glasses. While my back was turned to the girl, I dropped little white pellet into her glass then I filled it with Scotch and handed it to her. I said "Have a snort, kiddo. Then you can wait here while I go get your ring."

She downed her snifter without question. I took a couple of quick ones myself. Then I went and got my hat and coat. I said : "I'll be right back, baby. You wait here." I went out.

The instant I got to the downstairs lobby of the apartment-house, I dived for the phone-booth. I dropped a buffalo; dialed the home number of Sid Grainger, the guy I'd played golf with that same afternoon. He was president of Cosmotone Pictures, the outfit that had Chloe Cabot under contract.

1 finally got Grainger on the wire. I said: "Sid, how about meeting me at your studio right away? I want you to run off a reel of film for me."

"Sure, Turner. Meet you there in fifteen minutes."

I went down to my basement garage, got out my jalopy. I drove over to Parapet Street, where Cosmotone's lot was located. Sid showed up a few minutes later. He said: "What film do you want to see, Turner?"

"Any reel in which Chloe Cabot appears in decolletage," I told him.

He took me past the gate-keeper outside the lot We went into a private projection-room usually used for 'rushes' and pretty soon Sid dug up a Chloe Cabot reel. He ran it off. The Cabot girl stalked across the screen in an evening gown cut low. I studied her—hard. I saw that little mole. I saw something else, too. She was left-handed. And the dame in my apartment was right-handed!

That was all I wanted to know. I said: "Thanks, Sid," and went pelting back to my coupe. I drove like hell for Beverly, where Chloe Cabot's home was located. It took me seventeen minutes to get there. I jammed my thumb on the bell.

The door opened. A sour-faced butler looked at me. He said: "Yes, sir?"

"Is Miss Cabot in?" I asked him. I flashed my tin.

His eyes widened when he saw the badge. "Miss Cabot hasn't been home in several days, sir," he said.

I brushed past him, went into the house. "Show me where her safe is located," I said. I put plenty of authority in my voice.

THE butler led me to a study, pointed to the circular steel door of a safe set in the wall. I went to it, studied it. It had no dial, no knobs. But I saw what looked to be a series of tiny holes drilled into the face of the polished steel. I whipped out the diamond ring which the maid had given me, and I fiddled around with it until the oddly-cut stones matched up with those tiny holes in the steel. Then I pressed the ring hard against the holes.

Something clicked inside the safe. There was a buzzing sound. The door swung open. The whole thing was an ingenious electrical mechanism. By fitting the ring against those holes, an inner contact was made and the safe was unlocked.

I saw some papers inside the circular strong-box; dragged them out. I couldn't find any Cosmotone Pictures stock; but I did discover something else. It was Chloe Cabot's contract with Cosmotone. It called for four pictures to be made within the year— at a salary of two hundred and fifty grand per production. In other words: a million-buck contract.

My mental cogwheels clicked. If one more factor happened to come out right, I knew I'd see daylight. I shoved the contract in my pocket, leaped out of the house. I scrambled into my jalopy, headed for Hollywood Hills. I was looking for a certain spot; and pretty soon I found it. A small-sized Neon sign twinkled:

SUNAIRE SANITARIUM

I parked. I sneaked around to the rear of the one-floor, sprawling bungalow. I found an unlatched window; raised it. I hoisted my legs over the sill, dropped down inside a kitchen. Everything was dark. I flicked on my pencil-flash light, found a door. It led to a corridor.

I started down that hallway. There were closed doors all along one side. I opened the first two; didn't see anybody in the rooms. The third door I came to was locked. I always carry a ring of master-keys; and now I tried them. The fourth key worked. I opened the door.

There was a dame on a bed, sleeping. Her night-gown was cut plenty low in front, and one shoulder-strap was down over her bare arm so that my flash-light's thin white beam revealed the tiny mole I was looking for; and when I looked at the dame's face with its tumbled frame of honey-colored hair I knew I was coming to the end of the trail. This was Chloe Cabot, the movie star. The genuine Chloe.

I went over to the bed, touched her shoulder. She didn't stir. Her breathing was uneven, slow. I pried open one of her eyelids. The pupil was dilated, the eyeball rolled back. She was doped. I saw pin-pricks on her arm where she'd had several injections.

I knew there wasn't a chance in the world of snapping her out of her sleep just then. And there was no time to be lost. I slipped my arms under her, lifted her. I carried her out of the room, down the corridor. She was a dead weight, and I had a hell of a time getting her through that open kitchen window. But I made the grade.

I SNEAKED her around to my parked coupe, put her inside. Then I climbed in alongside her and gunned hell out of my motor; headed my jalopy toward town.

After a while I pulled up in front of headquarters. I leaped up the steps. "Tell Dave Donaldson to come out," I said to the desk-man.

In a minute, Donaldson appeared. He said: "Turner! Have you found out—"

"Yeah," I told him. "Come on with me. We're heading for my apartment. I think the guy who murdered that Filipino cutie will be coming to my joint pretty soon. Maybe he's there now. Let's get going."

Dave piled into my coupe, alongside Chloe Cabot's limp form. When he saw her he said: "Who the hell is this?"

I said: "Dave, this is Chloe Cabot. That diamond ring belonged to her. She's been kept in a private dippy-house the past few days—under narcotics. She's drugged right now. The guy that did it to her is the one who wanted the diamond ring. He's the one who killed the Filipino girl."

Donaldson said: "I don't get any part of it, Turner. What's it all about?"

"It's simple enough," I told him. "In the first place, that diamond ring is really a key to Chloe Cabot's private safe in her home out in Beverly. The murderer wanted that key. He wanted something out of her safe. Ho wanted it so badly that when he saw Chloe's maid coming into my office he followed her and killed her in an attempt to get it. He failed. Then he sent a dame to impersonate Miss Cabot; sent her to my apartment. She tried to get the ring-key away from me, but I didn't fall for it."

Donaldson said: "What the hell was the killer after?"

"Something that affects the financial set-up of Cosmotone Studio," I said. "Something that could change its ownership."

"What happened to the dame who came to your apartment?"

1 said: "I fed her a sleeping-pill in some whiskey.

She's probably still at my joint—out cold. That's why I think the murderer will go to my place. He'll be looking for the impersonator. He'll be wondering why she's staying so long, and he'll be looking for her to see if she got the ring-key from me."

"But how the hell did you find out where the real Chloe was being kept, Turner?"

"The other woman let that slip," I told him. "The dame who impersonated Miss Cabot fed me a story that was half true and half lies. But she *did* mention a certain sanitarium."

Before Donaldson could ask any more questions, I braked to a quick stop in front of my apartment-house. We left the drugged Cabot girl in my jalopy; locked her inside.Then we started upstairs, not making any noise. We reached my door. I grabbed Donaldson and said: "Sh-h-h! Listen—!"

From inside my flat I heard a man's rasping voice. "You damned yellow-haired slut! You let Turner pull a fast one on you! He probably had that diamond-ring in his pocket all the time—and you let him get away! I've already killed one dame in this mess; now I've got a good notion to bump you, too. . . ."

That was all I needed. I slapped my shoulder against the door, crashed it inward. Donaldson was at my heels. He had his service .38 in his fist. I said: "Okay, Sid Grainger. Lift the flippers—high!"

THAT'S who it was. Sid Grainger, president of Cosmotone. When he saw us, he tried to drag out his roscoe; but Donaldson was too fast for him. In two seconds, the nippers were on Grainger's wrists and I was holding the honey-haired girl who had tried to fool me a while before.

I said: "Well, Grainger, the jig's up. You had a million-buck contract with Chloe Cabot. But she was washed up as a star. Her pictures didn't pay. If you fulfilled her contract, your studio would be bankrupt—would fall into the hands of bankers. Block knew that. And he wanted control of Cosmotone. That's why he tried to bribe me to give him Miss Cabot's ring-key. He wanted her contract to hold over your head as a whip—to make you sell out to him for practically nothing.

"For a while I thought maybe Block was the guilty one. But when I found that contract in Chloe's safe, I knew you were the man. You were the only one with a strong enough motive. You had Chloe abducted, drugged. She managed to sneak that ring-key to her maid and send it to me. You saw the maid coming into my building downtown—it was right after you'd left me at the curb. You followed the maid to my office, killed her. And then you sent this dame up to me in an effort to get the ring. That's the straight of it, isn't it?"

Grainger didn't answer.

I picked up his roscoe; looked it over. I turned to Donaldson and said: "Here you are, Dave. It's a .44

with two shots fired out of the clip. This gat will match up with the bullet in that Filipino maid's heart or I miss my guess."

Donaldson said: "Yeah," and went over to my phone to put in a call for a squad car.

When he had taken his prisoners away, I went downstairs to my jalopy and drove the real Chloe Cabot to a legitimate hospital for treatment. When she got better, I collected a grand from her—for services rendered.

SILVERSCREEN SPECTRE

It's impossible; but it's so! Dan Turner takes up the case of the haunted movie, in which an accidentally electrocuted wife comes back to plague her director-husband

SOMETHING went *"spang!"* against my coupe's bullet-proof windshield. A spider-web of cracks circled the shatterproof glass. It made a beautiful design, but I wasn't in the mood to appreciate it.

I said: "What the hell!" and jammed on my brakes. I slammed myself out of my jalopy and went leaping into the night to look for the bird who had fired that shot. But there was no trace of anyone on the sidewalks or the street. That section of Beverly Hills seemed as deserted as King Tut's tomb. The hour was close to eleven.

I saw that I had parked almost directly in front of Adolph Maenzer's home. Maenzer was a former big-shot director for Altamount Pictures who was somewhat down on his luck. Just thirty minutes before, he had phoned me at my apartment and begged me to come see him right away. His voice had sounded so pleading over the wire that I had agreed to call on him at once. And now, here I was in front of his Spanish stucco house—and some sharp tomato had pushed a lead slug against my jalopy's windshield.

From the direction the bullet had taken, I had a sneaking hunch it had been fired from somewhere close to Maenzer's joint. I walked up to his front door and rang the bell.

NOTHING happened for maybe three minutes.

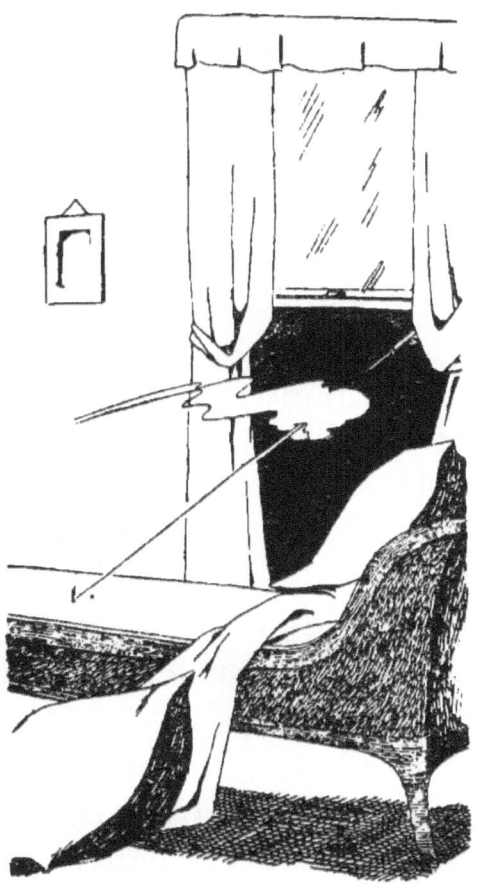

Then all of a sudden the door opened, and a little old lady peered out. She was short and dumpy, with a wrinkled face and a kindly, gentle expression. But right now I could see she had a grade-A case of the drizzling jitters. Her face was the color of watered milk, and she had a 1915 German-army Luger automatic in her wavering fist. She was aiming the Luger at my belt-buckle as she opened the door.

I don't like people to point their hardware at me. It makes me peevish. Besides, I'd been asked to come here. It got me sore to have a bullet thud into my windshield and then walk into the nasty end of a miniature cannon. That's no way to greet a man.

The little old lady glared at me and started jabbering something in German which I didn't understand. I saw her finger getting tight on the Luger's trigger, and I knew I had to do something about it before she bored a tunnel in my belly. So I took a long chance and yelled: "Hey—look out! Behind you!" Then, when she started to turn around, I made a dive for her gun-wrist and twisted the big automatic out of her grasp.

She shrank away from me, whimpering. Just then I heard footfalls in the house behind her, and a man came racing to the front door from one of the rear rooms. It was Adolf Maenzer himself, and he was saying: "What's this? What's this?"

I said: "Take it easy, Mr. Maenzer. I'm Dan Turner. And I wish to God you'd tell me what this is all about."

Maenzer took the little old lady in his arms and spoke soothingly to her in German. Then he turned to me. "I am very sorry, Mr. Turner. This is Mrs. Hasdorf, my housekeeper. She has been in my family for years—long before I ever came from Berlin to Hollywood. She thought you were an enemy, and she was trying to protect me."

The wrinkled little Hasdorf dame grabbed my hand and clung to it. She sobbed out something I didn't understand; but I gathered that she was apologizing. So I patted her shoulder and said: "That's okay, lady. Forget it." She turned and tottered back into the rear part of the house.

When she had gone, Maenzer said: "I am glad you came so quickly, Mr. Turner. I have a very important investigation for you to make. I will pay you

ROBERT LESLIE BELLEM

well—but I warn you, there may be danger."

I said: "Yeah. Somebody's already tried to put a slug through me."

Maenzer's pan got sort of greenish. "Gott!" he whispered. His eyes started darting around in a furtive, hunted way. For some reason, he reminded me of a weasel—or a cornered rat.

Then he reached out and grabbed my arm. "Come upstairs, Mr. Turner. I will show you what has been troubling me."

AS I followed him to the second floor, my mind went over Maenzer's history—as much as I knew of it. He had been in Hollywood about eight years. In that time, he had become a top-flight director for Altamount. Then, about five or six months ago, tragedy and bad luck had commenced spotting him behind the eight-ball.

First his wife, a lovely blonde actress named Vesta Delorme, had died under shocking circumstances—and that's not intended as a pun. While taking a bath, an electric heater had accidentally fallen into her tub. There'd been a short circuit, and Vesta was electrocuted.

After that, Maenzer had gone all to hell. He'd started hitting the bottle, and it was rumored he also had tried a crack at the needle, too. In any case, he'd lost his berth with Altamount; hadn't worked for maybe four months—until just recently.

61

Within the past thirty days, a quickie outfit on Poverty Row had hired Maenzer to make one picture. He was supposed to be working on it now; and it

might be the means of his getting a new toe-hold on suc-cess.

That was Maenzer's story as I remembered it. We reached the second floor, and he guided me into a leather-lined den. I noticed a small, silvered movie-screen set up at one end of the room; and opposite the screen I saw a projecting apparatus.

Maenzer said: "Mr. Turner, it is always my habit to view the 'rushes' of my pictures here in the privacy of my home. When a day's scenes have been shot, I have the negatives developed and prints made so that I may see the results by myself."

I nodded. "So what?"

His little rat-like eyes darted around the room. "Mr. Turner," he whispered hoarsely, *this latest picture of mine is haunted!*"

I said: "Haunted? What the devil are you getting at?"

"Wait. I will show you," he answered in his accented English. He switched off the room's lights and snapped a button on his projection machine. A square of brilliance danced on the silvered screen at the other end of the den. Then a movie scene splashed into view.

It was an em-cee-you—a medium close-up—of Carlotta Cordova, the Spanish star who was playing the lead in Maenzer's new picture. She was a lush brunette wren, with plenty on the ball in the way of tantalizing curves. She was going through her emotional paces in a solo scene as I watched the picture unwinding before me. And then, suddenly, I drew a sharp breath and said: "What the hell!"

SOMETHING was happening to that picture on the screen before me. Carlotta Cordova was fading out, as if in a dissolve shot; then, replacing her, I saw the feature of someone else. Another girl. A blonde girl—

Vesta Delorme, Adolf Maenzer's wife who had been accidentally killed several months ago by electrocution in her tub!

Her image grew clearer, sharper, on the screen. She seemed to be looking straight out with accusing, haunting eyes. Then, as suddenly as she had appeared, she vanished; and Carlotta was back in the picture again.

Maenzer snapped off the projector, clicked on the room's lights. He was sweating, and his eyes were glassy. "Now you know what I mean when I say this picture is haunted!" he rasped.

"Each night for a week, now, the same thing has happened! I bring the day's 'rushes' home to my private projector—and always my dead wife's face appears on the film! It is driving me mad, Turner! I'm going insane!"

"Wait a minute," I told him. "This looks like a gag to me. There are several ways it could happen. Your cameraman might be making a double exposure— filming someone who looks like your dead wife before photographing the scenes you direct. Or it might be somebody in the developing room who's superimposing an old shot of your wife on this new footage. It might even be a film editor or cutter."

"*Ja*. I have thought of all those things, Turner.

And I have checked them. But the theory falls down. I have found out that nobody—"

That was as far as he got. From the door behind me, a shot cracked out. I felt a slug pluck at my sleeve and then plock into the wall beyond me, chewing out pieces of plaster. I whirled around. In my fist I still had the Luger automatic I'd taken away from Maenzer's housekeeper. I raised it and took a flying dive for the doorway.

The second-floor hallway was dark, but I thought I caught a flash of something white at the far end, in the shadows. I yelled: "Stand still or I'll let you have a load of lead!"

The blurred white shape kept on going; vanished through an open doorway at the end of the hall. I squeezed the Luger's trigger but nothing happened. The damned gun was empty. Even as I hurled myself forward, I sniffed its muzzle. There was no trace of burned smoke.

That told me one thing. It proved that Mrs. Hasdorf hadn't been the one who'd fired a shot at my coupe's windshield a while before. I dropped the Luger and dragged out my own .32 automatic from its shoulder-holster. I reached the doorway through which the blurred white shape had disappeared. I slammed myself into a bedroom.

There was an open casement window opposite me, and I heard a scratching, scrambling sound just outside. I also heard what seemed to be a muffled feminine moan of fright. I leaped to the window, peered outward and down.

The side of Maenzer's house supported a wooden lattice-work trellis covered with rambler rose-vines. There was a girl clinging to the trellis, just below my reach. She was dressed in white, and I knew she must be the blurred shape I'd been chasing.

BUT now she was in a hell of a mess. Somehow, the bottom of her dress had got tangled in the thorny rose-vines; and her whole frock was up over her head, trapping her. She couldn't wriggle her arms and shoulders free of the dress, and it was up over her face like a billowing tent, smothering her cries. From the shoulders south she was as naked as a picked goose except for skin-tight, glove-silk snuggies.

I couldn't see her face, of course, because it was covered by her updrawn frock. But I could see plenty of the rest of her. She wasn't hard on the eyes, either. Her squirming, kicking legs were plenty nifty; and the way her swelling hips filled out those snuggies made me feel years younger, made my mouth water. She was hanging by her hands; and her arms being over her head made her breasts pout out like taut marble cones. I noticed that she was losing her grip with her left hand; and when I looked closer, I saw why.

She had a gun in that left hand. A small, nickel-

plated revolver! And there was a thin wisp of smoke still issuing from the muzzle!

I tried to grab her but she was too far below the windowsill for me to reach her. I said: "Baby, you're caught. And you'd better hang on where you are until I run downstairs and get under you to break your fall. Don't let go until I tell you, or you'll drop twenty feet and bust your pretty form."

She just moaned through the folds of her skirt.

I turned, left the window, raced out of the room

and down the stairs. I barged out through the front door; but as I hit the porch I smashed into a lean, wolf-jawed guy who had evidently just come from the driveway alongside the house. We ploughed together like a couple of billiard-balls on a carom shot, and I went skittering sidewise. I recovered my balance, stared at the egg I'd bumped into. I recognized him. He was Barry Barkis, president of the outfit for which Maenzer was making a picture.

He knew me, too. He said: "Turner—what on earth—?"

I brushed past him. "No time to talk. See you later."

He grabbed my arm. "But listen—wait a minute—"

I shoved him away. I didn't like him anyhow. I dashed around to the side of the house and looked up toward the spot where I'd left the half-naked wren hanging on the trellis.

She was gone!

Her dress was still stuck to the thorns of the trellis; so I knew she must have managed to yank herself out of the frock and climb down to safety. Well, she couldn't get very far without her dress. I started looking around for her.

Then, all of a sudden I heard a sound that startled hell out of me.

It was a shot from inside the house.

I PIVOTED and sprinted for the front door. Just inside, I saw a sprawled form. It was Barkis, the quickie producer. He was flat on his face, and blood was seeping from a hole in the back of his noggin. His brains were splattered all over the place in a yellowish-red spew. Adolf Maenzer was standing over the corpse, looking sick.

"A shot—fired from outside—for God's sake do something, Turner—!" Maenzer gibbered.

Before I could answer, I heard a motor being gunned to hell at the curb outside. I recognized the sound. It was my own jalopy! I said: "Damn it to hell!" and made a spurt across the front lawn, just as my coupe got under way.

I managed to catch my fingers in the luggage-rack behind the rumble-seat as my jalopy gathered speed; and I dragged myself up on the slippery, curved rear turtle-deck as the car went flying around the next intersection on two wheels and a prayer.

I peered in through the rear window; and I caught my breath. My jalopy was being driven by the dame who had clung to the trellis on the side of Maenzer's house. Now she was nude to the waist. I could see her gleaming shoulders, her coal-black hair. I caught a flash of her face in the rear-view mirror. I said: "For Cripes' sake! Carlotta Cordova!"

That's who it was, all right. The leading woman of Maenzer's latest picture!

I scrambled toward the left running-board as the

Cordova cutie fed soup to the motor. She evidently didn't know I'd boarded the machine; because when I finally managed to reach the running-board alongside her, she turned and gave me one scared look. Then she said: "Oh, God!" and almost put us up on somebody's front porch.

I grabbed for the wheel, straightened it out. Then I jammed my automatic into Carlotta's neck and said: "Slow down and don't do anything rash, baby. Otherwise I'm likely to blow your head off."

She sobbed and cut down her speed to about twenty. "Wh-what are you g-going to d-do?" she whimpered.

I said: "I'm going to take you to my apartment and ask you some questions. And you'd better a damn' sight answer me straight, if you don't want to spend the rest of your life on the inside looking out!"

I KEPT her covered with my roscoe, forced her to drive to my apartment. When she parked in front of my joint, I reached inside the coupe and found her nickel-plated revolver. I shoved it in my pocket and said: "Come on, kiddo. Get out of there."

"I can't! I—I haven't any d-dress on!"

I slipped out of my coat, handed it to her. "Put that around you, though it seems a shame. Then we'll go up the back way so nobody'll notice your bare legs." My temperature went back to normal,

70

with all that seductive loveliness covered.

I prodded her up to my flat, opened the door and made her go inside. Still keeping her covered, I managed to set fire to a gasper and pour a couple of slugs of Vat 69. I gave her one, drank the other myself. Then I hauled her down on my davenport forcibly and said: "Now, then, Carlotta. Just exactly what was your idea in trying to shoot a hole in my windshield when I first went to Maenzer's house? And later, why did you try to plug me when I was with him in his den?"

"I—I refuse to talk!" she flashed at me defiantly.

I reached an arm around her, yanked my coat away from her shoulders. Then I looked her over. She was damned easy on the optics. Her bare legs were smoother than the soft pink silk of her panties, and her thighs were as white and creamy as a celibate's dream. Up above her slender waist, her lovely body swelled outward in two enticing little hillocks of flesh—and as an old connoisseur of feminine charms, I'd say that Carlotta Cordova was just about perfect.

She shrank away from me. "Don't touch me!"

I said: "The hell I won't touch you! I've got some questions I want answered, and unless you unbutton your tongue I'm going to work you over."

"I—I won't answer any questions!"

"Then I'll make you, by God!" I said, putting the accent on the *"make."* And I hauled her against me, clamped my mouth over her lips, and started giving her the works.

She struggled and squirmed. "No— No—!"

I grinned into her flashing black eyes. I said: "Sister, I've got one certain way of making dames talk. It never misses. Now, either you spill the information I want or else. . ." There was no mistaking my meaning.

Very deliberately she laughed at me. "If that's your system, go ahead!" she taunted me. She drew up her arms over her head, so that I could see the smooth curves of her armpits and the contours of her breasts where they swelled outward.

I THOUGHT she was trying to run a bluff on me; and I don't fall for bluffs. So I kissed her again, hard. I was holding her by her bare shoulders, and my fingers strayed down her arms. She was beginning to pant a little.

I shoved her back among the cushions of the davenport and whispered: "Baby, either you're going to talk or you're going to be sorry. . . ."

"You can't scare me. You wouldn't dare. . . ."

"Wouldn't I?" I held her so tight that she couldn't get her breath. I could feel those firm little mounds burrowing into my chest as she squirmed in my arms. I couldn't tell whether she was wigggling to get away from me or trying to snuggle closer. By that time, I didn't give a damn.

I'll admit I'd started out just to scare some information out of her; but holding her so close and smelling the scent of her hair and feeling her warm flesh against me—well, after all, I'm human. I forgot my original purpose for a few minutes. What the hell?

THEN, when I thought she should have learned her lesson, I said: "Okay, babe. *Now* will you talk?"

She grinned at me. "No. I won't talk. And there's nothing else you can do to scare me, is there?"

"Yeah. I could beat hell out of you."

"You wouldn't do that."

"Maybe I wouldn't. But there's one thing I sure as God *will* do. I'll turn you over to the cops for killing Barkis at Maenzer's house a little while ago!"

Her face got pale, and for a second I thought she was going to faint in my arms. "B-Barkis—killed?" she moaned.

I said: "Yeah. Killed. Bumped off. Rubbed out. And a half-minute after he was croaked, you tried to lam away in my jalopy. Now, how do you think you're going to explain all that?"

She grabbed me, held my arms. She was trembling so hard that I could see the quivering of her pert, perky little breasts—like bowls of moulded jelly. "L-listen, Mr. Turner!" she whispered. "I—I guess it's time for me to tell everything. I'll have to tell everything! And then you've got to help me send

Adolf Maezner to the noose for murder. For two murders!"

I said: "What the devil—?"

The words were gushing out of her now, like oil out of a million-barrel well. "This is what happened, Mr. Turner!" she panted. "A few months ago, Maenzer's wife, Vesta Delorme, d-died. Her death was accidental, everybody said. But I know better. Maenzer murdered her!"

"What?"

"Yes. I'm sure of it. In the first place, Vesta was my best friend. I l-loved her as much as if she'd been my sister. And I happen to know that she had a deathly fear of electric heaters in her bathroom. She would never allow one near her when she was bathing. Yet she was killed by an electric heater falling into her tub. That doesn't make sense, Mr. Turner. You know it doesn't!"

I said: "Okay. For the sake of argument, it doesn't make sense. So what?"

"So this: It's my firm belief that Maenzer deliberately knocked that electric heater into Vesta's bath! He murdered her—just as he murdered Barry Barkis tonight and then tried to blame it on me!"

"Why should Maenzer murder Barkis? That doesn't add up right," I said. "Barkis was giving Maenzer a chance to come back. Maenzer wouldn't bump the guy who was helping him get back on his feet. That's screwy!"

"No, it isn't screwy. Not when you know all the details. You see—Barry and Vesta had been . . . lovers. . . ."

"You mean Barkis was playing around with Maenzer's wife before she was killed?"

"Yes."

"And you think Maenzer found it out, croaked her, and then waited for a chance to kill Barkis too?"

"Y-yes. That's what I think."

I SHOOK my head. "Nix, sister. Maenzer's scared by that phantom picture of his wife that keeps bobbing up in his movie rushes. But he doesn't act like a killer. And he wouldn't have phoned to me to go to his house if he'd been expecting to bump Barkis almost in front of my eyes." I took her wrists. "Carlotta," I said, "you've been feeding me a lot of hooey to steer suspicion away from yourself. You're the one that shot Barkis!"

"No—no!" she wailed. "Take a look at the revolver you took away from me. You'll find only two shots fired out of it. One was the shot I tried to put through your windshield. The second is the bullet I fired at you when you were in Maenzer's den, just after he'd finished running that reel of film through his projector."

I said: "Oh! So you admit firing those two shots, do you?"

"Y-yes. I w-wanted to scare you away. I didn't

75

want you to take Maenzer's case."

"Why not?"

"Because that phantom picture of Vesta on Maen-zer's rushes . . . it's part of a plan that Barry and I cooked up. We were trying to frighten Maenzer into confessing that he killed Vesta. Maenzer's a spiritual-istic believer. We thought we'd be able to make him think Vesta was coming back to haunt him. N-now do you understand?"

Something clicked inside my bean. I said: "Yeah. I'm beginning to understand plenty. And I want you to go home to your apartment right now. Don't leave until I phone you. I'll lend you a topcoat to cover yourself. Take a taxi—and get going right now."

She gave me a funny look. "Wh-what do you plan to do?"

"Trap a killer!" I said. "Now get the hell out."

THE minute she'd gone, I grabbed my phone and dialed police headquarters. I caught my friend, Dave Donaldson of the homicide squad, before he left for the night. "Get up here to my joint right away!" I told him. "I'm going to have a job for you!"

It took him less than fifteen minutes to meet me outside the entrance of my apartment building. I piled into his official sedan and said: "Drive out to Maenzer's house in Beverly—and don't spare the mules!"

"Adolf Maenzer?" Donaldson roared at me. "Say, what the hell are you—a fortune teller or something? We just got a call from Maenzer's place about forty minutes ago. He said a guy named Barkis had been shot at his front door. I've got men out there now, cleaning up and asking questions. How in God's name did you know about it?"

I said: "I was there when Barkis was shot. Now fold up your face and pay attention to your driving."

It didn't take Dave long to get us to Beverly Hills. He braked to a stop in front of Maenzer's house, and we threaded our way past a lot of other official-looking cars until we gained the front door. I rang the bell.

The door opened. I saw Mrs. Hasdorf, the wrinkled little old housekeeper. I said: "We want to see Mr. Maenzer, please."

"Ja," she nodded at me. She led us into the downstairs study, where Maenzer was facing a battery of newspaper reporters.

Maenzer spotted me and drew a sighing sob. "Turner—*Gott sei dank!"* he whispered. "I need your help more than ever. . .!"

I said: "Yeah. But before anything else, I want to go upstairs and take another look at the window that girl climbed out of." To Donaldson I said: "Wait here for me, Dave."

I legged it up to the second floor. But I didn't go near the open window where Carlotta Cordova had climbed down the trellis. Instead, I snapped on my flashlight and found a closet. I looked inside; saw what I'd hoped to find—a tin trunk with wooden slats. I pried it open, started rummaging around. Just as I finished with the photograph album I'd suspected of being here—

Blooie! Something bounced down on the back of my skull with the force of a trip-hammer. I pitched forward, buried my schnozzle in the trunk. I wasn't out for more than three or four seconds; but when I got back on my feet, the photograph album was gone and there was nobody in the room with me.

I STAGGERED back into the upper hallway—and saw Maenzer standing at the head of the stairs with an odd look on his pan. "I was beginning to worry about you, Turner," he said.

I said: "I'm okay. Come on down-stairs." We went down together, and I buttonholed Donaldson. I said: "Dave, I think I've got your case solved for you. The person who bumped Barkis tonight is the same person who murdered Vesta Delorme a few months ago!"

Donaldson said: "But Vesta's death was an accident!"

"No. It was murder. The killer tossed a connected electric heater into Vesta's tub while she was bathing."

Maenzer was white. "But—but who—"

78

I looked him square in the eye and said: "I don't know for sure. But in thirty minutes I'll tell you the murderer's name—just as soon as I've had a chance to ask Carlotta Cordova one question!" Then I turned to Donaldson. "Come on, Dave. I want you to take me downtown to pick up a certain bit of evidence; then we'll get the Cordova cutie!"

Dave and I leaped out of the house; scrambled into his official car. We headed in Wilshire, hell-for-leather. Two blocks beyond LaBrea I said: "Okay, Dave—slow down. Here's the Gaylaird Hotel where Carlotta lives."

"But you said you wanted to go downtown first to pick up a certain bit of evidence."

"That was a stall. Come along." I led him into the Gaylaird, and we went up to the penthouse on the roof of the left turret, where Carlotta had her sumptuous quarters. I rang the bell, and a Chink maid opened the door. I shoved my automatic into the slant-eyed baby's face and said: "Don't make a sound or you'll be shaking hands with Confucius!"

The maid went pale under her yellow skin. I backed her into a corner and said: "Where's Miss Cordova?"

"In—bed, sir."

I turned to Donaldson. "Guard Miss Asia, here, while I go boudoir-delving." Then I made a bee-line for the rear of the apartment. I saw a door and opened it. I smelled expensive perfume; and in the room's dim light I saw Carlotta lying in bed, sleeping. One shoulder-strap of her pajama was down half way to her elbow, baring most of a delicious little breast. But I didn't have any time for such things. I saw a French window being slowly opened on the other side of the room; an automatic's muzzle poked in and aimed at the Cordova cutie's heart—

I JUMPED; landed square on top of Carlotta, knocked her out of bed. I went rolling over the floor after her just as that gun in the window went *"Chow-chow!"* Then I was on my feet. I smashed myself at the window, landed outside on the turret-roof terrace. I saw a running figure. I smashed into it.

"Gott verdammte!" my captive yelled in an insane whimper. Donaldson came charging toward me, flashing his heavy-duty electric torch. He sprayed light on my prisoner's face. He said: "God in heaven—it's Mrs. Hasdorf! Maenzer's housekeeper!"

I said: "Not just his housekeeper. *His mother, too!*"

The little, wrinkled old woman squirmed under me. *"Ja! His mutter!* He vas ashamed of me because I vas Cherman—because I could not goot English speak. But how did you guess?"

I said: "I found it out when I looked through your trunk in that upstairs room of Maenzer's house. From the way you'd acted, I had an idea you were more than just a housekeeper. You were too interested in Maenzer; no servant would take such good care of him. I went through your trunk, found an old photograph album. I saw pictures of you as a young woman, holding a baby in your arms. And other pictures of that baby as it grew to boyhood, manhood.

"The child was Adolph Maenzer. And there was one photograph of you yourself—autographed 'To my son, Adolf.' That was the tip-off. But just as I found the picture, you sneaked in behind me and biffed me on the head."

"You—you suspected me?" the old lady gasped.

I said: "Sure. I had most of the details figured out; but I had to trap you to prove my case. I realized that your son had been pretty much of a rat. He abused his wife, Vesta Delorme. And he forced you, his mother, to the status of a servant. You allowed that; but Vesta kicked over the traces. She took a lover—Barry Barkis—to get even.

"Then you discovered that Vesta was playing around. Being still loyal to your son, you killed his unfaithful wife by dropping a hooked-up electric heater into her tub while she was taking a bath. That's the truth, isn't it, Mrs. Hasdorf?"

The old lady said: "*Ja. Und* I vould do it again—!"

I set fire to a gasper and said: "Well, you got away with it for a while. The coroner called Vesta's death accidental, and you thought you were safe. But meanwhile, things began to happen. Carlotta, who had been Vesta's friend, got the idea that your son had murdered Vesta. So Carlotta cooked up the double-exposure scheme on your son's movie 'rushes'—made it appear as if Vesta's ghost was haunting the film. She did it with an old Vesta Delorme reel. And your son, being innocent, called me in to break the 'haunt.'

"Then, tonight, Barry Barkis showed up at your son's house. You recognized him as the man who had been Vesta's lover. So you shot him with the very gun you've got in your hand now!"

"*Ja*. He had despoiled my son's home. I killed him the virst chance I got!"

I nodded. "That's the way I figured it. But I had to pin it on you. So in your hearing I mentioned Carlotta as the key to the mystery. That made you scared of Carlotta. You realized she must be the one who was wrecking your son's movie; and you thought maybe she might spill something to incriminate you. Not knowing how much she knew, you determined to come here and kill her to keep her from talking. Isn't that right?"

"*Ja*. But you said you vas going downtown virst. I thought I vould have time—"

I said: "Sure. That's what I intended for you to think. You did as I expected—and now you'll spend the rest of your life in jail . . . unless they decide to hang you."

"*Nein!*" she screamed. Then, suddenly, she squirmed out of my grasp, ran to the parapet. Before I could stop her, she leaped far out into space; went hurtling downward. I heard her scream—just once. After that there was nothing but silence.

Dave Donaldson turned away. He coughed in his throat. I felt a little funny myself. I went back into Carlotta's boudoir—and after Donaldson left, I stayed around a while with Carlotta to get my mind off what had happened.

Carlotta managed to make me forget, after a while.

VEILED LADY

One of the biggest stars in Hollywood had been missing for two months. Now she turns up in Dan Turner's office willing to pay anything for vengeance against her kidnaper

I T WAS late in the afternoon. I was sitting behind my desk. My office door opened. A shapely wren ankled in. She was wearing a form-fitting topcoat and a heavy black veil.

She had a figure worth three fortunes. Her stems belonged behind footlights. The topcoat didn't disguise the lilt of her hips or the firm thrust of her breast. I couldn't see her face on account of the veil. She said: "Are you Dan Turner, the private detective?"

I said: "Yeah." Then I kicked my chair out from under me. I sailed around the corner of my desk. I took a flying leap at the veiled cutie.

I had plenty of reason for the move. She was carrying an oversized handbag. It was open. She had one tiny fist inside it. To me, that spelled trouble.

I barged into her with one hell of a thump. My arms went around hers, clamping them tight to her ribs. Her firm form flattened tinder the sudden impact of my chest. She staggered backward, slammed hard against the far wall. She let out a muffled yip.

I snatched her handbag. Just as I'd figured, there was a roscoe in it; a deadly little pearl-handled peashooter. I shoved the rod into my coat pocket. I said: "Pardon my rough exterior, baby. Dames with gats

make me jittery. Plant yourself in that chair and tell me why you wanted to puncture my peritoneum. What did I ever do to you?"

She sat down. She was shaking like a dog coughing beef-seeds. She said: "I w-wasn't going to k-kill you, Mr. Turner."

I said: "Sure not. You just wanted to feed me a sample of breakfast-food. The kind shot from guns."

"N-no. . .!" she whispered through the veil. "I—I carry that pistol for self-protection. . ." She acted plenty scared. Her tone sounded on the level.

I'm a fair judge of character. I've got to be, in my game. A hunch told me she wasn't lying. I said: "You mean you think somebody's got the finger on you?"

She nodded. "Y-yes. And I—I need your help, Mr. Turner. Desperately! I . . . I'm Carol Calvin."

I yelled: *"Carol Calvin!"* and leaped toward her. I felt as if a mule had kicked me in the kisser. Because Carol Calvin was one of Hollywood's biggest she-stars. She was Altamount's entry in the platinum-blonde sweepstakes. And for the past two months she'd been missing!

MY THINK-TANK raced over what I knew about the case. She had vanished from her Beverly Hills mansion about eight weeks ago. Nobody had seen her since. Of course the papers had slopped over with headlines about her disappearance. It had been a sensation.

Ike Brantham, head mogul-in-chief of Alta-mount, had practically gone screw-house over the mystery. Carol's vanishing act had occurred spang in the middle of her latest starring opus. It had cost Brantham close to half a million smells to shelve the production. Moreover, there was a rumor that he was goofy over her. Anyway, he had offered a re-ward of ten grand for her safe return.

And here she was in my office: ten thousand clams' worth of gorgeousness on the hoof.

I set fire to a gasper; took a deep drag to cover my surprise. I said: "Jeest, baby, you gave me a turn. Most everybody figured you must be dead."

"I am," she whispered. She let out a dry, choked

sob. She lifted her heavy veil.

I felt my innards turning a somersault. I almost strangled. The blonde frill's face was downright sickening. It gave me the drizzling meenies when I took a gander at her.

She'd been carved to hellangone. There were knife-scars on her cheeks, from temples to chin. Her nose had been slit down the middle. Her lips were sliced into a perpetual grin. The wounds had healed into livid scar-tissue.

I damned near swallowed my cigarette. I said: "Good God Almighty!"

She lowered the veil again. I was glad she did. She said: "Now you understand why I say I'm dead. I'm a . . . a living corpse. . ."

It was a worse shock than if I'd found her murdered carcass somewhere. I gulped when I remembered how lovely she'd been on the screen. I said: "Who the hell did that to you? Have you been to the cops?"

"No," she said. "I—I don't know who knifed me. And I haven't been to the police. That would mean publicity. And I don't want anyone to know I'm still alive. Not yet. Not until I find the person that kidnaped me and . . . cut me. . ."

I said: "I get it. You think the bird might be warned; might lam. Huh?"

She nodded. She opened her topcoat. She was wearing a simple linen frock. It was cut plenty low at the neck. She unbuttoned it. I could see the swell of her white breasts. She didn't seem to mind, though. She probably figured she didn't have much sex-appeal with a face like hers. But she was wrong. I got a hell of a wallop out of putting the focus on her.

She unfastened a roll of greenbacks pinned inside the frock. She peeled off five centuries; handed them to me. She said: "I want you to find the man who . . . killed me. Here's an advance retainer."

Her voice had a flat, deadly ring. Vengeful. I caught wise. I said: "Now look. kiddo. That won't work. You can't take justice into your own hands. I know you want revenge. I don't blame you a damned bit. I'd like to find the punk that did this to you, and slice myself a piece of his neck. But it's illegal. If you think I'm going to help you locate the buzzard, so you can bump him—"

She said: "No. I promise not to do anything rash. I'll let the law take its course when the time comes."

I believed her. I had a hunch she was leveling with me. I took the geetus she offered me. I said: "Okay, sweetheart. I'll play ball. Maybe you'd better tell me as much as you know. I'll need something to start on. Have you got any enemies?"

"N-no," she whispered. "And there isn't much else to tell. The night I was kidnaped, I was going to attend a sneak preview over in Pasadena. Naturally, I thought it was my regular chauffeur who was driving my limousine when I started out. But when he turned off into a back road, I caught a glimpse of his face. He was m-masked."

I lit another gasper. "Yeah. Go on."

"I got frightened. I tried to jump out of the car.

But the doors wouldn't open. The handles were jammed, inside. And I couldn't lower the shatter-proof windows; couldn't break them. The tonneau was filling with some kind of gas. Maybe chloroform or ether. I . . . lost consciousness. . ."

"Then what?"

"I WOKE up with sand all around me. It was late at night. I c-couldn't seem to remember anything. My brain was fuzzy; I didn't even know my own name. My face was b-bleeding. I realized I was out in the desert somewhere. I managed to stagger along a crooked trail until I found a shack near the mouth of a hillside gold mine. The miner took me in. He was an old man—a desert rat. He saved my life. Nursed me back to health. It was j-just two days ago that I recovered my memory. I found out I was a little way out from Twenty-Nine Palms. I caught a stage; came back to Hollywood. I still had my diamond rings. I pawned them for ready cash; bought a revolver for p-protection. . ."

All of a sudden her voice rose to a hysterical wail. She shrilled: "Oh, God! When I look at my face in the mirror, I wish that old man had let me . . . die!" She seemed to go stark batty. She spotted my open window; made a lunge at it.

I caught her just as she was straddling the sill. Her skirt rode up past her garters. She had damned nifty stems. Her thighs were smooth and creamy. Barring her scarred map under the black veil, she was plenty soothing on the optics.

I yanked her back into the office. I pinioned her in my arms. I said: "What the hell are you trying to do?"

"K-kill myself!" she moaned weakly. She tried to get away from me. "I'm no use to anybody. . .!"

Her topocat was open. Her dress was still unbuttoned, where she'd reached for her bankroll. Her taut skin was whiter than milk, softer than satin. Tiny blue veins showed through.

I decided to combine life-saving with pleasure. I said: "Don't be a damned sap, sweetheart. Who cares about a few scars on your face? You've still got everything." Then I kissed the hollow of her throat.

She stiffened; moaned a little. She wasn't expecting that kind of a play, apparently. I guess she must have thought no man would ever take a second squint at her again. But what the hell! As long as she wore her veil, she could park her chewing-gum in my cuspittoon seven days a week. I started caressing her snowy shoulders, where her frock had slipped down over her arms. . .

I smeared kisses all over her throat and shoulders.

It worked. It restored a hell of a lot of self-confidence. She wrapped her arms around me with soft, thrilling gratitude. I got plenty of belt out of the way she squeezed herself against me. Her body was damned beautiful.

Presently I said: "There, now. You see, sweet stuff? You've still got what it takes to drive a guy uts-nay. And a plastic surgeon can fix your scars. We'll put the nab on the louse that messed you up. We'll toss his jodhpurs into a cell. And after a bit of surgery you'll be on top of the heap again."

"You—you mean you'll really h-help me, Dan. . .?"

I said: "Yeah, if you promise not to try any more wild west gunnery stuff."

"I p-promise."

I took her downstairs to my jalopy. I drove her to my apartment, made her comfortable there. I said: "You stick here until I get back. I'm going skunk-hunting."

I left her.

I WHEELED my wreck over to the Altamount lot without wasting any time. There were some things I wanted to find out. I flashed my tin at the gate-keeper. He let me through. I headed for the executive office-building where Ike Brantham hung out.

Brantham was a typical movie biggie. He was hard to reach. In his outer office a pert little red-haired secretary gave me the up-and-down and the back-and-forth. She was a cute little dish with curve-some thems and thoses. She said: "Did you wish to see someone, sir?"

"Yeah. Mr. Brantham."

She said: "Sorry, sir. He's in conference."

I took another squint at her. Somehow I seemed to remember her face. Then I tabbed her. I said: "You're Mary Ogilvie, aren't you?"

"Wh-why, yes, sir," she tipped her eyebrows a notch. "How did you know?"

"They ran your picture in the papers when Carol Calvin disappeared. You used to be her room-mate when she was an extra-girl; before she got to be a star. Right?"

"Th-that's right," she seemed startled. "You've got a good memory."

I said: "Yeah. I need one. I'm Dan Turner, private snoop."

She turned a shade paler. "Oh-h-h—"

I reached down and patted her. I said: "Now maybe you'll let me into the Shrine of Shrines. I want to see Mr. Brantham about Miss Calvin. I've got news for him."

She drew a sharp breath. It struck me she was fighting down some inner excitement. She won the battle, too. She pulled away when I tried to pat her again. She gave me the frigid focus. "Mr. Brantham is in conference. He cannot be disturbed," she chilled me.

Just then an inner door opened. A guy barged out. I knew him. He was a friend of mine. He was Steve Fillene, publicity chief for Altamount. He spotted me and said: "Hi, Sherlock. How's tricks?"

I said: "Swell. Is His Majesty in there? I've got to talk to him."

"Brantham? No. He just went out the back way. Said he was going over to Sound Stage Four to look over a new set. What's up?"

I took his arm. "Lead me to said sound stage," I said. "I want to find out a few things about Carol Calvin."

"What about Carol? You figuring on having a smack at that reward dough?" We were strolling across the lot, threading our way past assorted Indians, cowboys and cuties in heavy ochre make-up. I said: "Yeah. But I've got to get something to start on. Maybe you can help me. Who hated Carol's guts here in Hollywood? Did she have any enemies?"

Steve shrugged. "No. She was the sweetest wren that ever made faces for the galloping screamies.

Why? You think maybe some enemy cooled her off?"

"It's possible," I told him. "Listen. Was there any truth to the rumor that she was Ike Brantham's lady-

love?"

He said: "Nix. That was just a lot of balokum. Ike's wife is jealous as hell. She started all that gossip. But she was fishing in the wrong pond."

"All the same," I said, "Ike was pretty friendly with Carol, wasn't he? He knew a lot about her private life?"

"Oh, sure. He discovered her, you know. Befriended her, made a star out of her. But that's as far as it ever got. Say—you're not hinting that Ike's wife—"

I said: "You never can tell." I walked away from him; ankled into the huge sound stage building.

OVER at the far end, there was a gigantic set. It represented a waterfront scene. It was built up around the edge of a studio tank—a big deep pool of water with practical-prop boats tied up at the docks. In the background there were a mess of houses and storefronts. A couple of cameras were placed at angles; microphone-booms dangled from several overhead spots, with wires leading up to the main soundbooth far above the set proper. None of the lights were on; nobody was working on the stage just then.

I tabbed a short, stoutish little guy who was taking a gander at things. It was Ike Brantham. He had a sensitive pan—almost womanish. His eyes were kindly. He had the hands of an artist. That's what he was; an artist in celluloid. And a millionaire to boot.

I strolled over to him. I said: "Can you spare a minute or two, Ike?"

"Why—hello, Turner. Yes. What's on your mind?"

I focused my glims on him; tried to bore holes into his brain. "Who hated Carol Calvin?" I barked.

He went a little pale. "H—hated her? Good God—

what are you getting at?"

"I'm getting at that ten grand reward," I said. "I know where Carol is."

For a minute I thought he was going to faint. He clutched my arm to keep himself from taking a fall into the tank. "God—!" You say you—you know where she is? Tell me! Quick, Turner! Is she—is she—alive?"

I said: "Yeah. Plenty. But messed up."

"M-messed up?"

"Her pan," I said. "All carved to hell, Somebody worked her over with a shiv. And I aim to find out who did it."

Sweat broke out on his forehead. "This—this is horrible, Turner! I've got to see Carol. Right away."

I said: "Nix. Not yet. And I don't want you popping off to the newspapers, either. She's staying under cover until I find the rat that used a scalpel on her. Now come through, Ike. I've laid my cards on the table. You do the same. Tell me who might have hated Carol enough to slice her."

His eyes darted all around the set, like a ferret's. "No!" he whispered. "There's nobody in Hollywood who'd . . . do a thing like that. Unless some maniac—"

I said: "Level with me, Ike. Were you and Carol ever . . . you know what I mean. The usual Hollywood stuff."

He shook his head viciously. "It's a lie! I never so much as kissed her! Not even once!" He looked at me. "Not that I didn't try. I did—lots of times. But she's a straight kid. Plenty of lugs will swear to that. Every bozo in pictures made passes at her, one time or another. They didn't get to first base. None of them."

HE ACTED as if he might be trying to cover something—or somebody. I didn't go for his furtive manner. I decided to take a wild shot in the dark. I grabbed his shoulders. I shook hell out of him. His teeth rattled like dice. I said: "Yeah. That's the answer. You didn't get to first base with her. So you carved her face. You fixed her looks so nobody else would ever fall for her."

"You damned fool!" he panted. "You think I'd toss away all the money she meant to me? You think I'd ruin the picture she was working in?"

I said: "Yeah. That's exactly what I think. Jealousy does funny things to a guy."

He darted a hand into his pants pocket. He came up with a pen-knife. It had a release-gadget with a spring inside. He flicked the button. The blade opened automatically. He took a swipe at my throat.

The knife grazed my cheek, drew blood. I grunted: "Damn you to hell—!" and bashed the thing out of his mitt. It sailed over into the tank, splashed in the water. Then I doubled my right duke, took a poke at his beezer.

He was fast. He ducked me. Then he went running hell-for-leather toward the entrance. He was yelling: "Police! Help! Grab that man—get him!"

I started after him. And then a harsh feminine voice said: "Wait a minute, Mister Big."

I pivoted.

A brunette, stately bimbo was undulating her shape toward me. She was pretty in a hard, mature way. Her hips were voluptuous. Her breasts were likewise, only more so. Her dress was too damned tight. It showed more than was necessary.

I said: "Who the hell are you, sister?"

"I'm Mrs. Ike Brantham," she said.

That almost floored me. I stared at her.

She said: "I was over behind that back-drop while you were talking to my husband about Miss Calvin. I heard everything you both said. And I've got something to tell you. I want you to meet me at the Gay-boy Hotel in thirty minutes. Room Seven-Fifteen." She turned, stalked off.

I blinked. What the hell did she have on her mind? I determined to find out. I made for the exit.

I saw a red-haired jane standing just outside. It was Ike Brantham's secretary, Mary Ogilvie—Carol Calvin's former room-mate. She looked all worked up. "Mr. Turner—" she called.

"Yeah?" I started for her. But just then somebody came whistling down the steep steps from a crucible high over-head. It was my friend Steve Fillene, the publicity pounder-outer.

He hailed me. "What the hell's the trouble, Turner? I thought I heard Brantham yelling his lungs out for a cop. What did you do, sock him?"

I said: "Don't be silly. See you later." I left him standing there; turned back to the Ogilvie skirt. But she was gone. She must have taken a powder when she saw Fillene coming. Apparently she'd had something to say to me—but didn't want anybody else to give a listen.

I found my coupe, drove off the lot. I headed back to my own stash; walked in. Carol Calvin was looking out a window, puffing a pill. She crushed it out, lowered her veil before she turned to me.

"D-did you find out anything?"

I said: "I think so." I poured two stiff snorts of Vat 69, handed her one. We drank. I said: "Tell me something, kiddo. Were you ever Ike Brantham's sweetie?"

"No!"

"But his wife suspected it, didn't she?"

"Y-yes. She accused me. . ."

I said: "Okay. I think I've got a lead. When I talked with Ike just now, he acted as if he was trying to front for somebody. I'm guessing he was covering up for his frau."

"You—you mean Mrs. Brantham—"

"It shapes up that way. She was crazy jealous of you. She thought you were swiping her hubby. So maybe she kidnaped you and altered your puss so you wouldn't be so damned pretty."

"B-but . . . but how can you make sure?" she whispered. Her eyes glittered queerly under the veil.

I said: "I'm meeting the lady at the Gayboy Hotel in a few minutes. Room Seven-Fifteen. She asked for it. And I'll get the truth out of her if I have to squeeze her into a pretzel."

The Calvin cutie clung to me. "You won't let her c-come here and . . . hurt me . . . again?"

"Sure not," I said. I started to go out.

JUST then my phone jingled. Carol was standing near it. Her reaction was automatic. She answered it. She lifted the receiver and said: "Hello?" I yanked the instrument away from her; covered the mouthpiece with my mitt. I whispered: "You idiot— suppose somebody recognized your voice? You want to let the cat out of the bag?"

She paled; backed away. "I—I forgot—"

I uncovered the phone and said: "Turner talking. Give out."

"This is Mary Ogilvie, Mr. Turner. Remember? I'm Ike Brantham's secretary."

I said: "Oh, yes. What's on your chest, baby?"

"I've got something important to tell you. It's about Carol Calvin. I started to tell you back on the lot, but Steve Fillene came along. So I slipped away."

"Okay. Spill."

She said: "I used to room with Carol in the old

days, you know. And I just happened to remember that Fillene was crazy about Carol; used to call on her, take her out to supper a lot. She more or less gave him up after she got to be a star."

"Was he sore?"

"N-no. He took it gracefully enough. But—"

I said: "Thanks, cutie. It might be a lead, at that. I'll let you know." I rang off. I didn't put much stock in what the red-haired nifty had just told me. It didn't fit in; didn't add up right. I dismissed it; tossed a kiss at Carol Calvin.

I went out.

IT WAS dusk by that time. I drove over to the Gayboy, on Wilshire. I took a cage to the seventh; ankled down the corridor to Room 715. I rapped. Then I fastened my lunch-hooks on the .38 automatic I always carry in a shoulder-holster. If this was a trap, I didn't intend to be the cheese.

The door opened. Mrs. Brantham let me in. She was wearing a thin negligee. I could almost see through it.

I wondered about that. Hifalutin' married dames don't parade their attributes before strangers unless they've got a purpose. Mrs. Brantham had a purpose. I could see that from the way she was giving me a load of the old come-on stuff. The ivory smoothness of her flesh was inviting, and the sinuous sway of her hips was a direct challenge.

I closed the door. I said: "What kind of a deal are you after, lady?"

"Deal?" She handed me part of a smile. Her lips were red, pouting.

I nodded. I fished out a pill, lit up. I said: "Yeah. It's transparent as that thing you've got on. You're pretty nice, too. I might be interested—if I knew what you had in mind."

She laughed. It was deep, throaty; had fur on it, like a pussy-cat's purr. She glided toward me; took the fag out of my kisser. She inhaled a drag. "So you think you might be interested?" She whispered. Her dark eyes flashed.

I said: "Hell—I'm not made of ice." I ran my eyes over her contours.

She backed away. "Well. . . will you promise me something?"

"Promise you what?"

"To lay off the Carol Calvin case."

I'd been looking for some such crack. I swept her into my arms, smeared a kiss over her parted lips. I said: "We'll talk about that later, beautiful."

She ran her long fingers through my hair; hugged herself against me. Her lips were moist, sultry. She knew what to do with her mouth when she kissed. I could feel her breasts on my chest. Her whole body quivered.

I had just enough breath left to tell that she was wearing some imported perfume that must have cost a thousand seeds per drop. It was potent stuff. It seeped into my blood, charged my batteries. The thin silk of her negligee added lure to the sleekness of her flesh. . .

AFTER a while I said: "Tell me something, honey. Why do you want me to lay off the Carol Calvin matter?"

She sighed. "Because I can't have Ike worried. He's innocent; he never harmed that girl. And neither did I."

I stared down at her. "So you know I suspect you?"

"Of course. It's obvious. You tried to frighten Ike into implicating me, a while ago. And he did his best to cover up for me. Because he probably suspects me, too. But I didn't do anything to Carol Calvin. I'm telling you the truth, Dan."

I didn't believe her. She was a cat to the core. And cats are treacherous. I said: "Okay. If you didn't carve Carol, and your old man didn't, then who did?"

She laughed in my teeth. "Wouldn't you like to know?"

I started to pop her. I hadn't been able to get anything out of her with butter; so maybe a little rough stuff might work. I doubled my fist, aimed it at her jaw—

From behind me, a roscoe belched: *"Chow-chow!"*

The reports yammered from the open transom above the door. A pair of slugs buzzed past my left ear, almost nicked my cranium. Mrs. Brantham sagged back against the pillows of the lounge.

I said: "What the hell—!" and stumbled to my pins. I bashed myself at the door, twisted the knob. It wouldn't give. I hauled off four paces, hit the panels with every ounce of my two hundred pounds. The woodwork splintered. I sailed out into the corridor.

Some sharp apple had propped a chair against the door from the outside. That's what had delayed me. And now the gun-toter was gone. There wasn't a trace of anybody in the hallway. Not until a lot of other rooms opened up and people started spilling out to see what all the commotion was about. Then there was a hell of a mess.

I flashed my badge at a goof with grey whiskers. I said: "There's been a shooting. Call headquarters— quick, for Cripes' sake!" Then I hurtled back into 715, took a swift look at Mrs. Brantham.

The two slugs had drilled neat tunnels through her left breast. She was as dead as an iced catfish.

I put my brains into high gear. Who the hell had done it? Obviously it was some lug who knew she was in that room, talking to me. . .

But who knew of our date? I hadn't told anybody except Carol Calvin—

I said: "Goddlemighty!" and bashed myself out of

the room. I knocked down two bell-hops and a chambermaid; didn't wait to apologize. I plummeted into an elevator, shoved the operator aside. I jammed the control hard over; shot downstairs so fast my belly came up and squeezed cider out of my Adam's-apple.

MY COUPE was at the curb. I bounced into it, kicked hell out of the starter. I stripped three teeth off first gear, roared out into traffic.

Just as I reached the next intersection, a black sedan blocked me. It had: "L. A. P. D." lettered on the side. I slapped down on my brakes. Too late. My radiator whoosed into the police car. Metal and glass tinkled a tune of fifty bucks' worth of repair work.

I leaped out of my leaking Lena. The copper-jalopy was just dented; not badly damaged. A beefy guy in plain clothes started cutting up profane touches about my ancestry. I recognized the voice before I gandered his map. It was my friend Dave Donaldson of the homicide squad.

I said: "Hey—Dave!"

"Nuts to you, Turner!" he yelped. "I'm out on a murder beef. Just caught a flash over my radio. Out of my way, numbskull!"

I raced around his heap, piled in alongside him. I said: "Yeah. Bumpoff beef. I'm in it up to my left ventricle. Aim this can for my stash—and go like hell!"

He stared at me as he clashed his gears. He said: "What—who—"

"The missing Carol Calvin's in my flat!" I rapped at him. "Her mug is all carved up. I told her I thought Ike Brantham's wife did it. And now Mrs. Brantham is a corpse. For God's sake step on the juice!"

He did. He whammed past three stop-lights; sent drizzling jitters up fifty motorists' necks. That official sedan put skidmarks a block long in front of my apartment building. Dave and I were on the sidewalk before the car came to a full stop. We steamed inside, pelted up the stairs to the third floor.

The door of my stash was open. I heard a dame scream: "No—oh, God—*no!*"

I added speed; hauled out my equalizer. I bounced over the threshold.

CAROL CALVIN was crouched in a corner. Somebody had a roscoe jammed against her left temple; somebody with red hair and a green dress—

I fired from the hip; sent a chunk of lead through the murderer's gun-wrist. I said: *"Okay, Steve Fillene!* This is one time you'll crash the front pages—but it won't be a publicity gag!" I smacked into him, knocked him sprawling. I yanked off his red wig.

He frothed at the kisser. "Damn you—I thought I croaked—"

I said: "Yeah. You thought you plugged me when

you shot Mrs. Brantham at the Gayboy. But you missed me—which was just too bad for you. Because it gave me the tip-off that you were the louse I was looking for."

Dave Donaldson rasped: "What the hell is this?"

I said: "Fillene is the killer. *He was the only one who knew about my appointment with Mrs. Brantham*—except Miss Calvin here."

The publicity guy groaned and squirmed, nursing his shattered wrist. I looked down at him. "You were in love with Carol. I learned that from Mary Ogilvie, her former room-mate. Carol ditched you. You were crazy jealous. So you snatched her, drove her to the desert, sliced her face. You left her for dead. If you couldn't have her, you didn't want anybody else to make the grade with her.

"But she didn't die. She came back to Hollywood today; hired me to put the arm on the lug who'd carved her. And when I showed up at the Altamount lot, you got jittery. When I went on that sound stage to talk with Ike Brantham, *you sneaked up to the re-cording-booth* above the set. I saw you coming down from there, later. Up in that booth, you opened all the microphones on the set.

"Through the earphones, you heard what I said to Brantham. You found out Carol was still alive. You got scared. You knew you had to do something to clear your skirts.

"Then you heard Mrs. Brantham making that hotel date with me. You thought fast. You disguised yourself with a red wig and a dame's dress— probably to toss suspicion at Mary Ogilvie in case you were seen. Because you knew the Ogilvie wren had tried to tell me something as I left the sound stage building.

"Disguised, you went to the Gayboy; drilled Ike's wife from the transom. You tried to plug me, too.

"You took a powder; came straight here to my joint. You figured I probably had Carol Calvin hiding here—and you were right. You planned to bump her; maybe leave a fake confession note on her

corpse and the pistol in her mitt." As I talked, I frisked his pockets.

SURE enough I found a scrawled scrap of paper—

"To the Police:
I killed Mrs. Brantham to get even with her for the way she mutilated me. Now I'm taking the easiest way out.

Carol Calvin."

Fillene sagged when I found that forged note. He rasped: "I had to croak the Brantham dame. She got me fried one night; fed me enough kisses to make me admit what I'd done to Carol. She'd have tossed me to the wolves to save her old man. . ."

I turned to Donaldson. "Take this louse away, Dave. He stinks up my apartment."

After Dave had hauled Fillene downstairs I grinned at the platinum blonde sweetie. I said: "Well, that's that. Are you going to let me visit you once in a while, after a plastic sawbones mends your puss?"

She nodded; pressed herself against me. . .

She came through the operation in swell shape. She's prettier than ever, now. Occasionally I drop in to see her on rainy evenings.

DEATH'S PASSPORT

AT first I thought I must have sponged up too much Vat 69 at Abe Pilwyn's pre-wedding party before staggering home that midnight. At least I'd never gandered any spooks when I was sober. But I was certainly seeing one now.

I stepped back from my threshold and bleated: "Okay. I'll sign the pledge. I'll never touch another drop if you promise you won't turn into a pink elephant."

The guy's smile was cadaverous. "I'm not dead, Dan," he said from down near his shoelaces. And he barged into my stash, went to the cellarette, helped himself to a jorum of skee.

Then I realized he was genuine. For one thing, ghosts don't imbibe giggle-juice. Moreover, this bird had been a crony of mine in the old days; knew where I stored my Scotch. And he hadn't forgotten. "Len Kensington!" I whispered.

He downed his dollop. "Yes."

I irrigated my jitters with a nip of the same medicine. It's a hell of a shock to meet a bozo you've considered fish-food the past six months. By rights, Kensington should have been a skeleton festooning Davy Jones' locker instead of pacing my carpet like an underfed lion in a cage.

I could still see him taking off from Glendale Airport on the flight that erased him from this mun-

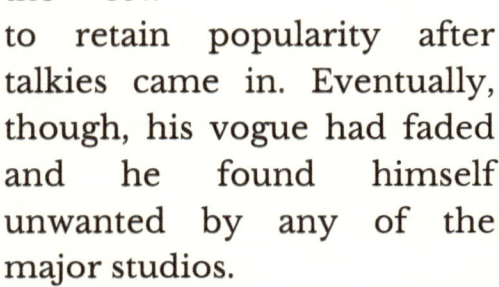

dane slate. He'd been a star since silent days; one of the few to retain popularity after talkies came in. Eventually, though, his vogue had faded and he found himself unwanted by any of the major studios.

That was when Pildex Productions, an independent outfit run by Abe Pilwyn and financed from a distance by an investment broker named Sam Dexter, decided to gamble on him. Casting him as a speed-demon flyer in a quickie aviation opus, they laid plans for the juiciest publicity coup that ever came out of Poverty Row.

IN PRIVATE Kensington held an amateur pilot's license. So Pildex Productions bought a Lockheed monoplane; announced that their star would attempt a non-stop record flight to Honolulu and back. The story hit the headlines simultaneously

with Kensington's takeoff and the quickie's release. It was swell timing; drew customers into the theaters the way a dead horse draws flies.

I'd been present when Len lifted his ship into the swallowing night. I'd watched Lanya, his curvesome brunette wife, blow teary kisses after him as if she never expected to see him again. I'd tabbed Abe Pilwyn, the producer, soothing her by putting his arm around her dainty waist. And that was the end of it.

The end of Len Kensington; but not of his aviation pic. Four days later the newspapers blatted: *"Flyer Missing At Sea" "Star Lost On Pacific Hop!"* It shoved the war news off the front pages—and it shoved audiences into movie houses from hell to Halifax. Everybody wanted a hinge at the hero who'd disappeared while on a genuine flight paralleling the one in his last cinema opus. Morbid curiosity, maybe; but it coined bales of lettuce for Pildex Productions.

It was still reaping copious shekels in the neighborhood dives six months later when Kensington had long since been given up for croaked. Only he wasn't croaked. He was alive, prowling my carpet and swigging my whiskey.

I said: "What the hell happened, Len? Did a boat pick you up? When did you get back?"

"I never left," he muttered grimly.

That didn't make sense. I said: "You must have a screw loose. I saw you take off that night!"

He flushed. "Yes. But you didn't see me land on the coast this side of San Diego an hour later and give my ship to another pilot."

"You mean—?"

"I was yellow," he said. "I was scared to go through with it. So I secretly arranged for a substitute flyer to take my place—a guy whose name I never even knew because he wouldn't tell me. He was down on his luck, glad for a chance to pick up five thousand bucks while I got the glory."

I began to get it. "This anonymous slob was to make the hop, bring the plane back to your hidden spot and turn it over to you?" I asked. "Then you'd have flown into Los Angeles, pretending you'd been at the controls to Honolulu and back?"

Kensington jerked me a nod. "I gave that poor

devil his passport to death, Turner. He didn't make the grade. I can't understand why, because the plane was okay. I went over it myself—"

A hunch nipped me. I said: "Did you have any enemies who might have wanted to bump you? Somebody who might have sabotaged the ship, thinking you were really going to fly it?"

"Impossible!" he shook his head. "Whatever happened was an accident. But that doesn't change things. The guy was lost and I'm responsible. I'll pay as long as I live. God knows I've already paid plenty. Six months of hell; of keeping under cover; hiding because my pride wouldn't let me show myself . . ."

"You haven't told anybody the score?"

"Nobody but you, now. Not even the girl who took me in and gave me a bed because she got a yen for me . . ."

I could understand that. If he revealed his identity he would have been forced to admit his cowardice; compelled to confess he'd sent another pilot in his stead. That would have branded him for life—and no dyed-in-the-wool actor, accustomed to feeding his ego on years of public adulation, could take that kind of rap. It was easy to see why Kensington had preferred to let the world consider him defunct.

"Then why the hell come to me now?" I asked him.

"I'm tired, Dan. Tired of taking charity from this poor little jane who's been looking after me. I'm hungry, not for food but for my wife. You're a friend of mine; a smart private dick. I—I thought you might help me regain what I've lost . . ."

A sudden brainstorm slugged me. I yelped: "Suffering tripes, I've got to move fast!" And I grabbed my hat, lunged at the door.

"Wh-where are you going?"

"Stay here and don't ask questions!" I said. "I'll be back soon—I hope." Then I hurled myself out of the flat. I had less than thirty minutes in which to stop Len Kensington's wife from committing Arizona bigamy with Abe Pilwyn. It was their elopement shindig I'd attended that evening, just before coming home to find Kensington himself haunting my portal.

A SLENDER blonde wren was passing along the corridor as I arrowed out. I smacked into her before I could drag anchor. The impact knocked her upside down. I stumbled over her kicking stems, landed on top of her. She unleashed a gasping moan as my weight flattened her resilient curves.

For an instant I was all tangled up in slim legs and bare thighs and fluttering skirt. The sensation was pleasant enough but I didn't have time to enjoy it. I scrambled upright, pulled her with me, steadied her. When I got a swivel at her startled puss, I recognized her. She was an extra chick around the studios; I'd been on a few parties with her in the old days.

"Vonnie Vale!" I said.

She pushed the mussed golden hair out of her glims, tugged at her girdle, twisted her brassiere back into position beneath the bodice of her frock and gasped: "Hello, D-Dan. You're so impetuous! You ought to carry a Klaxon."

If I'd had more time I might have volunteered to help adjust that brassiere; its plump contents intrigued me. But there were other matters more immediately pressing right then. I said: "Sorry, babe. I'll get in touch with you some rainy evening and make amends. Just now I'm in a hell of a yank." Then I blew her a kiss, hurled my heft downstairs to the basement garage and aimed my jalopy toward Glendale Airport.

A BLUE-PAINTED private monoplane was just trundling off the tarmac as I gained the field in a shower of sparks. An attendant with a badge tried to halt me at the gate and I dished him up a helping of knuckles, sent him skidding on his pistol pockets. I catapulted across the runway, waving my arms and yelling fit to split my adenoids.

The blue plane's motor coughed, died; its wheels locked to a stop. I wrenched the door open and said: "Pardon my rough exterior, folks, but the wedding is off."

In the cabin's rear twin-seat, Abe Pilwyn sat with a fat arm around Lanya Kensington's waist. Up front,

Sam Dexter—the money guy behind Pildex Productions—twisted away from his controls; glued the focus on me. "Turner!" he said. "What on earth—"

I poked a thumb at his partner and Lanya. "They can't get hitched in Yuma tonight. Or any other night. Her husband's still alive."

Lanya's dark lamps widened; her tempting kisser made a startled crimson zero. I could see the sudden

surge of her gorgeous whatchacallems under her fawn jersey frock; they swelled until I thought the material was going to split open—which would have been jake with me. She had a figure that was damned pleasant medicine for the orbs. "Len alive?" she gasped. "Oh-h-h, thank God! Thank God!" It sounded sincere enough.

A wheezing oath of frustration erupted from Pilwyn's pudgy throat. "You're crazy!" he choked. "Kensington's dead! We collected his insurance; I'm marrying Lanya. You can't tell me—"

"But I *am* telling you," I said. And I spilled the story as Len had given it to me.

Pilwyn yeeped: "He can't have Lanya! She's mine!"

"No, Abe," the brunette twist spoke for herself. "Len's the one I love. I was marrying you because I thought he was d-dead . . . and because you'd been good to me. But everything's changed now." She popped out of the plane in a flurry of fawn jersey skirt and a twinkling of silk-smooth legs; grabbed at me. "Where is Len? Take me to him. Please!"

I drew a thrill from her nearness; envied Kensington the kisses he'd garner when the reunion took place. Lanya was a choice morsel in any man's book. "He's at my tepee," I said. "But we've got to dope up a scheme to bring him back to the public without making a heel of him."

SAM DEXTER turned his ship over to a ground crew and we all went to the depot's waiting room. Abe Pilwyn growled: "Who the hell wants him back?"

I said: "You will when I show you how to make a stack of geetus from the publicity." Then I set fire to a gasper, went into details.

We could fake a note in a bottle, I pointed out,

and have somebody pretend to find it. The note would ostensibly give Kensington's position on some south sea island. Pildex Productions could then outfit a rescue yacht, go through the motions of saving their lost star from his Robinson Crusoe jam.

Of course he'd be on the yacht all the time; but the newspapers would go wild when he was brought back to Hollywood. That aviation pic could be reissued; a new quickie made with Len in the leading role. It was a natural.

Sam Dexter thought so, too. So I said: "You go attend to the note in the bottle. Abe can see about chartering a boat. Lanya will go home and I'll bring Len to her so she can hide him out. Okay?"

They chorused okay and lammed. I felt like a boy scout as I went toward my rambling wreck. I'd fixed it for Kensington to resume his career, get his wife back. And I'd probably earned a fat fee for myself in the bargain; Pildex Productions would certainly cut me in for a slice of the cabbage they stood to make. That was an important item; I'm trying to save up a retirement fund before some sharp disciple whittles my name on a bullet.

The future looked so damned rosy I didn't even get sore when that airport gate-guard tried to put the arm on me as I left the field. He was boiling because I'd bopped him; wanted to take me down to the gow on an assault charge. It cost me an argument and a ten-spot to poultice his bruised dignity; but what the hell? I had time to spare and dough in sight.

Presently he subsided, turned me loose. I climbed into my heap and drove home. I opened the door of my stash and called: "It's all set, Len—Good *God!*"

Len Kensington would never need to be rescued from a desert island. He was sprawled on my floor with three .38 slugs in his guts. The slugs had rendered him deader than the 1918 Armistice.

THE APARTMENT was infested with plainclothes cops captained by my friend Dave Donaldson of the homicide squad. Dave piped me entering and yowled: "I've been waiting for you to turn up, dammit! Maybe you can explain what goes on here!"

My elly-bay was doing nip-ups and I had to fight to keep from jettisoning my pancakes. "He's dead!" I whispered.

"You must be psychic," Donaldson sneered.

I said: "Who chilled him?"

"That's what I crave to know!" Dave roared at me. "Your next-door neighbors heard three blasts and saw a blonde frill powering down the stairs. They put in a quick beef to headquarters and this is what I found. You got anything to spill, Sherlock? Such as who this lug was, and what he was doing in your dump, and who had the curse on him?"

I shook my noggin. It took a couple minutes for

Dave's information to seep into my soggy grey matter. Then a hunch sneaked up my leg. I said: "A blonde wren, hunh?" and pivoted to the door; slammed myself out of the apartment.

Donaldson tried to block me but he was too slow on his dogs. I pelted down to the basement, climbed into my bucket and souped the kidneys out of it; bored a hole through the night with my radiator ornament. Pretty soon I parked in front of a bungalow on a side street near Rampart; raced toward the porch.

The cottage was where Vonnie Vale hung out. I kept remembering how I'd smacked into her in the corridor of my apartment stash a while back; how startled she had seemed. Maybe she hadn't merely been passing by; maybe she'd been eavesdropping on my conversation with Len Kensington . . .

. . . Len had mentioned a jane who'd taken him in, given him a bed. Which might possibly add up to Vonnie Vale being the she-male in question. If my guess made a bull's-eye, hell was about to pop. I don't like corpses strewn around my living room; especially when they leak lots of juice. It costs coin to have your rugs cleaned.

RINGING THE bell, I schemed up a campaign. In itself Vonnie Vale's presence outside my door a little earlier wasn't conclusive proof of her connection with the Kensington kill; wouldn't warrant an actual accusation. Even if the neighbors fingered her as the chick who had lammed out of the building after those shots were fired, she could still defy the police to pin anything on her chemise.

But if she *had* been in on the croaking, I knew a way to find it out. All I had to do was watch her reactions.

I jingled again. This time she opened up. "Why— why, hello, Hawkshaw!" she said in a voice that quavered around the fringes.

I moved in; fastened the appreciative focus on her. She was embellished in a nightgown three shades thinner than watered whiskey and a lot more potent. Through the gossamer material I could tab her various tempting thems and thoses—including a pair of tapered white gams, a set of lyric hips, and a duet of curves that made my fingers tingle up to the elbows. Some damsels are built that way: just looking at them makes you pine for your vanished youth.

"Hi, kiddo," I said. "Did I disturb your slumbers?"

"W-well, I *was* asleep." Which was a lie and I knew it. She still had her makeup on, and I know she would never go to bed without cold-creaming her piquant puss. She added: "What brings you here at such an hour, Dan?"

I perched on the divan, pulled her alongside me. "I just wanted to apologize for ramming into you tonight," I said.

Her rouge became more noticeable as her cheeks whitened. "Oh, th-that's all right. I'd forgotten all about it."

I said: "Have you forgotten all about this?" and slipped an arm around her; hunted for her lips with my kisser.

She didn't try to fight me off. She gave me what I wanted—but her heart wasn't in it. The kiss was mechanical. She was just going through the motions.

I poured on more coal; pressed her backward and started to examine the quality of the nightie she was wearing. "Nice piece of goods, babe," I remarked. My hand touched more than silk as I said it.

"I—I'm glad you like it, Dan." Her voice was tight, edgy. Then she made a weak effort to push me up. "Let's n-not wrestle tonight, do you mind?"

"It's been a long time," I reminded her. I danced my fingers over her shoulders and down her smooth bare arms. "Can I help it if I'm human?"

She struggled for a phony smile. "All right, handsome. I guess we're b-both human . . ." She let me take her lips again; cuddled close to me when I began hunting a spot to pat with my palm.

It was nice to snuggle her that way. She was soft, feminine; her hair smelled good. For a minute I almost forgot my original purpose in starting the joust. If she hadn't been so damned passive, I might have got my arteries steamed up.

But there wasn't much fun to it when she merely

relaxed on the cushions and let me do all the leading. Competition is the life of trade—and this was like taking candy away from a baby. So I pulled her shoulder straps back into place and said: "Maybe I've lost my technic."

"Oh-h-h, no . . ." She didn't mean a word of it.

I said: "Or maybe you've got a boyfriend you like better."

"N-not any more . . . I mean—"

"You mean you haven't got a boyfriend because you croaked him!" I snarled. And I stood up, jerked her to her feet. "I was testing you—and you reacted just the way I expected. I knew damned well you wouldn't be in any mood to pitch woo with a murder on your conscience!"

The rouge-spots were ugly splotches against her colorless cheeks. "My God—you don't th-think I k-killed him? No, Dan! I didn't! Oh, please—you've got to believe me—"

I said: "So you admit knowing he's dead. Which means you're the jane I'm looking for. You're the one who gave Len Kensington a home. You loved him. Tonight you followed him to my wikiup; heard him asking me to help him get back to his wife."

"Y-yes, but—"

"Sooner than give him up to another woman, you creamed him. Deny it and I'll feed you a meal of your own teeth!" I commenced shaking her until her thingumbobs jiggled like mounds of aspic in an earthquake—

SHE CLAWED at my map; broke free. "It's not so!" she whimpered. "I didn't shoot him! I admit I went into your apartment after you left—"

"Why?"

"To talk Len into coming back to me. We argued a long time. Then somebody knocked. Len thought it was you. He thought you were bringing his wife in to see him—"

"And?"

"He didn't want her to catch him with another woman. So he pushed me into the bedroom, shut me in there. Then I heard him opening the front door of the flat . . . and there were three shots . . . someone fell . . . someone also ran away . . ."

The story rang true. I said: "What happened then?"

"I came out of the bedroom," she said tonelessly. "Len was on the floor, d-dead. I got panicky. I was afraid I'd be suspected. I raced out of the building and came home . . ."

"You didn't see anybody who might have done the triggering?"

"N-no . . ." She came close to me, clung to me like a terrified child. "Please believe me, Dan! I—I'll do anything to prove I'm telling the truth!" And she jammed her pouting figure against my shirt-front; offered me the bribery of her lips, her body.

It wasn't necessary. I had a hunch she was leveling. I said: "Okay, sweet. If what you say is true you needn't worry about a murder rap; somebody else pulled the kill and you'll be in the clear if you come clean with the bulls."

"I've got to go the p-police?"

"It's best," I told her gently. "You want Len's murderer nabbed, don't you?"

"Y-yes."

"So maybe your evidence will help," I said. "Get your threads on an' let's go."

She went into the boudoir, and started to dress. Don't blame me if there was a mirror placed where I could tab each little movement; after all, I'm as curious as the next slob.

WHEN SHE was frocked and shod we piled into my chariot; I headed for home. Just as I expected, Dave Donaldson was still on deck when we ankled in—although Kensington's corpse had been taken away in the meat wagon. Dave rasped: "So you came back. I thought you would, so I waited. Who's this number?"

"The blonde the neighbors saw lamming," I said. "Go ahead, Vonnie; spill your story to the nice apoplectic detective before he blows a fuse."

She faltered out her side of the mess; then I added what I knew. When I got through spouting, Donaldson growled: "So the dead guy was Len Kensington, hunh? That's all I need to know. It hands me the killer, by Gahd!"

"How come it does?" I asked him.

He said: "Kensington left a message before he kicked the bucket; wrote it on your rug with his own blood."

Vonnie Vale moaned quietly; sagged against me. She'd been through hell that night; she was still going through it. I supported her and kept listening to Donaldson.

"I discovered the message after you rushed off," he told me. "But up until now I couldn't savvy the connection." And he pointed to a wavery brown scrawl on the floor.

I leaned forward; stared. The gooey finger-marks spelled out a lower case *"p-i-l—"* ending in a squiggly round hieroglyphic that trailed off to nothing.

"You see?" Donaldson crowed. "He tried to tell us it was Abe Pilwyn who drilled him."

I said: "Yeah?"

"Yeah! P-I-L spells the start of the name, doesn't it?"

"Could be," I said.

He snapped: "The whole thing's plain as hell. Pilwyn wanted Kensington's wife. He couldn't stand the thought of losing her to a guy that was supposed to be dead. So he decided to make her a widow—a real widow this time. That was his motive—"

Before I could interrupt him, my phone-bell jangled. I unforked the receiver and said: "Dan Turner talking. Make it brief. I'm busy."

"Dan—this is Lanya Kensington. Come quick—bring Len with you—Abe and Mr. Dexter are fighting here—Abe's threatening to k-kill him—"

I yowled: "The hell you yodel!" and hung up, whirled around. I grabbed Vonnie Vale, gestured at Donaldson. "Let's go thumb a killer!"

We whooshed down to the street. I jammed Vonnie into the tonneau of Dave's official police chariot, wedged myself beside her while Dave took the wheel. He said: "You better be taking me to Abe Pilwyn, by Gahd!"

"I am. Goose this thing." And I gave him Lanya Kensington's address.

I'LL SAY one thing for Dave Donaldson: when he scents a pinch in the offing he can drive like a maniac. He blooped that sedan up to seventy from a standing start; kicked the everlasting tripes out of it. The yellow-haired Vale cutie shivered against me like a cat coughing lamb-chops; she must have thought she was headed for the pearly gates. Her even little teeth chattered like pennies in a Salvation Army tambourine.

I snuggled her, told her not to worry. But I didn't sound very convincing. Especially when we zipped around a corner on two wheels and a miracle. Vonnie and I resembled two hunks of popcorn rattling around in a hopper and I didn't like it a damned bit. I couldn't even hold onto her where the holding was nicest because she kept bouncing so much I wasn't able to pick my spots.

It was a hell of a wild ride; but pretty soon we were at the end of the line. Dave slammed to a halt in front of Lanya Kensington's modest shebang, scuttled from under his wheel and said: "Now what?"

I stuck a match in my mouth, tried to light it with a gasper. When my nerves quit screaming I ordered Vonnie Vale to stay in the car; then I dragged Donaldson toward the house.

Len Kensington's cuddly brunette widow was on the porch to greet us. She looked pale, jittery. "Wh- where's Len? You promised to bring him—"

I ducked the issue. "Take us to Pilwyn and Dexter." She led us inside, pointed to a closed library door. From within the room I could hear Abe Pilwyn snarling: "You're going to do as I say, Sam."

"And toss away a fortune?" That was Dexter's worried voice. "Don't be foolish. Put away that gun."

"Like hell! When Kensington shows up, we're going to hand him a fistful of cash, send him on his way. He can be bought. He's *got* to be bought! I won't let him have Lanya, understand? I'll croak him first. And you too if you—"

I yanked on the knob, bounced over the threshold, whipped out the .32 automatic I always carry in a shoulder holster. On the far side of the library Abe

Pilwyn was aiming a roscoe at his partner. I shouted: "Hold it, Abe. Save him for the gas-chamber!" Then I said: "Dexter, you're under arrest for murdering Len Kensington."

The finance man of Pildex Productions gave me a wild-eyed glare; edged toward the French window behind him. "I don't know what the hell you're talking about!"

I said: "You shot Kensington because you didn't want to disgorge the insurance fortune you collected when he was declared legally dead—a policy you took out on him before the Honolulu hop. You made the profit because you own Pildex Productions; Abe Puwyn is just a front man."

"That's not murder proof."

"Kensington left his own proof. He wrote your name in blood before he signed off."

Donaldson said: "Cripes, Dan, it was Pilwyn's name—"

I shook my head. "It all goes back to an insurance swindle pulled by Dexter. He wanted to collect on Kensington's policy without actually killing the guy."

"How could I do that?" Dexter sneered.

I said: "By arranging for Kensington to vanish and having him declared croaked. But he refused to stay vanished, so this time you were forced to bump him.

"You were one of the only four possible suspects who knew he was in my apartment. The other three

were Vonnie Vale, Lanya Kensington, and Abe Puwyn. Want me to tell you how I eliminated them?"

"Help yourself."

I SAID: "It was simple logic. Before he died, Kensington wrote 'pil' without capitals, and another letter that looked like a zero. The only way you can

make a word of that is by adding a 't'—and then you
get 'pilot'."

"What pilot?"

I said: "Obviously the anonymous one who had
doubled for him on the Honolulu hop. In other
words, a man he didn't know by name. Which
cleared Vonnie and Lanya. Of the four persons who

knew Kensington was at my stash, only you and Abe Pilwyn were left.

"But Abe wasn't a flyer. And he'd been at the air-port when Kensington started that Honolulu jaunt. So you, Dexter, were the guy with the roscoe.

"As financial backer of Pildex Productions you'd always stayed away from the studio; Kensington had never met you. Therefore he didn't suspect your identity when you told him you were an out-of-luck aviator. He turned his plane over to you and went into hiding. That was the crux of your scheme. You sank the plane in the ocean, got back to shore and allowed the world to believe Len Kensington had been lost at sea.

"You figured he wouldn't dare show himself after that. You were safe in having him declared defunct so you could collect the insurance. But he fooled you. He turned up. So you had to bump him. He still didn't know you, even as you were shooting him. He merely realized you were his substitute pilot—and that's the word he tried to write. Satisfied?"

Dexter grinned in my teeth. "Sure. I'm satisfied you can't prove a word of it, even if it were true."

Somehow I'd been anticipating that. So I said: "You're wrong, rat. An eye-witness saw you do your triggering. She was in my bedroom at the time and she's outside in a police car now, ready to put the finger on you."

That got him. "You dirty son!" he yelled; and he

hurled himself backward through the French window in a shower of glass.

I launched my bulk across the room. Dave Donaldson made his move at the same instant. We collided. I said: "Damn you for a clumsy ox!" and landed on my hands and knees. By the time I got going again, Dexter was a blur in the distant shadows. I saw him making for Donaldson's sedan; saw the glitter of a cannon in his duke— The cannon yammered: *"Kachow! Chow!"* and vomited twin flame-streaks at Vonnie Vale in the car's tonneau. But even as I saw it, more gun-thunder roared from behind my shoulder. That was Donaldson's service .38 doing its stuff. Up ahead, Sam Dexter screamed and pitched forward on his smeller.

By the time I reached him he was as dead as a Hitler promise. Vonnie Vale was whimpering inside the car, bleeding from a bullet-nick in her arm.

I grabbed her, snagged a strip from her dress, bandaged the scratch. That ruined the frock; left a lot of loveliness on display. She moaned: "Oh-h-h, Dan . . . I th-think I'm going to faint! Please . . . take care of me . . ."

So I took her home and cared for her.

DRUNK, DISORDERLY, AND DEAD

She loved her husband, yet she was determined to create a public scandal. Dan Turner might not have minded so much being her partner in the scene except that her husband was his friend. There was no way for him to guess it was all leading to murder!

I DON'T like drunken dames, even when they're as gorgeous as Rhoda Ashworth was. To me, a swacked she-male is an abomination. And the Ashworth cutie was obviously plastered to the gills.

I could tell it the instant I drifted into the Cafe LaBomba that evening and saw her fastening the glassy glimpse on me. She was sitting at a ringside table with her hubby of six months' duration, Walt Ashworth; and as soon as she tabbed me, she caterwauled: "Dan Turner, the Hollywood Sherlock! C'mon over, lover. Wanna dance with you. Wanna be held in your arms!"

A fine business, I said to myself. Especially that lover part. Hell, I'd never even considered a pass in her direction. In the first place she was barely twenty; I always toss that size back in the brook on account of the game laws. Besides, her marriage to my friend Walt Ashworth, studio still-photographer, was supposed to be a movietown idyll—one of those genuine love matches full of hap-piness and honeysuckle. Or at least that had been the score

until recently. Then, apparently, something had
gone haywire in the Ashworth paradise.

RHODA'S present drunkenness in the Cafe
LaBomba was a good sample of it. This made the

fifth or sixth time in less than a month that she'd
made an unholy show of herself in public—which is
downright dynamite for a jane who plays sweet in-
genue roles in the galloping snapshots. Calling me
lover in front of her husband and a cabaret full of

picture personages was the nastiest faux pas of all; especially when Gordon Maxim was sitting at the very next table, where he couldn't help overhearing it.

Gordon Maxim was the big cheese of Tec-Vox Pix, Rhoda's home lot. And to make matters worse,

he had Dahlia Mannerling with him; the same Dahlia Mannerling who wrote a daily Hollywood gossip column syndicated from hell to Hawaii. Dahlia was a lassie who could purvey scandal with both fists when she wanted to.

"Wanna dance with Turner!" Rhoda Ashworth

kept bleating. "Wannim to kiss me." Then, with everybody in the joint staring at her, she added: "I know what'll gettim."

Whereupon she started doing a strip-tease peel out of her blue satin evening gown.

Even the orchestra missed a downbeat when that happened. And no damned wonder. In a town full of choice cookies, Rhoda was the sugar frosting on the cake. She had coppery red hair cut in a page-boy bob, the lower waves waterfalling around throat and shoulders of snowy delight. Her glims were a peculiar violet color made darker now by the excited dilation of the pupils, her kisser was a ripe red blossom, and she was built like the illustration on a bachelor's calendar.

I've pasted the optic on many a cinema sweetie in my day, but this Ashworth dish topped them all. Her gams were long and slender, her thighs were sleek columns under clinging satin, and her lilting hips melted into a wasp-thin waist-line that didn't require corsetry. From that point on the scenery became even more spectacular. Right now she was worrying her shoulder straps down her arms; in another instant there would be plenty on full display.

Screwily enough, her groom wasn't doing a damned thing about it. He just sat there pouring the last slug out of a private rye bottle. He must have been fried to the hat, I thought. Otherwise he'd have made some move to stop the show Rhoda was furnishing. With his fishbelly face and lusterless lamps he looked like a fugitive from his own funeral.

I hastened my pace, made for his table. That was when Tim Sullivan, the LaBomba headwaiter, appeared out of nowhere and put the grab on the Ashworth babe.

He yanked her costume back where it belonged; tried to whisper some sense into her ear. Maybe he figured he still meant something to her; she had been a cigarette girl in the joint prior to being discovered by a Tec-Vox talent scout, and Sullivan had been her immediate boss.

But evidently he didn't drag much weight now. She kicked at his shins, jerked away from him and yeeped: "Get your Irish paws off me. Those days are gone forever!"

At that juncture I barged up. Sullivan handed me a harassed look and lammed. I said: "Hi, folks. Nice evening. Did I hear myself being paged?"

"You did," Walt Ashworth nodded glumly; downed his snort. "Definitely!"

Rhoda opened her arms. "Dance with me, Dan. Dance with me!"

WELL, what the hell? The music was languorous, the night was young and the Ashworth chicken felt damned nice in my embrace. Moreover, she'd already created a big enough scene; if I refused her invitation she might have stirred up a juicier stink.

So I whirled her out across the polished floor.

She did surprisingly well for a wren with a snoot-ful. And the way she pressed herself close to me would have got us both tossed neck-over-tincup out

of a lower-toned dive. She welded her body to mine until I could practically feel the circulation coursing through her veins. Her skin was the color and texture of heavy cream, her hair was faintly fragrant and her gown slashed plenty low in front. My temperature commenced to bound toward the higher brackets.

I whispered uneasily: "Not so ardent, sweet stuff. You'll manufacture a scandal. Not to mention the wear and tear on me."

"I want a scandal!" she came back at me. Her voice wasn 't the least bit bleary.

That didn't add up to make sense. "Look," I said patiently. "You're just a kid. You're still damp behind the ears. You've got a career ahead of you. Gordon Maxim—"

"Phooey on Gordon Maxim."

I didn't like to hear her talk that way about the Tec-Vox mogul. He was an inoffensive little bald-head with a withered right arm, the result of polio in childhood; and he'd invested copious geetus to make Rhoda a star. "Is that a way to show your appreciation?" I said.

"Don't preach to me, please."

I said: "I'll preach and you'll listen. Once the gossips of Dahlia Mannerling's kidney get their hooks in you, they'll rip your rep to shreds. You'll be washed up."

"So what?"

"So quit shoving up against me before Walt gets the idea I'm on the make," I told her.

"Walt isn't even looking," she said tremulously. "Dan, I-I w-want you to t-take me home."

"And run out on him?"

She bit her lower lip. "Yes. Maybe it'll bring him to his senses. I'm not drunk, Dan. I never have been drunk, even when people thought I was. I've been trying to shame Walt into getting a grip on himself. I want him to think that if he goes to hell in a hand-basket, I'll go right along with him—even if it smashes my career."

I said: "Oh-oh! A reform act, eh?"

She nodded. "Because I love him so t-terribly much."

"And how-come he needs reformation?" I said.

"I—I've found out he's . . . on the needle," she whimpered woefully.

CHAPTER II
Gone for a Ride

THAT was news to me. It hit me like a bash in the teeth. So Walt Ashworth had turned out to be a hop-head! And his sweet little frau was determined to shame him into the straight and narrow, no matter what the cost. I admired her for it; and determined to help her if possible. I said: "Okay, soldier," and piloted her back to her hubby just as a lady lenshound from the Hollywood *Cita-del-News* exploded a flash bulb to snap a shot of the glittering gathering.

Sullivan, the Irish head waiter, had just handed Walt Ashworth an uncorked fifth of pleasure-water. "With Mr. Maxim's compliments, sir," he said. Walt took the bottle, nodded sullen thanks to the bald little Tec-Vox executive at the next table, and sloshed out a generous tipple.

Sliding back into her tipsy act, Rhoda grabbed the glass away from him; raised it to her own crimson lips. "Wanna drink to my latest love," she announced. "Wanna drink a toast to Dan Turner." She skidded the skee past her tonsils.

Ashworth shrugged, filled another jorum, tossed it off. "Sure," he mumbled. "To Turner." Nothing seemed to disturb him; not even the intimation that Rhoda and I were chiseling.

Then Gordon Maxim and Dahlia Mannerling left their table; came over to us. Dahlia looked more like a jeweled Earl Carroll showgirl than a syndicate columnist for a string of metropolitan blats from coast to coast. She was hefty, blonde; but her curves were properly proportioned. She packed considerable poundage but no fat.

It was rumored she had no use for men, which was a shame; her complexion was the peaches-and-cream you sometimes see on Junoesque yellow-haired dames, and she wore a green metallic creation that adhered to her form as if she'd been electroplated into it. I'd often wondered what it might be like to grab a handful of the Mannerling contours, et cetera, but opportunity had never knocked.

It wasn't knocking now. She didn 't even seem to realize I was present. "Better let me take you out of here, Rhoda darling," she drawled throatily. Her affected manner was as spurious as sunstroke at the South Pole.

Rhoda lurched a little; grabbed at my arm for support. She said: "No. Wanna go with Dan. Wannim to—hic—take care of me." Her alcoholic histrionics were damned convincing.

Walt Ashworth favored me with a sour grin. "Go right ahead," he said with politely drunken gravity. "Take care of her. Don't mind me."

Then Gordon Maxim worriedly whispered something to the luscious Mannerling frill and they both faded out of the picture. I couldn't help casting a wistful glance at the blonde babe as she ankled off. The sway of her hips fascinated hell out of me. Her height dwarfed Maxim; made him appear incongruously gnome-like. What she really needed was a bozo my own size, I meditated.

BUT I had other affairs to attend to. I slipped an arm around Rhoda Ashworth's slender waist; steered her toward the exit. She stumbled as she crawled into my jalopy, out on the parking lot; I had to hold her or she'd have taken a nose dive against the instrument panel. I said quietly: "You can cancel the inebriety act now, hon. We haven't got an audience here."

She sagged against me when I slid under the wheel and kicked the starter. "It's not . . . an act . . . now. Funny, but . . . I really am crocked! And I'm so . . . unhappy.

Tears were in her glims; her mouth trembled forlornly. I couldn't resist stroking her shoulder to soothe her. And when I did that, she melted into my arms like a kid scared of the dark. "Oh-h-h, Dan!" she wailed.

I kissed her. Not on the lips, but on the forehead. Even the yielding of soft curves upon my shirt-front failed to touch off my fuses. She was just a youngster in love—and in trouble. A guy would be a heel to take advantage of a situation like that. "Never mind, sweetness," I said. "Everything will turn out all right."

"B-but when I think of Walt using m-morphine—!"

"We'll straighten him out," I told her. "If you can't do it by making him jealous or shame him by pretending to go on public benders, we'll find another way."

She hiccuped jerkily. "I'm not pretending . . . about the bender . . . this time," she mumbled.

I AIMED my coupe out Sunset; headed for her stash

down at Malibu. "That last snort must have tagged you off third base," I said. I reached past her to crank down the window on her side.

My elbow brushed swelling firmness where her gown dipped low. It was mighty nice; but it was also hands-off territory as far as I was concerned. Besides, I was uneasy. When we started winding through the hills and canyons beyond Beverly, the fresh air didn't seem to help her a damned bit. She swayed around as if all her bones had turned to sponge rubber. Her head lolled, her peepers were closed and she was breathing stertorously.

"Passed out," I whispered. Then I yelled: "Hey! What the hell—!"

A big black limousine without headlights was crowding me over to the side of the deserted highway. It had overtaken my chariot with hissing silence; now it was cutting athwart my bows like a sinister shadow.

I jammed down on my brake pedal; twisted the wheel. Rubber smoked off my tires as I skidded to a stop. I squirmed around; dug a hand under my left armpit where I always carry a shoulder-holstered .32 roscoe.

My move was a split second late. A hulking lug in chauffeur's uniform had already barged out of the limousine's tonneau and planted his oversize brogan on my running board. He had an improvised handkerchief mask over the lower section of his pan and a blue-barreled automatic in his duke. He said: "Freeze, snoop, or I'll perforate you like a canceled check."

His voice sounded ugly, menacing; his roderick looked capable of blasting my teeth into the next township. I froze, as requested.

"Get out," he said.

I got out.

He kept me covered; reached in and fastened the grab on Rhoda Ashworth. He hauled her toward himself. He was a husky monkey; he put his free arm around her, lifted her like a sack of feathers, and backed toward the limousine.

He wasn't alone in his snatch act. His confederate was at the black car's steering wheel, crouched low and muffled by darkness. All I could see was a slender, ring-studded white hand on a chromium wheel-spoke. Then I couldn't even tab that much. The masked bozo furnished me with a free ticket to obliteration; slugged me across the noggin with his heater. I wasn't expecting it; didn't have time to duck. The blue steel muzzle kissed me on the cranium; filled my think-tank with fireworks. Then the pinwheels and skyrockets and Roman candles were blotted out by thickish billows of fog that drifted into my brain and lulled me to sleep.

I COULDN'T have been unconscious very long. But when I swam out of the anaesthetic, the black chariot was gone. So was Rhoda Ashworth. I couldn't even find any tire marks to indicate where the kidnap buggy had been.

My head ached to beat hell; there was a lump over my left ear the size of a Georgia watermelon. Outside of that, though, I was all in one piece; barring a slight wooziness I seemed to be ticking as usual.

Genuflecting to the ancestors who'd bequeathed me my thick skull, I scrambled dizzily into my rambling wreck; sat there for a minute to gather my bashed wits together. I fished out a gasper, set fire to it, sucked the smoke into my bronchial cavities. Then I asked myself who the hell had snatched the Ashworth filly—and why.

The answer eluded me. All I knew was that the kidnap car hadn't turned around and headed back toward town; not at that spot, anyhow. There were no wheel-traces on the soft shoulder to mark such a maneuver. Therefore the snatchers must have continued on toward the ocean. I goosed my cylinders and set forth in the same direction; hoped against hope that I might run into something.

I did—and how! About three miles farther along, the spray of my headlamps broomed a highway curve where it snaked through a canyon; reflected momentarily upon a blue-and-white object reposing inertly on the road's shoulder. The white portions were feminine flesh; the blue was satin evening gown.

A dirty premonition crawled up my pants, bit me under the hip pocket. I tossed out my four-wheel anchors.

I was out on the smooth asphalt before my pile of iron had stopped rolling. I catapulted my bulk toward the ditch; whipped out a pencil flashlight and showered its ray on the thing that had caught my eye. I felt my scalp crawling, my innards churning, and my cookies trying to come up.

Rhoda Ashworth was sprawled nastily in the sparse underbrush. There was an ugly raw gash on her left shoulder where she'd impacted against the jaggedness of a chunk of rock. Her glims were wide open, staring; her lower jaw hung loosely agape. I didn't need a second gander to know that she was deader than a last year's Christmas tree.

CHAPTER III
Dragnet for Turner

FOR an instant I was too flabbergasted to do anything but stare at her. I could see the marks in the soft earth where the defunct wren had hit and rolled before smacking into that boulder. Now she was grotesquely sprawled, with the blue satin skirt hiked up above her thighs. They'd been damned tasty thighs, once. But now they were skinned and rasped by friction-contact with the paving; her stems were askew in laddered chiffon. One shoulder strap of the blue evening gown was broken; the satin bodice ripped to reveal the upper slopes of her breast. It was still a flawless sample of creamy beauty; no blood had welled from the gash above it to mar its milky perfection. I leaned forward; pressed my palm under that firm hillock. I couldn't feel a trace of heartbeat.

"The dirty rats!" I whispered, thinking about the people in the snatch-car. Anybody could see what had happened. Rhoda's form had been tossed out of the black limousine while it was whooshing hellity-blam toward the coast highway. The marks in the earth indicated that she had landed with terrific force; had ploughed into the undergrowth and car-omed off that jagged rock like a cue ball making a two-cushion bank. And now she was a corpse. She 'd play no more heroines for Tec-Vox.

I started to lift her. Then a white beam of light sliced at me; tires screeched shrilly and metal snarled on paving. I straightened up, pivoted, blinked into the blinding illumination. A voice that sounded like the cop said: "Hold everything, mister. This thing I've got in my hand is a gun."

He was a motorcycle bull; a county highway hero. He rested his chug-bike on its prop and edged toward me; came into the light. He looked hardboiled; his jaw stuck out like a concrete buttress and he outweighed me a good twenty pounds. "What's cooking?" he growled. "Who's this dame?"

"Rhoda Ashworth, the movie star," I said. "And nothing's cooking. It's already cooked. The lady is extremely deceased."

He said: "Yeah. So I see. Rhoda Ashworth, eh? H-m-m-m. What's your name and why did you croak her?"

I stiffened. Until then, it hadn't dawned on me that my own spot might not smell so appetizing. Maybe that was because I'd still felt a little fuzzy from being maced over the conk by that masked chauffeur. But when the brass-buttoned minion tossed his verbal bombshell at me, I saw I stood a damned good chance of being put in the middle and squeezed.

Plenty of people had seen me leaving the Cafe LaBomba with the Ashworth quail; but there hadn't been any witnesses when she was abducted from my bucket. I could explain until I was green around the adenoids—but would my explanation hold water?

"Listen," I said quickly without giving my name. "What makes you think I cooled this morsel?"

He told me he wasn't blind. "Any dope can see the story. You were riding along with her. You went on the make. She put up an argument. You hauled her; tore her dress. Still she wouldn't listen. So you opened the door on her side; tossed her out. Then you stopped; backed up. You got out to see how much damage you'd done. That's where I came in."

I said: "You're as nutty as a fruit cake, pal. In the first place, the fall didn 't croak her. She was dead long before she ever landed in the ditch."

"How come?"

I pointed to the gash on her shoulder. "See any pool of blood, wise guy?"

"No."

"There's your answer," I said. "If she'd been alive when she was given the heave-ho, she'd have bled from that gash. But she scarcely leaked a drop of juice. Therefore she was already meat for the undertaker when she went wafting through space."

The highway bull lifted his thick shoulders. "So okay. So you creamed her before you ditched her. Let's try on these nippers for size."

I WAS over the well-known barrel. If we'd been inside the city limits I might have stood a chance; one of my best friends is Lieutenant Dave Donaldson of the L. A. Homicide Bureau. But out in the county I generated less than zero horsepower. The sheriff's division hasn't got too much use for private snoops, anyhow.

There was only one thing for me to do. I did it. I stretched forth my wrists for the bracelets; let the motorcycle slob snick them on me. Then, while his attention was still on that jib, I balled both maulies; brought them rocketing at his plough-share chin in a sizzling twin uppercut.

The Turner knuckles collided with the guy's button. He said: "Glph-mmph!" and his knees caved under him like boiled noodles. Then he stretched out on the road-side for a nice long snooze.

I got his keys; unmanacled myself. My hands freed, I lunged over to Rhoda Ashworth's body; lifted it and dumped it into my coupe. I crawled under the wheel; souped my carburetor.

Driving back toward Hollywood with a dead wren propped against me wasn't my idea of a hilarious evening. But it had to be done. I wanted to know how the Ashworth chicken had met dissolution; my personal future depended on the answer.

The obvious solution was that her kidnapers had bumped her. In which case, I'd be in a sweet fix— because I couldn't prove she'd been kidnaped out of my chariot before getting the works. The law would try to put the finger on me for the job. I'd find myself languishing in the gow with no chance to hunt for the snatchers who were actually guilty.

My sole hope lay in a sneaking hunch that her death hadn't been murder at all. There was a bare possibility Rhoda had passed to her reward via the acute-alcohol-ism route; kicked the bucket in the snatch car from too much joy-juice previously imbibed. Her abductors, upon discovering that she was no longer among the living, had thereupon consigned her remainders to the breeze and taken a hurried powder for parts unknown.

If this second theory proved correct, I'd be in the clear—even though I couldn't hang an abduction rap on anybody. The mere tossing of her corpse into a convenient ditch wouldn't be regarded as a major crime, no matter who did it; not as long as death itself had been from natural causes. Therefore, it behooved me to get an autopsy performed—and damned soon.

It was a county coroner's job, of course. But I wanted to work it through the city police department, where I had some influence. To monkey with any other division would be sticking my neck out, inasmuch as I'd bopped a sheriff's cop. That's why I was blasting my wreck back toward town with a cadaver for company.

Once Dave Donaldson got me the findings of a medical examiner, I might be free to make some moves of my own. Mainly I hankered to catch up with that masked chauffeur; I owed him a swift poke in the mush for the way he'd bludgeoned me. And if I turned him up, I could probably clear myself with the sheriff's office.

BY NOW I was within the purlieus of Hollywood proper. I drove my heap into the basement garage under the apartment shack I call my home; went upstairs to my tepee. Then I phoned Headquarters, asked for homicide.

Dave Donaldson answered. I said: "Turner talking. Listen. I want you to get a morgue wagon and ferry it post-haste to the garage beneath my stash. By yourself. And keep your blabber buttoned whilst accomplishing same."

"That's a hell of a queer request," Dave growled suspiciously. "What's behind it? Delirium tremens?"

"No," I said. "I've got a nice fresh stiff in my jalopy."

"You what?"

I said: "A stiff. Rhoda Ashworth, the Tee-Vox cutie. And I want her autopsied to get me out from under a bump-off bleat."

Donaldson gave issue to a bellowing snort. "So you're the gazabo! By cripes, this takes the fur-trimmed wienie!"

"Meaning what?"

He said: "There's a county dragnet out for you, Sherlock. It's on the radio right now—short wave, long-wave and God-knows-what-wave! A sheriff's putt-putt gendarme claims that some anonymous gent laid the slugs to him after committing killery on that Ashworth doll. Now every dick in the area is hanging out the eye for a vee-eight coupe containing the villain and his victim!"

I said wearily: "I'm the anonymous gent; and my chariot contains the cadaver in question. But it's all a horrible mistake. This is how it happened." I gave him the complete box score, omitting no details. I added: "So now you see why I need that autopsy report to jack me out of the grease."

"Yeah. I see," he said. "I'll be right over. Don't go away."

I told him I wouldn't, and rang off. I ambled over to my cellarette; broached a virgin fifth of Vat 69. I was just tilting a tumblerful down my gullet when somebody rapped on the front door.

I opened up. Tim Sullivan, the Cafe LaBomba headwaiter, waltzed close to me. He had a nickel-plated .22 lady's gun in his right mitt. He said: "You stinking louse!" and pulled the trigger.

A bolt of lightning smacked me in the heart. All my wires short-circuited; all my lights went out.

CHAPTER IV
The Real Truth

I WOKE up in Hollywood Precinct emergency ward. Dave Donaldson was leaning over me and saying: "It's damned near time."

My chest felt as if a locomotive had hit it. I was all wound up in yards of adhesive tape; my left lung felt like one great big bruise. But I knew I was alive. Heaven didn't contain any Donaldson-type angels.

I squinted up at him. "Where were you when the thunderbolt struck?" I said.

"So you're ready to talk," he grated. "That's fine. You're going to need a lot of words to get you out of this mess."

I tried sitting up; found I could manage it. I said: "What am I doing here and why am I alive,"

"You're here because when I went to your apartment I discovered you laid out on the living room rug with a neat little bullet hole in your lapel. I brought you in for first aid," Dave said. "And you're

alive because you happened to be wearing a shoul-der-rigged gat when somebody tossed a .22 pill at you. Your rod stopped the slug. Barring a black and blue chest you'll pull through. Now, who tried to ventilate you'?"

I said: "Skip that for a minute. I want to know if you got Rhoda Ashworth's corpse out of my jal-opy."

"Sure. And I just received a stomach-contents analysis from the coroner's toxicologist." Donaldson shoved his beefy puss close to mine. "Why did you poison the Ashworth bim?"

I slid my dogs over the side of the bed and yelped: "Did you say poison?"

"Yeah. I said poison. The report calls it gel-semium rhizome, whatever that is. What made you do it, Philo? You must have been off your damn' trolley!"

"Off my trolley, hell! I didn't croak that wren, you crazy ape!" Then there flashed through my think tank a fleeting picture of bejeweled white fingers. Ideas meshed and clicked. "I didn't do it, but I bet I know who did! And maybe there's another corpse ready for harvesting right this instant!"

"Whose?"

"Walt Ashworth," I said. "Listen—"

Donaldson favored me with a fresh-laid titter. "I knew your brain would crack some day, snoop. Walt Ashworth was alive enough fifteen minutes ago when he came down here to identify his wife's body. He was sick as a horse, but that was hangover and shock. We sent him back home."

This tidbit of information stopped me for an instant. It didn't quite line up with my theories. Just the same, I figured I was on the right track; Ashworth's survival was an accident. It had to be. I said: "Let me out of here. I've got things to do."

"You'll stay put," Dave growled. "Or didn't you realize you're in custody on suspicion of murder?"

I hated to biff him. He's a friend of mine. But sometimes he gets nutty notions. And this was one of the times. By holding me, he was allowing a murderer to run loose; closing a case that was as wide open as the mouth of a coal mine. So I whapped him.

His teeth clicked together. He fell across the bed. I pelted to a closet; found my threads and climbed into them. Then I opened the hospital room's window; wafted myself outward into the night. I started running.

AT THE next corner I hailed a cruising hack; gave the cabby the Rampart Street address of Dahlia Mannerling, the blonde columnist. From now on, I had to work fast. I'd cold-cocked two minions of the law's majesty; I was under the gun for Rhoda Ashworth's kill. Unless I fastened the elbow on the genuine bumper-offer I was a gone goose.

The Mannerling skirt lived in a pretentious two-story dump that spelled prosperity in italics. I went to the door, kicked a few blisters on it. A hulking slug in butler's uniform opened up for me after the third kick.

I tabbed him from his general outlines. He was the bozo who had worn chauffeur's garb and a mask, earlier that evening; the one who'd caressed my cranium with a cannon. "So you also buttle," I remarked. Then I bashed him a Loney, full in the kisser.

He folded. That put me even with him. I leaped over his sprawled bulk; took to the staircase. An upstairs door opened and Dahlia Mannerling said: "What's all the commotion?"

"The name is Turner and I'm about to raise the lid off hell," I told her. I put my two palms on her chest and shoved.

She staggered backward into her rose-tinted boudoir. She was wearing a nightie and a negligee, both thinner than the tissue of a Christmas present; and what I saw through gossamer silk made me forget the pain in my bruised chest. How could a guy think of his own bosom when he had a chance to cop a swivel at Dahlia's?

She was like a Viking goddess straight from Valhalla. Her long yellow hair cascaded to her waist. The swelling flare of her hips melting into gorgeous white thighs and tapered stems gave me a sudden attack of the speechless jitters.

She backed away from me as I ankled over her bedroom threshold. "This is going to take some explaining," she said. The words might have carried more threat if her voice hadn't quavered quite so much.

I moved in on her. I said: "Sister, you spoke a spoonful. Do you smoke?'

"Why—yes."

"You aren't going to like the taste of cyanide fumes in the gas house," I said. "It won't be like Turkish tobacco."

Considerable color departed from her peaches-and-cream cheeks. "Are you crazy, or just drunk!"

"I'm neither. I just happen to be accusing you of kidnaping and murder—both of which are punishable by death in this neck of the forest."

Her diamond studded fingers went to her kisser. Her peepers bulged. "My God! You don't think I—?"

I dug my fingers into her snowy shoulders. "I think you croaked Rhoda Ashworth. Yes." Then I added: "You and Gordon Maxim."

"But—but that's insane! It's—"

"Sure. You're going to claim it was accidental. I'm afraid that won't wash, baby. Listen. The way I add it up, Maxim was worried because Rhoda was getting drunk too often in public. It threatened to ruin her as a star—which would wipe out the investment he had in her."

The Mannerling dish whispered: "Of course Mr. Maxim was concerned. Who wouldn't be, under those circumstances?"

"Being concerned," I said, "Maxim made up his mind to do something about it. He blamed Rhoda's drunkenness on her husband; he figured Walt was dragging her down to the gutter. If he could remove Walt from the picture, Rhoda might reform."

She sucked in a deep, quivery breath that arched out her loveliness. "No! Gordon Maxim never even considered Walt Ashworth as the cause of—"

I SAID: "Clam up, sister. I'm doing the gabbing. Maxim determined to bump Walt Ashworth. So he put some poison in a bottle of rye and sent it over to Walt's table with his compliments."

"P-poison. . . ? So that's what was wrong with Rhoda—" The blonde quail tried to bite back the words, but it was too late.

"So you know there was something wrong with her," I grinned.

She skipped that. "Listen, Mr. Turner—Dan— It's true Mr. Maxim sent Ashworth some whiskey. But it wasn't poisoned. It couldn't have been. We'd both had a drink out of that bottle before we sent it—"

"If you interrupt me again, I'll feed you a clap across the mush," I growled at her. "I say the whiskey was poisoned. Walt started to drink a dollop of it. Just then Rhoda snatched the glass out of his hand; downed the snort herself."

She nodded.

"So that scared the living bejaspers out of Gordon Maxim. He wanted to get Rhoda out of the cafe—fast. He wanted to administer a quick antidote before it was too late. His scheme had backfired; his poison had gone down the wrong hatch. That was why you and he offered to take Rhoda home."

"N-no. That wasn't our reason—"

I stung her across the puss with my left palm. My fingers put red prints on the whiteness of her cheek.

I said: "When Rhoda refused to go with you, things looked bad. You and Maxim blew the joint; got into your limousine. When I brought Rhoda to my jalopy and started for Malibu with her, you followed. You jammed me off the road; put the snatch on her. Unfortunately, she kicked the bucket while you were taking her to a doctor." I stared into Dahlia's widened optics. "Am I right?"

"Only p-partially," she choked. "You've got the truth so twisted around that . . . why, you really could send me to prison!" Fear sent tremors through her; I could see her flesh rippling. Then, all of a sudden, she wrapped her arms around my neck and jammed herself against me. "You can't arrest me! You can't!"

"Why can't I?"

"B-because I'm going to make you listen to the real truth!" she said. Then she mashed her parted lips to my startled mouth.

CHAPTER V
One More Dead Man

HER kissing technique was marvelous. I'm an old osculatory expert myself; but the Mannerling number taught me some tricks I hadn't known about. She didn't kiss with her lips alone; she tossed her whole damned framework into the job.

It amazed me. She had a rep for being strictly untouchable; the Hollywood wise guys claimed she wouldn't give a man a second look. Yet here she was feeding me a workout that would have had the Hays office screaming for the scissors. The succulent sweetness of her labial pressure sent steam sizzling past my epiglottis; it was like a shot of high powered voltage crackling through my capillaries.

Her nightie and negligee had somehow drifted from their anchorage to reveal a pink expanse of shoulder and arm; she moaned when I poured a kiss to the hollow of her throat. "Dan . . . oh-h-h, Dan. . .!"

Well, what the hell? When a dame whimpers to me in that tone of voice, I'm human enough to listen. Especially when I know that the lassie in question wouldn't come near me under ordinary conditions. Something was forcing her to do the things she was doing; something damned important. In spite of her fervor I sensed a hidden reluctance, an undercurrent of sheer desperation.

I released her before I lost the last of my self-control. I said: "You're faking, aren't you?"

"F-faking?"

"Yeah. Putting on an act. Trying to soften me up so I'll listen to what you've got to say."

She caught her lower lip between her teeth. "Not only listen. I want you to *believe.* . . ."

I hung the swivel on her. "Okay, baby. Spill your story. You've got my attention. Or anyhow you will have when you pin that negligee together and cover the distractions."

She blushed and drew the silk-and-lace edges shut. "In the first place, I didn't know anything about poison being in that bottle of whiskey," she quavered. "Neither did Gordon Maxim. In fact, there couldn't have been poison in the rye when Maxim sent it to Walt Ashworth. Maxim and I had each had a drink out of the bottle beforehand."

"Then why was the bottle sent to Walt?"

"To get him even drunker than he already was. We didn't want him to interfere when we offered to take Rhoda home. You see, Dan, we were planning to whisk Rhoda to some sanitarium; make her take the liquor cure. That was Maxim's idea, and I had agreed to help him—because I liked Rhoda. I hated to see her career spoiled. Besides, Gordon Maxim has been a good friend of mine. Rhoda represented a big investment on his part; an investment he stood to lose if she kept making a fool of herself in public."

I thumbed a match, ignited a pill. "Go on talking!"

"When Rhoda insisted on leaving the cafe with you, we decided on the kidnaping stunt. It's true we followed your car. My butler-chauffeur was the one who did the actual snatching; I drove the limousine."

I said: "Yeah, I know. I tabbed the rings on your fingers when your hand was on the steering wheel. But the connection didn't click in my gray matter until later. When it did click, I came right here. But go ahead with your story."

"We t-took Rhoda away from you; started toward the beach. She was unconscious. Then, suddenly, Mr. Maxim yelled at me from the limousine's tonneau, where he and my chauffeur were holding Rhoda. Maxim told me she was d-dead. . ."

"So you got panic-stricken and dumped her, eh?"

She said: "Y-yes. That was Maxim's idea. He was afraid people might accuse us of—"

"Of murder," I supplied.

THE word seemed to give her the shuddering mee-mies. "But it wasn't murder! At least, Maxim and I had nothing to do with it We were only trying to straighten her out. Why should a movie executive kill his most promising star—a girl who meant a fortune to him?"

I said: "He wouldn't. It was an accident. He was

trying to bump her husband, the way I figure it."

"No, Dan! You're wrong! I saw that whiskey bottle being opened. I had a drink out of it. Then it was handed to that head waiter, Sullivan—oh, my God!"

I peered at her. "Now what?"

"Tim Sullivan used to be in love with Rhoda when she was a cigarette girl at the Cafe LaBomba. Maybe he blamed Walt Ashworth for her drunkenness. Maybe he slipped poison into the bottle before giving it to Walt!"

It might have been a good theory, except for the fact that Sullivan had later tried to gun me down. I'd already reconstructed his reason for that particular bit of vengeful skulduggery; and it didn't match up with Dahlia Mannerling 's present accusation.

I shook my head. "Wrong number, kiddo. But I'll hand you this much: I don't think you had anything to do with Rhoda Ashworth's untimely demise. As far as I am concerned, you're in the clear."

"Th-thank you, Dan." She glided up to me, put her arms around my neck. The kiss she fed me wasn't of the passionate variety; all it contained was gratitude.

But I drew a bigger bang out of it than I'd got from her previous lip-work. This time the gesture was at least genuine.

I backed away from her. Another salute like that one and I might forget my manners. She whispered: "Wh-what are you going to do now?"

"See some suspects," I told her. "And just to make sure you don't phone a warning to anybody, I believe I'll salt you down." Before she knew what was up, I unpocketed my handcuffs; fastened one around her left wrist. I attached the other bracelet to a bedpost. "You may be uncomfortable, and I'm sorry," I said. "But I know dammed well you can't reach your telephone now." Then I blew her a kiss; lammed from the room.

Downstairs, the butler-chauffeur was still listening to the birdies. I trussed him with his own galluses for safe-keeping; went out to look for a night-owl cab.

I found one; had myself ferried out to Gordon Maxim's hovel in the Miracle Mile district on Wilshire.

By this time there were extras on the street, head-lining my arrest and subsequent escape; evidently the heat was on me plenty, now.

I damned the cops for their numb-skull mulishness; if they'd been willing to cooperate with me instead of trying to nab me, my work might have been easier. As it was, I had to play a lone hand; had to steer clear of arrest while playing it. Maybe it sounds easy, but it wasn't.

GORDON MAXIM was a live-alone-and-enjoy-it bachelor with one outstanding eccentricity: he did

170

not allow his servants to remain under the same roof with him overnight. By the time I rang his doorbell it was pretty late; there weren't any lackeys around to let me in. The house was dark; Maxim himself didn't answer my bell-blast.

That struck me as queer. He wasn't a gadabout; didn't approve of staying out after midnight. It would take something damned important to keep him away from his downy couch at this hour, I thought.

Then I heard a dim, persistent jingling within the joint; a phone was ringing and nobody was answering it. On impulse, I dug out my ring of master keys; found one that worked the lock. I let myself in.

My flashray guided me to the stairs; the tinkling phone sounded from the upper floor. I followed my ears; came to a closed bedroom.

When I shoved the door inward, the phone-bell got louder, shriller. The instrument was alongside the bed.

I started toward it. Then I froze and whispered: "What the hell—"

Gordon Maxim was stretched across the bed in his pajamas; there was a roscoe near his withered right hand and a bullet-tunnel in his temple. He was deader than the proverbial chicken in a hard-boiled egg.

CHAPTER VI

A Lesson on Poison

I TOOK another gander at his corpse; gulped three or four times. Then, because the phonebell's harsh clatter was rasping my frazzled nerves, I uncradled the instrument and said: "Yes?"

"Gordon?" a she-male voice quavered. "This is Dahlia Mannerling. That private detective, Dan Turner, may be on his way to see you. He was just here. He left me handcuffed to my bed. He tied up Grimes, the butler, too. But Grimes got loose and came upstairs; broke the bedpost and freed me. Oh, Gordon—it's terrible! Turner accused us of having p-poisoned Rhoda Ashworth! You know we didn't do it. You've got to find some way of convincing him—"

I hung up on her. Listening to her terrified telephone monologue had cleared a lot of cobwebs out of my thinking machinery. Now I knew positively that Dahlia was innocent—and that Gordon Maxim was likewise beyond suspicion. Thinking she was talking to Maxim himself, the blonde babe would certainly have spilled her guts if there had been anything to spill.

I also knew she wasn't linked with Maxim's death. Had she been aware of it, she wouldn't have supposed that she was talking to him over the wire. Okay; then who the hell had bumped him?

It certainly wasn't suicide. The set-up was rigged

to make it look that way; but the killer had over-looked Maxim's crippled right arm. The bald little Tec-Vox biggie couldn't have wielded a heater with that withered duke; couldn't have triggered a slug through his own right temple. So the answer was murder.

Then I saw the motive for it. A scrawled note was on his pillow. I lighted it with my pencil flash:

"I poisoned Rhoda Ashworth with a dose of gel-semium rhizome. Now I'm following her to hell.
Gordon Maxim."

That confession was phoney. It had to be, to link up with the spurious suicide. In the first place, if Maxim had really been guilty of poisoning Rhoda, why hadn't he killed himself with a dose of the same medicine instead of messing up his brains with a bullet? And in the second place, I'd already tabbed the fact that he couldn't have used that gun with his right hand.

So the story was easy to figure. The real killer had hoped to cover his tracks and close the case by creaming Maxim and planting Rhoda's bump-off on the dead man's coattails. And where the hell did that leave me?

It left me in the soup. Because my fingerprints were all over the Maxim house where I'd let myself in and touched sundry doorknobs, banisters, or what

DRUNK, DISORDERLY, AND DEAD

have you. The law might damned well accuse me of croaking the Tec-Vox executive in an effort to get out from under that previous murder beef.

I said: "Damn!" and scuttled downstairs; slipped furtively into the night. One question kept bothering me. What the hell kind of broth was gelsemium rhizome?

For that matter, who might have access to the stuff in lethal quantities—plus the opportunity of introducing it into Walt Ashworth's whiskey?

TIM SULLIVAN'S name seemed to slip into the answer column of that mental questionnaire. He'd been sweet on Rhoda Ashworth in her cigarette-girl days. He'd seen her public drunk acts. And he might have blamed her apparent downfall on her husband. It would have been easy enough for him to dope the bottle of rye while carting it from one table to the other. Then, by accident, Rhoda had imbibed some of the stuff—

But that didn't explain the head-waiter's subsequent attack on me. Nor could I understand why Walt Ashworth himself hadn't gone to glory after drinking a dollop from the poisoned bottle. For once in my life I was up a stump. No matter how I added it up, two and two kept making five instead of four. The main trouble was, I'd never been tangled in a poisoning case before; most of my homicides had been shootings, stabbings and so forth.

Then I thought of my crime library. There were some toxicology handbooks in my apartment stash; maybe I could learn something from them. I nailed another Yellow; got out a block from my dive. I approached carefully; I knew the neighborhood would be infested with plainclothes cops hoping to put the arm on me. But maybe they'd forgotten to cover the rear-alley entrance to the basement garage. It was worth a chance.

Luck smiled. I sneaked in without being tabbed; legged it upstairs. Then I froze into an alcove as I saw a hulking blister parading up and down past my front portal.

His back was toward me. I didn't wait for him to turn around so I could get a hinge at his puss; didn't need to. I ducked around an elbow in the corridor; reached my kitchenette door. I went in that way.

I didn't snap on the overhead lamps; my flashlight was good enough. I opened my bookcase, dragged out Trumper's *Memoranda on Toxicology*, turned to page 184. Then I whispered "Well, I'll be go to hell!"

My puzzle was unriddled!

The paragraph I'd read cried out for a drink. I inhaled about six fingers of Vat 69; wondered how the hell I was going to trap the killer. Then the skee started coursing through my arteries, nudging my brain-cells. An idea hit me. I grabbed my phone; dialed it softly. A voice said: "Hollywood *Citadel-*

News."

"Is Peaches Vanner, the photographer, there?"

"I will connect you." There was a buzzing wait, then: "Miss Vanner talking." Her tone was sweet and dulcet to match her disposition. She was a nice little red-haired trick, even if she did snap photos for a living. I'd been on more than one party with her in the old days; knew she could be damned accommodating at times.

I said: "This is Dan Turner, the great lover. Remember me?"

"Great lover . . .! Good heavens, Dan, do you know the bulls are looking all over hades for you?"

"Yeah," I sighed. "I know all about it. Nuts to them. I want to ask you a question."

"If it's the usual one, why ask it? You already know the answer."

I said: "This is business, not pleasure. Didn't I see you in the Cafe LaBomba early this evening, making candid shots and popping off flash bulbs?"

"You did if you were there. But what—?"

"Listen, honeybunch. Have you developed any of those negs yet?"

"No. I was just about to start. Why?"

"I hanker for the reel out of your candid gadget," I said. "It may mean getting my neck out of a sling."

She drew an audible breath. "If you're on the level, I'll do anything you want. Or is this a gag?"

"No gag." I told her. "Meet me in ten minutes at

the corner of Yucca and Las Palmas. It'll be good and dark there. Bring that spool of film with you—and keep your fingers crossed for me." I rang off.

My next move was to riffle the phone-book; find Walt Ashworth's number down at Malibu. I whispered the call to a toll operator; listened for the ringing signal. Presently Ashworth answered. He sounded logy, surly. "Well, what is it?

"I'm not giving any newspaper interviews."

"I don't want one, Walt. This is Dan Turner."

His voice choked up. "Dan! My God, man—where've you been and what did you have to do with Rhoda's d-death? The reporters are claiming that you—"

"Never mind what they claim. They're all damp. But I'm about to clean this thing up, once and for all. And I'll need every bit of your help."

"Wh-what do you mean? If you know anything, for God's sake tell me!"

I said: "It isn't what I know now. It's what I'm about to find out. Have you got a darkroom down there at your beach place?"

"Yes, certainly. Photography's my business."

"Good," I said. "I'll be seeing you soon. And I'll have some undeveloped candid negs with me. One of them is going to show a snapshot of Rhoda's murderer in the act of putting poison in the whiskey." Then I broke the connection.

I went into my bedroom, opened a bureau

drawer. I dragged out a spare automatic to replace the one that had stopped Tim Sullivan's slug.

I hefted it; went out through my kitchenette.

The hulking geezer was still parading past my front door. I slid up behind him; poked my rod into his kidneys. I said: "Don't do anything foolish, Sullivan. Unless you're hoping to become suddenly dead."

CHAPTER VII
Antidote for Death

THE headwaiter from the Cafe LaBomba stood petrified in his tracks. I turned him around, slowly; frisked him for his .22 gat. "Have you been waiting long, pal?" I asked him.

His glare called me a dirty name. "Damn your soul, snoop—!" he whispered.

"Cork it," I told him. "Justice is about to catch up with somebody; the somebody might be you. Do I make myself clear?"

He just stared at me with glims that sparked profanity.

I prodded him toward the rear stairs. "So you found out from the headlines that your bullet hadn't croaked me," I murmured. "You also saw where I'd lammed from the law. So you hung around my stash hoping I'd show up; hoping to get another chance to use me for a clay pigeon. You've got a filthy disposition, Sullivan."

His muscular frame jerked. "And you are a—"

"Don't say it," I snapped. "I know what's on your mind, so keep the words to yourself. This is going to be the payoff. Down the stairs with you; no noise. Cops are probably all around; but if you yell for them, I'll blow you to glory."

We descended. The basement garage was evidently unguarded. I made Sullivan get behind the wheel of my jalopy; told him what to do and explained what would happen to him if he didn't. He heeled the starter, gunned the motor. We whammed up the slanted ramp, doing a good thirty-five in second gear; a harness flattie was at the entrance and he damned near got knocked into the corner pocket. The scratches are still on my left fender where it scraped the brass off his buttons.

He yelled blue murder. Then he pumped a slug at us. But we were on the street and under way by that time. A bullet nicked my bucket's rear deck; scared the toenails off Tim Sullivan. He mashed the throttle as far down as it would go.

WE MADE it to Las Palmas and Yucca in nothing flat; I kept my roscoe up against Sullivan's brisket the whole time. Presently I said: "Stop here."

Peaches Vanner was parked in the shadows; sitting in a 1933 clunk that looked ready for the scrapyard. She got out when we pulled up alongside.

"Dan—" she said.

She looked cuter than hell in a slanted hat and man-tailored tweeds. Her ankles had just the right chiffon sheen of slimness; her curves were all to the mustard. I beckoned. "Give me the films, babe."

"Here they are. Can't you tell me—?"

"Not now. But I'll need your chariot. There'll be a radio bleat out for mine by this time. Do you mind?"

She shook her head. "You're welcome to the old bus, Sherlock. How's about letting me in on the doings?"

"Sorry, hon. No can do. But I'd like one more favor from you. I want you to phone Dahlia Mannerling; tell her I'm going to make the big pinch. Got that?"

"Yes. That is, I—"

"Tell her hell's going to pop at the Ashworth joint in Malibu. That's all." I got out of my crate; kissed her while still keeping Tim Sullivan covered. Then I motioned for him to take the wheel of the other car.

He did. I crawled in beside him. "To the beach, pal," I said. "And let's not linger."

The Vanner doll's wreck rattled forward. Fifty was its top speed, but that was okay. It spelled less chance of being stopped by some nosy motorcycle slob. I kept my roscoe and one lamp on Sullivan; the other on the road. The payoff was coming up.

We wound through the canyons beyond the Will Rogers Memorial polo field; zipped into patches of fog and out again. Now the road began to dip into its last slant where it joined the coast highway. Malibu lay to the north. I felt sweat beginning to form in my armpits. Would my trap work?

Hell, it *had* to work! Otherwise I wouldn't be able to prove a damned thing. All I had was a theory. It was ironclad and steel riveted; but it wouldn't stand up in court. Not unless I got a confession to back it up.

I nudged Sullivan with my rod. "Remember you're to keep your trap corked. I'm going to have you under the gun every minute. If you make one wrong move, you're in a hell of a fix."

He just grunted.

Then we were in front of the Ashworth stash. I got out; kept Sullivan alongside me. I rang the Ashworth bell.

Walt opened up. His eyes narrowed when he saw the headwaiter. "What's all this?" he asked.

He looked like a walking cadaver; his map was pasty, his glims sunken, his kisser dry and parched. He didn't observe that I had Tim Sullivan under duress; that was because the rod was in my pocket where it wouldn't show. I said: "You can ask questions later, Walt. There's work to be done now."

"What kind of work?"

With my free hand I produced the roll of exposed film that Peaches Vanner had given me. "This," I said. "When you've developed it, you'll have a snapshot of your wife's killer."

"How do you mean!"

I said: "A newspaper photographer was on deck at the Cafe LaBomba tonight. She snapped a series of magic-eye shots just as Gordon Maxim sent that fifth of rye over to your table. Remember the flash bulbs flaring just around that time? Well, this reel will show the bottle being carried *and the poison being dumped into it—*"

THAT was like prying the lid off of hell. Tim Sullivan let out a raging bellow! Walt Ashworth dragged a .38 Spanish from his hip pocket. Walt said: "Give me those films, damn you!" and made a grab for the spool. "You'll never gas me!" He drew a bead at my noggin.

I ducked as his cannon yammered: *"Chow-chow!"* Tim Sullivan gave vent to a squeal of pain as a slug nipped him in the left arm. I went hurtling at Ashworth; tripped over a rug. It threw me. My cranium collided with a wall. For a split instant I was stunned.

Then Sullivan and Ashworth came together. Sullivan had only one duke to work with; the other arm was hors du bullet. But he did good work with the tools at his command. He wrenched at Ashworth's hog-leg, tried to snatch it. Ashworth fought like a maniac. "I'll kill you—both of you—!" he foamed.

From the front doorway, a dame screeched. My

glims cleared enough to let me see Dahlia Mannerling coming into the room with two sheriff's patrolmen flanking her. Then, somehow or other, Sullivan twisted Ashworth's rod around—just as it went off.

Ashworth coughed, stiffened, and went down. Red juice leaked out of his chest, stained his shirt. The two highway cops lunged at Tim Sullivan, disarmed him, pinioned him. One of them said: "What the hell goes on here?" Then he said: "Why, I'll be damned! *You're* the son who slugged me on the road tonight!" He pointed a finger at me.

"Take it easy," I told him. "If you arrest anybody, it'll be Walt Ashworth, here. He's the murderer. Aren't you, Walt?"

Ashworth writhed on the floor. "You . . . snooping . . . louse. . .!"

I said: "It's funny what the needle will do to a man. It made a killer of you. When Rhoda learned you were a hop-head, she tried to reform you. She pretended to get drunk in public; pretended she was having love affairs with mugs like me. Her tactics made you sore; you began to hate her because she wanted to straighten you up.

"Maybe she went so far as to threaten you with other things—such as proclaiming your dope addiction to the world. She was nutty about you, pal. Too damned nutty for her own good. Her attempts to make a man of you backfired. You determined to

183

kill her—so you could go on with your needlework without being nagged.

"You chose the poison route; being a photographer, you had access to chemicals. And you selected gelsemium rhizome because it would give you a swell alibi. A book on toxicology gave me the tip-off, Walt. Gelsemium kills by respiratory paralysis—asphyxiation. But its first symptoms are exactly like the signs of ordinary drunkenness: dizziness, double vision, staggering gait, loss of speech and so on. You could dose Rhoda with it, and everybody would think she was merely plastered. And you could take some of it yourself without it harming you, except to make you somewhat sick. *Because the only antidote for gelsemium is morphine—and you were already saturated with that!*"

A blood-bubble formed at his lips; burst. "You think ... you're. . . smart. . .!"

I LIT a smoke. "Sure I'm smart when I can read the answers in a book. You figured to drink the same poison you gave Rhoda; but she was the only one it would kill. Then you could claim somebody had tried to croak both of you. By a freak of luck, the whiskey you used came from a bottle sent over to your table by Gordon Maxim. Later, you decided you could pin the works on him by creaming him and making it look like a suicide confession. But I trapped you, pal. I did it with a reel of film. You thought the negatives might show you in the act of pouring your poison in the rye bottle.

"That caused you to go off the deep end; and now you're finished, thanks to Tim Sullivan."

Ashworth didn't answer me. He couldn't. There wasn't any more breath in his lungs. It had all leaked out through that bullet hole.

Sullivan growled: "I'm glad! I wish I'd washed him up with my bare hands!" Then he looked at me. "I—I'm sorry I went gunning for you, Mr. Turner."

"Skip it. You knew Rhoda had left the cafe with me. When you heard she was dead, you thought I'd killed her. You loved her, and you wanted revenge. I realized why you tried to ventilate me; that was why I never once suspected you of Rhoda's kill. If you'd been guilty of poisoning her whiskey, you wouldn't have thought I was responsible. That's nothing but simple logic."

He nodded. "Anyhow, I got the revenge I wanted. . . ."

I said: "Yes. And Dahlia Mannerling gets a hell of a big story for her column. I guess everybody ought to be satisfied."

The big blonde bim gave me a quivery smile. "Will you take me home, Dan?"

Her eyes were thanking me for clearing up the mess. And I sort of gathered the idea that if I took her home she might show her appreciation in other ways. . . .

I slid an arm around her waist. The morning was

young; a lot could happen before the sun came up. I said: "Let's go, kiddo." After all, what the hell?

STAR CHAMBER

The girl had paid Dan five centuries and asked him to meet her at eight. Now her ex-husband was trying to hire him, and setting the same hour for an appointment! The whole set-up smelled to Dan, and behind it all was the stronger smell of cooking opium

T HE GRANDSTAND was jampacked. It was the last day of the racing season at Santa Anita; the final race of the afternoon. I was standing at the rail, watching the beetles through my binoculars, when somebody suddenly blammed into me from behind; almost knocked me tail over tincup.

In my game you learn to expect trouble at unexpected times. I whirled around, braced myself. My hand started toward the .32 automatic I always carry in a shoulder-holster.

Then I unlaxed.

It was a dame who had barged into me. She was an auburn-haired, curvesome cutie with violet glims, bee-stung lips and a figure like seven million bucks.

She was dressed in a tweed sports outfit that was tailored to her shapely form like melted wax. The fabric fondled her rounded curves, left no doubt about the sleekness of her hips and thighs. She had the kind of gams a bachelor dreams about but seldom sees.

She said: "I—I beg your pardon!" in a loud, apologetic tone. Then, in a tense whisper, she added: "You're Dan Turner, the private detective, aren't you?"

I said: "So I've been told," and took another gander at her. "And you're Folly Hempstead, the Cosmotone star."

She got pale. "Sh-h-h-h!" she whispered frantically. She shoved a crumpled bit of paper into my mitt. "Listen. Can you meet me at eight o'clock tonight in room 513 of the Galsworthy Hotel in Hollywood?"

That surprised me a little. I don't get hotel room invitations from gorgeous she-males every day in the week. When I grabbed a third squint at the way her bonbons bulged against the tweed, I couldn't help saying yes. I could think of plenty of nice ways to pass the time with her in a private room . . .

She must have read my thoughts. "It isn't that, Mr. Turner. It's a matter of . . . life and death! The door will be unlocked for you. Don't fail me—and don't tell a soul!" Before I could answer, she squirmed through the mob and lammed.

I FORGOT to watch the horserace; didn't even see which goat copped the duke. I was too busy wondering what the hell Folly Hempstead wanted with me—and why she'd been so damned mysterious about making the date. Maybe there was some explanation in the wadded scrap of paper she'd slipped into my hand. I looked at it.

It was a five-century note. A cool half-a-grand, all in one lump!

That spelled plenty. In a way, I was disappointed. It told me the Hempstead lovely wasn't inviting me to a boudoir joust. She had a job for me; an important job. People don't fork out five hundred plasters for nothing. Moreover, she was scared. She didn't want anyone to know she was hiring me.

Mentally I added up what I knew about her. She was the daughter of Cyrus Hempstead, president of Cosmotone Productions. But she was a damned sweet actress in her own right; had gained stardom in her latest pic. The public went for her in a large way.

She'd been married for a while to Fenimore Bray, the scenario writer; but the hitch-up had gone haywire about six months before. There had been a Reno divorce. Now the gossip columnists were saying that she was holding hands with Mack Martyn, former production chief of Cosmotone, who'd recently lost his berth because of a fuss with old man Hempstead.

There was a rumor that Folly was talking her dad into reinstating Martyn pretty quick. But there was no scandal linked to the romance. Martyn was a bachelor, and it wouldn't be long until Folly's divorce decree would become final.

Then she'd be free to marry the discharged production chief—provided her old man didn't object, which didn 't seem likely.

But why the hell did she need a private gumshoe?

It was too much for me. I followed the crowds down under the grandstand, stopped at the bar for a quick snifter of Vat 69. Over the rim of my glass I

spotted two guys lapping up suds at the other end of the mahogany. I almost choked.

One of the men was Fenimore Bray, the scenario writer—Folly Hempstead's ex-hubby. And the bozo with him was Mack Martyn—her next, if the gossip was correct.

It struck me funny that they'd be drinking together in such a friendly way. Fenimore Bray was talking, laughing. Martyn was partially deaf, but apparently he had no trouble catching Bray's remarks. He wore an electrical ear gadget, with a tiny microphone slung near his binocular case.

Just as I finished my jorum, Martyn spotted me. He raised his hand and yelled: "Hi, Sherlock! Come join us in a snort."

I never turn down a drink. I ankled down the bar. Marten said: "Dan, meet Fenimore Bray. Fen, this is Dan Turner, heaven's gift to the detective industry."

FOLLY HEMPSTEAD'S former husband was tall, muscular. He gave my hand a hell of a squeeze; almost twisted my wrist out of joint. "Glad to know you, Turner. This is a damned lucky meeting. I need a private dick. Could we get together tonight—say around eight o'clock?"

I said: "Sorry, pal. I've got a date. How about tomorrow morning at my office?"

He seemed disappointed. "Well, okay then."

I tossed off another short Scotch, kidded around

for a minute and went on about my business. Driving back toward Hollywood, I tried to guess what might be on Bray's mind. It was queer he should want to see me at eight o'clock that night, when I had a secret date with his ex-wife at the same hour. It was probably coincidence, I figured; but damned odd just the same. Almost as odd as his being with Mack Martyn, who had replaced him in Folly's affections.

I had supper at the Brown Derby. Then, a little before eight, I drove my jalopy around to the Galsworthy Hotel on Franklin Street.

Just as I parked, somebody came pelting hell-for-leather out of the alley alongside the hotel. It was a jane. I caught a fleeting swivel at her pan; saw that she was a Chink cutie—and pretty as a picture. She wasn't wearing a coat; and I noticed her silk dress was torn open in front. She was holding the edges together to keep herself covered.

There was a taxi in front of my bucket. She slammed herself into it, her nifty stems twinkling; said something to the cabby. The hack lurched away. Out of habit I put the focus on its rear license plate; made a mental note of the number. Then I looked at my strap watch. It was practically eight o'clock. I went into the hotel, took the elevator to the fifth floor.

I barged down the corridor to room 513. The door was unlocked. There was a light inside. I ankled in. Then I froze.

Folly Hempstead was stretched across the bed, stripped to her step-ins and brassiere. My throat tightened up. I said: "What the hell—!"

Her piquant puss was mottled, her throat bruised to hellangone. Her tongue stuck out like a chunk of spoiled sausage and her eyes were wide open, glassy, staring up at the ceiling without seeing it.

She was as dead as a salt mackerel. She'd been creamed.

I LEAPED to the bed, dug my fingers under her breast. Her flesh was still warm, resilient; but there weren't any heart-beats. Her lovely shoulders were black and blue and so was her cuddly torso. There were added bruises on her perfect thighs and legs, as if somebody had kicked the tripes out of her before choking her to death.

Her ripped dress was over in a corner, in shreds. She must have put up a whale of a fracas before her murderer got his fingers around her gullet. From the grotesque angle of her noggin I could tell that her vertebrae had been snapped. The killer must have had damned powerful hands.

There was a phone on the wall. I dashed to it, un-cradled the receiver, dialed police headquarters. I asked for my friend Dave Donaldson of the homicide squad; got him. I said: "This is Dan Turner. I just stumbled into a bump-off."

"That's a nasty habit you've got. Who was croaked this time—and why?"

I told him to flag his trousers to the Galsworthy Hotel; gave him the room-number. Then I rang off, set fire to a gasper, waited.

Donaldson didn't waste time getting on the job. He blammed into the room before I'd finished my third coffin-nail. He took one startled gander at Folly Hempstead's corpse and almost tossed his muffins. "Jeest—!" he gulped.

I said: "Yeah. Exactly."

"What's the low-down?" he barked at me.

I shrugged. "I don't know. She ran into me at the racetrack this afternoon; handed me five centuries, and asked me to meet her here at eight o'clock tonight. She told me to keep my kisser buttoned. She acted scared. When I got here, I found her remainders on the bed the way you see them now."

"Did she say what was on her mind, this afternoon?"

"No."

"Well, then, did you spill to anybody that you were going to meet her here?"

"No," I repeated.

Dave said: "Well, dammit, somebody found it out! Say—could anybody have overheard her talking to you at the track?"

"Impossible. She whispered."

"Then maybe she blabbed it herself before she came here."

I said: "I don't think so. From the way she acted, I gathered she was keeping everything absolutely mum. I'm telling you, she was scared gutless."

Dave grunted. "Well, whatever she wanted to see you about, it's all washed up now. You're five hundred clams to the good. And I've got another stink to unravel. Nuts!"

THERE didn't seem much I could do to help him. I

said: "I think I'll toddle home. If you want me, phone me." I went down to my chariot, drove to my apartment stash.

I was just fitting the key in the lock when somebody tapped my shoulder from behind. It startled the clabber out of me. I spun around, balled my maulies, stared.

It was Fenimore Bray, Folly Hempstead's ex-spouse. He looked pale, drawn. "I've got to see you, Turner. Tonight. Right now. I know you told me to wait until morning, but—"

I said: "Okay. Come in." We went into my joint. "What's eating you?" I asked him.

He paced the rug. "You've got to help me get Folly out of trouble," he said.

That stiffened me. Didn't he know she'd been cooled off? No; of course not. The newspaper extras wouldn't be out for another hour. Meanwhile, maybe he might spill something that would give me a lead to her killer. I said: "What kind of trouble?"

He averted his peepers. "Listen. Maybe you'll think I'm a damned fool. Folly divorced me; but I still love her. I hate to see her going to hell in a handbasket."

"Meaning what?"

"She's been leaning on her elbow," he muttered.

I jammed a gasper into my teeth to cover my surprise. "Hitting the pipe?"

"Yes. Opium. Some lousy rat got her on the stuff.

It'll ruin her; wreck her. I want to hire you, Turner. I want you to find out the Chink dive where she does her dreaming. Then I want you to give your information to the Feds."

The minute he mentioned a Chink dive, I got a funny feeling in the pit of my elly-bay. I said: "Damn me for a numb-skull!" and shoved Bray out of my apartment. I followed him. "Beat it, cousin. I've got a job to do!"

Then I left him standing flatfooted while I sprinted downstairs to the basement garage and piled into my coupe.

LUCK was with me. When I jammed on my brakes in front of the Galsworthy Hotel, there was a Yellow parked at the taxi-stand. I looked at the tag. It was the same hack I'd seen a while before.

I flashed my tin at the jehu. "Got a question to ask you, bud."

"Okay, shamus. Shoot."

"About an hour ago you drove a slant-eyed wren away from here. A cute little cookie with her dress torn. Where did you take her?"

"That's easy, brother." He mentioned the address of a bungalow on Curson street.

I thanked him, piled back into my wreck. I souped the motor up to sixty and then added ten more for luck. In a few minutes I was standing on the porch of a little cottage. There was a light in one of the back rooms. But when I rang the bell, the light went out. Nobody answered.

I twisted the knob, pressed my weight against the cheap pine door. It was flimsy. It gave. I went bouncing over the threshold.

I had my roscoe in one hand, my flash in the other. I started for the rear room where the light had been—

Spang!

Something glittered toward me in a flat arc. It was a shiv. I ducked sidewise. It sliced past my ear, buried itself in the well behind me. I said: "Damn!" and bored a pencil of light into that back bedroom.

A cutie in pajamas was crouched in a corner. She was whimpering. I recognized her yellow complexion, almond optics. She was the Oriental frail who had run out of the alley alongside the Galsworthy Hotel.

I smacked into her, grabbed her.

SHE couldn't see my pan because my flash-beam was in her eyes. She wriggled, twisted, tried to fight me off. She was slim and straight as an arrow. I could feel her solid little whatcha callems panting up and down against me. As I shoved her backward, her knees hit the edge of the bed. She lost her balance. I mashed her down with my weight, sensed yielding flesh against me in the darkness as I dropped my flash and went to work on her.

I said: "Toss knives, will you?" and smacked her across the mush. Then I gave her a belt on the other cheek for good measure. She went limp, quit struggling, started to moan. All of a sudden her bare arms snaked around my neck.

"Don't kill me!" she quavered. Her English was perfect. "Don't kill me do . . . anything . . . if you . . ." The words stopped as she fastened her succulent lips on my kisser.

I've run up against expert pash in my time; I know most of the answers. But that Chinese filly fed me a brand that was new to me. Her mouth battened on mine in a manner that made my tonsils curl up and sizzle. Her arms tightened about my brisket, and her breath scorched me like a firecracker.

I couldn't help running my fingers over her. In the darkness her skin was like velvet. She was thin, but she had curves enough to suit anybody. I found plenty of them.

It's funny how an unexpected opportunity like that can sidetrack your original purpose. For the moment I forgot about Folly Hempstead being bumped; couldn't even remember my own name and telephone number. This Oriental cupcake was teaching me things I never knew before. And after all, I'm as human as the next guy . . .

IT WAS a long time before my think-tank got back to normal. Then I grated: "Why did you slam that shiv at me, baby?"

"I—I was afraid you'd k-kill me like you killed Miss Hempstead . . ."

I jumped up on my pins. "Say! How the hell did you know she was chilled? And who do you think I am?" I found the wall-switch, clicked it; jammed my .32 against her tummy. "If you know who croaked the Hempstead quail, start spilling!"

She blinked at me in the light. Her dark, slanted peepers got wide when she saw the badge under my coat. "You—you're a detective—?"

"I'm Dan Turner. Quit stalling before I start shooting dice with your front teeth."

"D-Dan Turner . . .? Then I can tell you . . . everything!" She grabbed my arm. "Listen. Miss Hempstead took me to the Galsworthy Hotel tonight to meet you—"

"Did you know in advance where you were going?"

"No. She wouldn't tell me until we actually arrived there. She said nobody knew the meeting-place except you and herself. She wanted me to tell you about the opium-joint where I used to work, and Lystra LaSalle, and . . . the others. We waited in room 513 for you to come. Then a masked man walked in.

"He grabbed at me, tore my jacket. I got away from him. He hit Miss Hempstead with his fists; started choking her . . . I got out through the window, went down the fire-escape, came home. J-just now, when you broke in, I th-thought you were the same man—"

I broke in: "What about an opium-joint. What about Lystra LaSalle? Who was the masked man?"

She started to answer me. Suddenly she looked past my shoulder, toward the bedroom window; let out a bleep of terror. Some sixth sense told me she wasn't fooling. My hunch made me dive for the floor. I tried to drag the Chinese cutie down with me.

I was too late. There came a hell of a clatter as a window-pane smashed inward. A roscoe sneezed: *"Chow-chow-chow!"* and one slug caught the slant-eyed wren smack in the breast. She collapsed on top of me, coughing ketchup. The second bullet hit the overhead electric light, put it out. The third was aimed at me, but it splatted into the Asiatic frill instead. I could feel her corpse jerk under the impact. It wasn't pleasant.

I cursed, tried to worm out from under her. By the time I made it, there wasn't anybody at the smashed window. There was nothing outside but darkness.

I found a phone in the front room, called Dave Donaldson, told him what had happened. Then I lunged out to my parked vee-eight.

A front tire was flat. Some bright apple had let the air out of it.

I WAS five minutes putting on the spare. Then I climbed under the wheel, started rolling. My noggin was buzzing like a hive of hornets. I tried to piece things together. In the first place, Folly Hempstead had wanted to talk to me about an opium-joint; had wanted the Chinese chick—a former employe of the dive—to spill some information to me. That linked up with Fenimore Bray's story. He claimed his ex-wife was hitting the pipe.

In the second place, Folly hadn't told a soul that she was meeting me at the Galsworthy Hotel. She hadn't even let the almond-eyed jane in on that—until they actually reached the place.

Yet somebody had found out where Folly was going to meet me. Armed with this information, he had gone to the hotel; choked Folly to glory. Now, how had the killer discovered where she was going to be at eight o'clock?

I couldn't add up the answer to that one. And until I did get it figured out, I wouldn't have a line on the murderer. I shifted my grey matter into high gear; fished around for another angle. Suddenly I remembered something the slant-eyed cutie had said to me, just before she got plugged: ". . . tell you about the opium-joint where I used to work . . . and Lystra LaSalle . . . and the others . . ."

Lystra LaSalle was a brunette vamp in Cosmotone pix; a top-ranking star. I'd known her in the old days, when she played bits at fifteen clams a day.

We'd been on parties together. But I hadn't seen her recently, except on the screen. I didn't even know where she hung out. Just the same, she might be a lead. I decided to look her up.

I was in a residence section by that time. There wasn't a phonebooth in sight. Then a thought hit me. Mack Martyn lived just away from where I was; and until recently he'd been executive head of Cosmotone. Maybe he could tell me what I needed to know. I drove to his drop, thumbed the doorbell.

He opened the door himself. "Why—hello, Sherlock! What brings you here?"

I noticed he wasn't wearing his electrical ear gadget. I raised my voice. "I want Lystra LaSalle's address. Have you got it?" I framed the words slowly, so he could read my lips.

He nodded, smiled. He told me a number on Crenshaw. Then he said: "Is Lystra in dutch about something?"

I didn't bother to answer him. Apparently he didn't know about Folly Hempstead's death. And I didn't have time to go into details. So I said: "Thanks," and lammed back to my heap; headed for Crenshaw Boulevard.

THE LaSalle frail's wikiup was a big two-story affair on a corner lot. As I drifted up, a black sedan purred down out of the driveway, made a U-turn, headed for town. I got a gander at the driver; and a funny feeling bored through me. It was Fenimore Bray.

Now, what the hell was Folly Hempstead's former hubby doing, coming out of Lystra LaSalle's place?

I legged it to her front porch; jingled the buzzer. A maid let me in. I said: "Is Lystra home?"

"Yes, sir. But she has already retired—"

I pushed past her, went upstairs. The LaSalle dame's boudoir door was open and she was sitting before a dresser, in negligee. Her black hair was hanging down over her shoulders; made startling contrast to the whiteness of her skin. She was plenty gorgeous in a mature way, but I noticed hollow circles under her glims; and her complexion wasn't as clear as it had been a couple years before. She was thinner, too. She still had plenty of yumph, though. It showed through the thin chiffon when I tabbed her reflection in the glass.

She spotted me; jumped up and turned around. "Dan Turner, of all people! What—"

I grinned, went to her. "Long time no see, hon. I thought I'd drop around to find out if you'd gone high-hat."

She must have remembered some of the good times we'd had together in the old days. She laughed, pouted out her red lips, arched her generous creampuffs. "I'd never go tall millinery on you, handsome. Why haven't you looked me up before this?"

I shrugged. "Just one of those things. How about a

kiss to make up for lost time?"

She gave it to me without any argument. She hadn't changed much on that score. And the way she melted against me put ideas in my mind. Her negligee was fluffy, perfumed, provocative; didn't hide much. Her flesh felt warm and nice through the sheer chiffon. I felt my temperature coming up. . . .

AFTER a while I whispered: "Jeeze, I'm jittery."

"Need a drink to restore the vitality!"

"It takes more than a drink to fix me, these days," I said.

"Meaning what?"

I whispered: "Joy-smoke."

She got stiff in my arms. "Good God—you, too?"

"Yeah. But the law knocked over my Chink joint last week. I haven't located another place yet"

Lystra said: "That 's funny."

"What 's funny?"

"You being on the pipe. And Fenimore Bray coming here to ask me about the same thing, a while ago."

I said: "Bray?" and pretended to be surprised. "Is he—?"

"No. But he told me that Folly's on her elbow these days. He wanted to know if I could tell him where she puffs it."

"Did you?"

She said: "Certainly not!" in a harsh rasp. "He'd

have the place raided if he knew about it. I'm not cutting my own throat."

"But you do know a joint, don't you?" I made my voice sound dry.

"Yes. Are you leveling with me about wanting to cook a pill?"

I said: "Sure I'm leveling. Would I admit a thing like that for the fun of it?"

She drifted out of my arms. "Wait till I get a dress on. We'll go buy a dream."

I watched as she slipped out of the negligee, slid into satin panties and brassiere, wriggled frock over her noggin. She put her bare tootsies into pumps, jerked a coat over her shapely shoulders. "Let's go."

We went in my jalopy. She directed me over to a street just off Sunset; pointed to an old-fashioned frame residence. I parked, let her steer me to the stash. She knocked on the door. It opened. A Chinese maid smiled. "This way, Miss LaSalle."

We angled down a hallway. There was a pungent, acrid, bittersweet odor everywhere; the stink of burned *ahpien*. We passed an open door. I took a hinge into the room, saw people lying on couches, drug-dreaming. I recognized a lot of them. They were actors, actresses, Hollywood biggies; Cosmotone biggies, mostly.

The maid opened another door. "In here, Miss LaSalle." Then she turned, padded away.

Lystra went ahead of me; stepped over the threshold. I saw a flash of dull metal; heard a choked moan. Then the LaSalle wren was on the floor with her conk bashed in—and I was staring into the business end of a gat!

A guy was holding the roscoe on me; a tall bozo with big mitts and a black hood that masked his puss.

He said: "Come into my star-chamber, Mr. Turner. The chamber where stars dream sweet dreams—and snooping gumshoes meet death!"

STAR-CHAMBER was right—in the medieval sense of the word, meaning a torture-room. I was in a jam; a damned nasty jam. I knew it.

I knew I didn't stand the ghost of a chance to draw my own .32 heater. The hooded bird would plug me before my duke moved two inches. There was only one hope. Maybe he wouldn't want to shoot me because of the noise. Maybe he'd try to mace me the same way he'd bludgeoned Lystra La-Salle.

There was a closed window behind him. I got a wild idea. I said: "Why should you croak me, mister'?"

"You know too much."

I tensed my muscles, fed him a blast of words. I said: "You're damned right I know too much, *Mr. Finemore Bray!* For one thing. I know you murdered your ex-wife, Folly Hempstead, with those powerful hands of yours! *You killed her because she was going to spill what she knew about you running a dope-den!"*

He said: "You son of a witch!" and reversed his rod, started to blam it down on my dome. That's what I'd been hoping for. I swerved, ducked—and catapulted full-tilt at the window. I took the whole damned sash with me, glass and all. I went sailing out into the night before he could get his artillery back into firing position.

I landed on my shoulder-blades in a back yard. There was a gate in the surrounding fence. I scrambled upright, catapulted toward it, made the grade. Then I was in a black alley, running like hell.

At the next corner there was a druggery. I dived for the phonebooth, dropped a jitney in the slot. I dialed Dave Donaldson, got him. I said: "Turner talking. Blast yourself out here to Sunset and Maltman—fast! Pick me up. We're going places!"

It took him twelve minutes to reach me. I scrambled into his official heap while it was still moving. While waiting for him, I'd looked in the phonebook; found Fenimore Bray's address. Now I said: "Step on it, for Cripe's sake!" and told him the street-number I wanted.

He didn't ask questions. He just drove. He kicked the kidneys out of his motor, didn't bother about traffic signals. In nothing flat we skidded to a stop in front of Bray's bungalow. There was another chariot parked up ahead. I grabbed Donaldson's arm. "Come on!"

We plunged to the front door. Just as we reached it I heard a rodney sneeze: *ka-chow!* I said: "Too late!" and hit the portal with my poundage.

IT smashed open. Dave and I launched ourselves toward an open bedroom. I saw Fenimore Bray lying on the bed with a bullethole in his temple, a gat near his hand, a black hood-mask on the pillow under him.

Donaldson said: "Bray! He browned himself! That proves he must have murdered—"

"Suicide hell!" I yelped. I lunged toward the bathroom with Dave at my heels. Somebody was trying to get out through the window. Donaldson pulled his service .38, squeezed the trigger. The guy at the window gasped and sagged backward, I said: *"Okay. Mack Martyn. That settles your hash!"*

Dave Donaldson's pellets had made sieves of the former movie executive's lungs. He coughed up blood. "Damn . . . you . . . "

I said: "Old man Hempstead fired you from Cosmotone. You wanted to get even. So you started an opium joint. You got a lot of Cosmotone biggies hitting the poppy. You made love to Hempstead's daughter, Folly. You put her on her elbow, too. That was your revenge on Hempstead for giving you the boot. You planned to wreck his studio by making

hopheads of his best people—and his daughter!"

Donaldson stared. "I'm damned!"

I went on: "Yeah, Martyn. Then Folly found out the truth about you somehow. She realized you were wrecking her father's outfit. She was going to spill the words to me. You croaked her before she could talk, there at the Galsworthy Hotel. But that Chinese maid got away. So she was your next victim. You blasted her through her cottage window just as she was about to belch the low-down to me."

Martyn spat red. "You—you—" He writhed on the floor.

I said: "You figured that Lystra LaSalle would maybe take me to your dope-joint—because I asked you for Lystra's address. So you went there, waited. You conked Lystra, tried to conk me too. But I fooled you—and laid a trap for you. I pretended to think you were Fenimore Bray, before I escaped.

"When I powdered, you knew you were in a pickle. There was only one way out. You planned to come here, bump Bray, plant the hood-mask on him as evidence and make it look like suicide. That's exactly what I figured you'd do. Only I thought I could get here in time to save Bray. I didn't; so that's another killing on your doorstep." I looked into the bedroom, at Bray's remnants. Poor devil; he had loved Folly Hempstead. Maybe he'd be with her in another world.

Dave Donaldson said: "But how the hell did you

figure out that Martyn was guilty?"

"It was simple—and I was too damned dumb to get it at first. The whole thing hinged on how the killer had known about Folly meeting me at the Galsworthy Hotel tonight. She hadn't told anybody; neither had I. Yet the murderer knew it.

"Then I remembered that Martyn was partially deaf: He had an ear gadget—but like all deaf people, *he could also read lips!* He was at Santa Anita today. He had binoculars. He must have been watching Folly through the glasses when she spoke to me. That's how he knew about our appointment. *He read her lips through his binoculars!*"

Martyn choked: "Smart . . . dick . . . damn you to . . . hell . . . " He croaked cursing me.

RIDDLE IN THE RAIN

Dan had his own private quarrel with the man who tried to sell him a commission in the army, but when the lug was killed, the whole affair took a different complexion

A T FIRST I thought the blonde cupcake was plastered. No sober wren would stand hatless in the pouring midnight rain, the way she was doing. She didn't even have a topcoat over her thin blue frock.

It was her face that jolted me, though. Light from a street lamp sifted down on her dripping golden hair, threw her delishful features into sharp relief. She was as pale as a slice of Monterey cheese; and as I rolled by in my jalopy, I got a gander at her glassy glims. They held no more expression than the windows of a vacant house.

I whispered: "What cooks?" and drew toward the curb, put my gears in reverse and backed up to the motionless cutie; opened the door on her side. But she didn't stir, didn't slip me a tumble. 1 might as well have braced a marble statue.

Her silence, her frozen stance with the rain slapping at her, gave me the creeps. There was something weird about it; unnatural. Particularly when I recognized her and knew there was no good reason for her to be in this condition.

I said: "Hiya, hon. Pardon my freckled tonsils, but

aren't you Vestra Valentyne, the Altamount starlet?"

She pinned the lackluster focus on me. "I don't know. Am I?" Her voice was as dull as a two dollar phonograph.

THE screwball response flabbergasted me. How could a jane be unsure of her own identity? It didn't add up right; didn't make sense. In fact, the whole thing had a nightmare quality of coincidence when you considered the fact that I'd

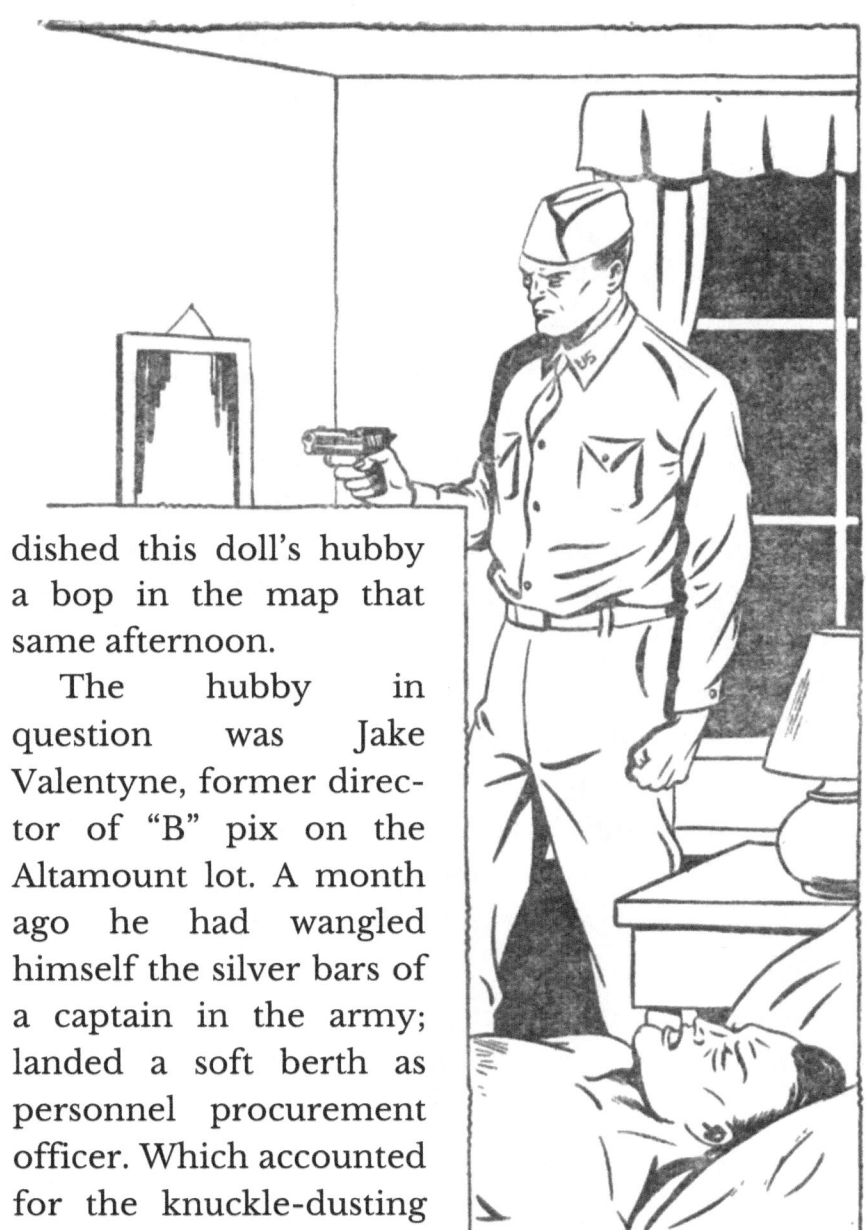

dished this doll's hubby a bop in the map that same afternoon.

The hubby in question was Jake Valentyne, former director of "B" pix on the Altamount lot. A month ago he had wangled himself the silver bars of a captain in the army; landed a soft berth as personnel procurement officer. Which accounted for the knuckle-dusting I'd doled him.

I had barged into his quarters, intending to enlist. Whereupon he hinted he might get me a lieutenant's commission if I greased his palm with geetus. Instead, I fed him a lump on the kisser. Bribery has no place in the military service when there's a war going on.

So now it was past midnight and here stood Jake's blonde and fragile frau, soaked to the rind and acting as if she'd lost her mental marbles.

I said: "Sure you're Vestra Valentyne. Also, you're flirting with pneumonia. You waiting for somebody?"

"I—I don't know," she answered in a tone that reminded me of a scared kid dreaming up goblins in the dark. "I d-don't even know why I'm here. Wh-where is this?"

"Melrose and Cahuenga," I said. "The town is Hollywood. And I'm Dan Turner, private snoop. Get in and I'll drive you home."

She shook her head like a dame in a drunken daze. "I—I don't remember if I've got a home. I—I feel so—" The words trailed off and her knees began to buckle.

I catapulted out of my coupe, caught her before she hit the pavement with her piquant profile. As I lifted her, I lamped the bruise on her temple; a big blue bump that had been hidden until now by her wet yellow hair. From the dimensions of it, somebody must have bunted her with a length of lead pipe.

I said: "Jeest!" and quit wondering why she was

suffering a dose of amnesia. It was a miracle her conk wasn't caved in.

SHE sagged limply as I hefted her into my bucket. I slid in alongside her, drove with one mitt, propped her steady with the other. But my mind was strictly on the job in hand.

I had a mighty sick chick on my hands and an idea in my think-tank. Going back to my brawl with Jake Valentyne, I realized it had been a haywire play. Several witnesses saw me cork him; which placed him in a position to do me dirty. He could sue me for assault and bashery; or he might make it tough for me to enlist.

I didn't want that to happen. There was a chance he hadn't actually meant his hinted offer to sell me a commission. Maybe he'd been testing me to see if I was as unscrupulous as Hollywood thinks I am. By pasting him, I'd laid myself wide open for a future full of gloom.

But now the setup had changed. Jake's wife was in a bad way; needed help. If I took care of her, the guy might call off his grudge. So I aimed my heap toward Sunset, where his tepee was located.

The clouds were still leaking copious amounts of juice when I dragged anchor in the driveway of the lavish Colonial wigwam. There was an army jeep under the porte-cochere, and I parked behind it; toted the blonde quail to the front porch.

A tall, skinny punk in khaki with two chevrons on his arm was ringing the doorbell. He copped a squint at me through the darkness and said: "Can you tell me if anybody's home, sir? I'm Corporal Lorton, Captain Valentyne's clerk. I've been trying for ten minutes to— *Hey!* What's the matter with the lady?"

"She passed out from a knock on the noggin," I said.

He shoved his youthful map closer to mine. "Say, I know you! You slugged Captain Valentyne this afternoon. I was there."

"Were you?"

"And this is the captain's wife!" the punk growled. "Listen. If you've hurt her—"

I said wearily: "Lay off. All I'm trying to do is get her indoors so she won't croak with influenza. Ring that bell again. I haven't got all night."

He rang but nothing happened. I ran my hand through the Valentyne frill's pocketbook; couldn't discover any keys. "Here, bub," I grunted to the kid in khaki. "Hold her for me while I pick the lock."

"That's illegal, mister."

"So it's illegal! You can blow if you don't like it."

"No. I have a communication for Captain Valentyne. Official business." He tried to sound important but I could tell he wasn't sure of himself.

I festooned the blonde cutie on his brisket. He had to hold her or she'd have gone sprawling. Then

I dug out my master keys, tried a couple. Presently I discovered that the lock was already unlatched. I pushed the portal open, ankled in, found the light switch and flipped it.

SIMULTANEOUSLY, Vestra snapped out of her trance. "Where are w-we?" she quavered.

"You're home, hon," I said. "Come upstairs and I'll blot you into some dry threads."

Corporal Lorton yeeped: "Wait a minute. You can't take that kind of liberties with an officer's wife."

"Ah, go climb a string," I snarled. And I half steered, half carried the bewildered blonde lassie to the second floor with Lorton trailing along behind.

In the upper hallway there was an open door with dim pinkish light glowing beyond it. The room looked like a she-male boudoir, so I nudged the Valentyne doll inside. Then, suddenly, she froze; stiffened against me and started shuddering like a kitten coughing brickbats.

I copped a swivel over her shoulder and came near tossing my tomatoes. There was a stubby, hairy-chested character on the bedroom rug, garnished only in the southern portion of a set of silk pajamas. His unpeeled torso was stickily crimson from a stab wound where some sharp disciple had rammed him with a skewer and twisted it around.

He was Captain Jake Valentyne, and he was

deader than a slab of barbecued beef.

I GASPED: "What the —!" and tried to get a grip on my fluttering elly-bay. And then the defunct bozo's shivering blonde wife emitted a shrill bleat, yanked herself away from me. Whirling, she made a wild dash for the door.

She moved plenty fast in spite of the way her wet, clinging skirt impeded her shapely stems. I was a fraction faster, though. I reached out, spun her around, and hauled her toward me.

I jammed her up against the wall and growled: "Okay, hon. Out with it. Did you butch this baboon?"

"What do you m-mean?"

"I'm asking you if you killed your husband."

Her kisser twisted, writhed. "I d-don't understand. I n-never saw him before, as f-far as I know!"

"Don't feed me that stuff!" I rasped. "Come clean before I belabor the custard out of you."

From behind me, a cool voice said: "You won't belabor anybody, mister. Put your hands up."

It was the corporal punk. Only he didn't look like a punk when I pinned the startled focus on him. His youthful puss was set in grim lines, like a Commando at bayonet drill; and he had an army automatic aimed at my adenoids.

"Hey, nix!" I yodeled. "What's the idea?"

"You know what the idea is. You hit Captain Valentyne this afternoon. You threatened him."

"What of it?"

"He's dead, that's what of it. Murdered."

I said: "You think I beefed him?"

"It's not my job to think, mister. And it's not your job to put Mrs. Valentyne through the third degree." His peepers slitted. "I told you to get your hands up."

I shrugged. "Okay, sonny boy. My flippers are lifted. Better phone the gendarmes."

"I'll contact my commanding officer first. Don't be telling me my business." There was a telephone on the bed stand across the room, and he kept me covered as he backed toward it. "We'll find out whether you killed the captain or his wife did."

Just as the punk said this, hell frothed over. I was facing away from the hallway door; didn't hear anybody sneaking up the staircase. Vestra Valentyne was trembling against the wall at my left as Lorton dialed "O" for the operator—

Over my shoulder a roscoe sneezed: *Ka-chow!* and I saw the corporal lurch, stagger, go down. Vestra screamed. Then something hard and metallic maced me across the back of the thatch. I was senseless long before I landed on the rug.

WHEN I woke up, the premises were infested with cops in blue serge and army officers in olive drab. Later I learned how they came to be there. The skinny punk had dialed the phone operator just before he got drilled, and the operator, plugging in, heard the shot; reported it to police headquarters. Two harness bulls in a radio cruiser picked up the subsequent flash, investigated, spotted the wounded Lorton and realized the mess had a military angle.

So they sent for some colonels and majors in addition to the usual assortment of ordinary plainclothes dicks.

Naturally I didn't savvy any of this when I opened my optics and glommed a groggy swivel around the boudoir. The first thing I noticed was that the blonde Valentyne quail was absent. Next I lamped her hairy-chested hubby's remainders being loaded into a wicker meat-basket by a pair of morgue attendants. On the far side of the room an ambulance medico was bandaging Corporal Lorton's shoulder where a slug had dug a tunnel. And looming directly over me was my friend Dave Donaldson of the homicide bureau.

Dave had a sour expression on his mush, like a guy sampling green persimmons. He rumbled: "It's about time you swam out of your swoon, Sherlock. You're in the grease up to your nostrils this trip."

I staggered to my pins, fished out a crumpled gasper, set it afire. My noggin felt as if it had been massaged by a pneumatic riveter and I had a lump under my haircut the size of a spittoon. Dave's remark didn't help my disposition much.

"How come I'm in the grease?" I asked him.

"For opening Jake Valentyne and putting a pill in Corporal Lorton."

I took an irate hinge at the skinny non-com. He was conscious by this time, of course; had been for quite a while, apparently. Long enough to toss accusations at me, anyhow.

"So you claim I plugged you," I snarled at him.

His voice was steady. "Who else could have?"

I said: "Somebody in the hall. The shot was fired by my ear. Then I got clubbed. The knob on my dome proves it."

A potbellied major glared at me. "Criminals have been known to injure themselves for the sake of an alibi."

That fried my tripes. I whirled on Dave Donaldson. "Ask Mrs. Valentyne where the bullet came from."

"She isn't here," Dave said. "She must have powdered before the radio patrolmen arrived."

"Then give me the paraffin test. Or take a gander at my gat. It hasn't been fired for a month."

DOUBT slid into Donaldson's tone. "You sound as if you were leveling, Hawkshaw. Maybe you didn't plug the corporal. But did you stab Valentyne?"

"No. He was defunct when I got here. Lorton will back me up on that." I looked at the punk and he nodded.

Dave said: "You could have knifed the guy earlier. They say you tangled with him this afternoon."

"Yeah. When he tried to sell me an army commission."

A leather-complexioned colonel poked his horn into the conversation. "There may be some truth in that. G-2 has been watching Valentyne on suspicion of peddling commissions."

"So he was crooked," I said. "But I didn't croak him. I was hoping to soothe him by playing good Samaritan to his wife." And I explained how I'd brought her home.

Donaldson scowled. "Where is she now?"

I didn't know, and I started to say so. Before I could shove the words out, though, a homicide dick barged in.

"Lookit!" he sputtered.. "I been talking to an old gink that lives across the street. He seen Mrs. Valentyne and some monkey lam out of here a while back, right after a shot sounded. The guy helped her in a car and drove off with her."

Dave stiffened. "Did this neighbor spot the car's tags?"

"New."

"So now we've got a snatch on our hands as well as a murder!" Dave caterwauled.

I WASN'T so sure of that kidnaping angle. Several factors argued against it, and I pointed them out.

"Listen," I said. "If you were going to snatch a cookie for ransom, wouldn't you make sure there was somebody to fork out the payoff?"

"I suppose so."

"Well, Jake Valentyne's remnants were in plain view. Whoever grabbed Vestra knew her hubby was deceased. Nobody in his right mind could hope to get dough from a dead man."

Dave said: "Maybe the idea was to put the bite on Altamount Pix."

I shook my head. "Vestra's just a minor starlet; not important enough to rate a ransom reward from her studio. If she was kidnaped, it wasn't for financial reasons."

"Then maybe she knew the identity of her husband's murderer," Dave suggested. "Maybe it was the killer who grabbed her to keep her from belching."

I said: "If the guilty guy had craved to shut her up, he could have done it permanently with a bullet when he fogged the corporal and put a dent in my dome."

Dave mulled that over while the Lorton punk was being helped down to an ambulance for a trip to Hollywood Hospital. Meanwhile I worked my own mental cogwheels; tried to figure why the blonde cupcake had been spirited out of the stash.

Presently a hunch sneaked up my slacks. Maybe I'd been right in the first place. Maybe the Valentyne quail had bumped her hubby. And maybe there was someone who cared so much for her that he wanted to get her out from under the rap!

But who was the bozo that loved her, assuming there was such a person? Gossip had never smeared her, as far as I knew.

Then I remembered a certain brunette wren named Margo Dutton, a bit player on the various

Hollywood lots. This Dutton dame was Vestra Valentyne's closest friend; she would know about Vestra's private life if anybody did.

The instant I thought of Margo, I pinched a blister on Donaldson's arm. "Listen, pappy. Can I haul bunions now?"

He favored me with a bitter sneer. "No, you can't. You're not in the clear yet by a long distance."

"Oh," I said. "Look. What are these things?"

"Your knuckles. So what?"

"So this," I said, and slugged him. As he folded, I hurtled my hundred and ninety pounds out of the place before anybody in the room knew what was cooking.

I plunged down the steps, five at a clip; went sailing out into the dripping night like a comet with the hotfoot. Six leaps carried me to my jalopy. I kicked the starter, rolled backward off the driveway. Ten seconds later I was careening up the street, hellity-blam.

MARGO DUTTON lived in a bungalow court over on Yucca. I parked a block away; started hoofing toward the cluster of cottages. By the time I reached Margo's hutch I was drenched to the kidneys and my grinders were clattering like dice in a cup.

I thumbed the bell. Presently a light gleamed inside and the portal opened. The Dutton frill fastened the drowsy focus on me, then widened her dark

glims.

"Dan!" she said.

I gave her an apologetic grin. "Hiya, toots. My bucket broke down just now. I was only a block away, and I thought maybe you'd lend me your phone to call a cab."

"Oh, I see," she sounded disappointed. "Sure, come in." And she steered me into the tiny living room.

I pinned the admiring focus on her. She was embellished in a set of black pajamas to match her inky hair.

She asked me: "Don't you think you ought to have a snort of something to ward off bronchitis, handsome? You're dripping like Niagara Falls."

"I could use a nip. What kind have you?"

She gave me a funny look. "Vat 69—your favorite. I keep a bottle in stock the way some dames keep a candle in the window."

I should have remembered from previous visits that the Dutton doll never missed a trick when it came to playing hostess to her boy friends.

I hadn't visited her in quite a while, though. We'd been on any number of parties together in the old days; but recently I'd quit hanging around, mainly because some other lug had become her Number One boy.

Which was why I had used the excuse of a busted jalopy to get into her wikiup now. After all, if her current flame happened to be here, I didn't want to cause trouble.

However, it turned out that the trick hadn't been necessary. Margo was all alone—as she proved by the question she asked me when she came back with the Scotch. "Why not take off that wet suit and let me dry it, Philo?"

"That would be nice," I pulled my mouth down at the corners. "Especially if your boy friend should ankle in and catch me here."

She downed her drink. "What boy friend?"

"That Altamount press agent," I said. "Leo Linden."

"Leo stepped out of my life a month ago." She drifted closer to me. "Is that why you've been staying away?"

"Yeah."

"Then I'm glad your coupe broke down tonight. It gives me a chance to tell you I'm . . . back in circulation. In case you're interested," she added hopefully.

I DIDN'T like this turn the conversation was taking. What I actually wanted was information about

Vestra Valentyne; but if I came right out and asked, Margo would catch wise to my real reason for calling on her. And it might make her so sore that she'd clam up on me, refuse to tell me what I craved to know. She had a nasty temper when you rubbed her the wrong way.

It was a situation that demanded diplomacy in carload lots. As far as I'm concerned, there's only one way to deal with a dame in a case like that. Any quail's suspicions can be quelled by a few judicious kisses.

I slid an arm around her cuddlesome waist, pulled her against me. "You're a sweet chick, Margo. I go for you."

She shoved me off.

"D-don't!" she panted.

I said: "Scared of me, baby?" and crushed her close to me.

This time she didn't struggle. She just quaked in my arms, as if she had the emotional jitters. "Not scared of you, no," she insisted. "But I hate to be taken for a sleigh ride."

"Who's taking you for a sleigh ride?" I said.

She looked up into my peepers; seemed to be trying to read my thoughts. "I don't trust you, Sherlock," she said. "I don't trust any man. You're all heels. Kiss me some m-more."

I obeyed. I said: "You mustn't judge all men by any one bozo, hon. Can I help it if that Leo Linden louse gave you the brush-off!"

"But I c-cared for him, Dan." She wrapped her arms around me; dragged me toward her.

I said: "Hey, what is this? Am I supposed to be catching you on the rebound, helping you forget the guy?"

"Maybe. What do you care?" she gave me a crooked smile. "You help me pick up the pieces of my busted heart. I trade you a few minutes of necking. It's a fair exchange, isn't it? Sort of—well, friendly." She ran her fingers through my hair. Then she pursed her red lips for another kiss.

I whispered: "You've got funny ideas of friendship, sweet stuff. It's okay with me, though."

"Why shouldn't I have funny ideas about friendship? It was my best friend that took Leo away from me. Let's stop talking about it. Let's just think about . . . us. The present m-moment."

I tensed, pulled away, hung the startled glimpse on her. "Who was this pal that swiped your sweetie?"

"She didn't really swipe him. He happened to fall for her, is all. It wasn't Vestra's fault."

"Vestra Valentyne?" I yowled.

"Yes. What's the matter? Where are you going?"

I made a grab for my hat. "I've got work to do, sis. You just handed me the lead I've been looking for. Much obliged." And I made for the door.

She flurried after me. "You m-mean you're on a case? All the time, you were digging for information?

Pumping me? Why, you dirty stinking creep!" She grabbed up a heavy hammered brass ash tray; slammed it at my features.

I ducked in the nick of time and said: "Sorry, kiddo. I'll be seeing you." And I scrammed before she could find any more deadly weapons to heave at me.

DRIVING through the rain, I commenced piecing my puzzle together. This Altamonnt press agent, Leo Linden, was a guy I knew casually—a hulking, good looking slob with romantic inclinations. Every time he fell in love, he got the idea he'd found his perfect mate. Any wren who happened to be the object of his affections could have anything he owned, all the way down to his toenails.

So now he'd gone overboard for Vestra Valentyne. And he was just the type that would smash every law on the statute books to help a quail he was crazy about—up to and including an attempt to derrick her out from under a homicide beef. All my instincts shouted that Leo was the one who had glommed the Valentyne doll out of her igloo after plugging Corporal Lorton and swatting me on the scalp.

It was easy to guess why he whisked her out of the wikiup. He knew she'd croaked her hubby, and he wanted to save her from the consequences. But he made a bad mistake when he maced me; I don't take that brand of treatment from anybody. I made up my mind to put the finger on Vestra—and the way to do it was through Leo Linden himself.

I drove to his apartment stash on Franklin; knuckled the door. Just as it opened, I yanked my .32 automatic from the shoulder holster where I always carry it. Then, when Linden's handsome pan appeared before me, I shoved the rod up to his teeth.

"Hello, pal," I said. "Would you like a mouthful of slugs?"

He jerked backward, popped his lamps at me. "Turner! What in God's name is the idea?"

I followed him inside. "The idea is you shot an army corporal tonight and cracked me over the cranium. So now it's my turn."

His mush got pasty. "How—how did you know—?"

That was as good as a confession. I snarled: "Where's the Valentyne cupcake?"

"She—she—I don't know. What makes you think I could tell you where to find her?"

I barged close to him. "Cork the lies, chum. I know you took her out of that boudoir."

"Can you prove it?"

"I don't need to. I'll beat the truth out of you." And I hit him across the puss with my gat.

HE SAGGED into a chair, his cheek dribbling ketchup. "Please don't . . . I'll . . . talk."

234

"Make it snappy."

"I'll admit I shot that soldier and slugged you and got Vestra out of her house. I did it because you were accusing her of killing the louse she was married to."

"Sure she killed him. That's why I want her." Linden's map contorted. "You're wrong. Vestra isn't a murderess. Although I wouldn't have blamed her if she had stabbed Jake Valentyne. He was cruel enough to deserve killing."

"Cruel to Vestra?" I said.

"Yes. He was always beating her up. He did it early this evening in my presence. She asked him for a divorce so she could marry me. He went wild, struck her on the temple with a book-end. I knocked him down—"

"Ah," I growled. "So you're the one that skewered him!"

"No—! I left him unconscious; took Vestra away with me. She didn't know me, didn't even know her own name. That blow on the head had injured her mind. While I was driving her around in the rain, she suddenly jumped out of my car; ran off. I spent hours, searching for her. . ."

His voice sounded sincere, honest; I got the impression he was leveling. "Then what happened?"

"I finally decided she might have gone home. So I went there, found the door unlatched, walked in. I heard your voice upstairs, accusing somebody of

murder. I sneaked up the steps, looked into the boudoir and saw Jake Valentyne lying dead, as if he had
been bayonetted. . ."

"Whereupon you shot the corporal, bopped me,
and lammed with the jane, hunk?"

"Yes."

I yipped: "Where is she now?"

"In Hollywood Hospital. I took her there, registered her under an alias, left her for medical treatment."

All of a sudden I had the answer to my riddle.
I leaped over to Linden's phone, snatched it
from its cradle, dialed police headquarters and
got Dave Donaldson on the line. "Turner talking," I yelled. "Meet me at Hollywood Hospital
in a hurry. This Jake Valentyne kill is all washed
up!"

I rang off before Dave could pour a load of useless questions in my ear; whirled and started for the
door as fast as I could pelt. The Linden guy leaped
from his chair, blocked me. He raged: "Damn your
soul, I won't let you arrest Vestra! If you try to rail-
road her, I'll kill you!"

He made a dig for his hip pocket as if to pull a
roscoe on me. I nailed him on the chin with a
roundhouse haymaker; knocked him colder than
Siberia. Then I caromed from the flat, walloped
downstairs to my bucket, and souped the bejoseph
out of it.

NINE minutes later I pulled up in front of the hospital just as Donaldson arrived in his official sedan. He bounced out, lumbered toward me. "Okay, snoop. Stick out your fins for the bracelets," he bellowed.

I said: "Stew you, hideous. I'm about to hand you a killer. Come on, flag your diapers inside with me."

He hesitated, then wheezed along in my wake. I made inquiries at the information desk; turned down a long white corridor. "Hey!" Dave panted. "Who's here that we want?"

"Vestra Valentyne, for one."

"Then how do you figure to find her in the men's ward?"

I said: "I don't," and shoved my heft against the door of a private room; barged into darkness. I used my pencil flashlight to locate the wall switch; flipped it. A bedside bulb glowed to life, cast yellow reflections on a youthful face.

"The jig's up, Corporal Lorton," I said grimly. *"You're under arrest for cooling your captain."*

The skinny punk sat bolt upright; winced as pain nipped his bandaged shoulder. "Wha-what—?"

"A certain press agent just gave me the unwitting tip-off," I said. "He described Jake Valentyne's carcass as looking like somebody who'd been bayonetted. That clicked exactly with how I remembered Valentyne's wound; as if a sword has been jammed into him and twisted around before being pulled out. A sword—or a bayonet."

The corporal's Adam's-apple jiggled up and down. "So what?" he strangled.

"So that's how soldiers are taught to use the bayonet. You stab, twist, extract. In other words, it was an army guy who had bumped Valentyne."

"But wh-why pick on me?"

"You're an army guy," I grunted. "And you were at Valentyne's stash. You'd pulled your job of killery and were just leaving as I arrived with Jake's wife. So you thought fast; pretended you'd been ringing the bell, trying to get in. I should have known you were lying when I discovered the lock unlatched; but it didn't register at the time."

Lorton stared at me. "You can't prove I stabbed him."

"The hell I can't. Your motive was revenge. Valentyne was a crook. He'd been peddling commissions. The way I dope it, he had promised to make you at least a second lieutenant if you sweetened him with enough sugar. So you slipped him the lettuce, but he failed to deliver."

THAT was a shot in the dark on my part, but it struck home. The kid cringed, paled, let his jaw drop. Then I knew I had him. And after all, my theory was sound enough. I knew Jake Valentyne had been taking graft; so why wasn't it a logical motive for a croaking?

Lorton gasped: "That's no proof. That's just t-talk."

"So I'll give you proof," I said. "We found the check you paid Valentyne."

"That's a lie! I gave him cash. Five hundred dollars. And then he laughed at me, dared me too—h-h-h, my God!" the punk sobbed as he realized he'd dumped himself spang into the gas chamber. Only in his case it turned out to be a firing squad. A court martial saw to that. Personally, I think he should have been handed a medal for bumping Valentyne; but an army officer is an army officer, even though he's also a rat.

Anyhow, I let Dave Donaldson clean up the loose ends. In the meantime I hunted Vestra Valentyne's room; got there just as Leo Linden showed up. Leo had a mouse on his mush where I'd corked him; but he forgot his hurts when he copped a gander at the golden-haired quail.

"Vestra!" he said, and rushed toward her.

She opened the glims, and they weren't like the windows of a vacant house now. There was sanity in her expression and romance in her voice as she murmured: "Leo, darling."

They went into a clinch. I ankled out, left the building, got into my chariot and headed for that bungalow court where the brunette Margo Dutton cookie lived. Margo had lost Leo Linden, sure enough; but she still had me. . .

SLEEPING DOGS

Dan Turner was interested in good green folding lettuce, but once in a while a case turned d up which made the issue at stake worth more than the geetus in. volved. This was one of them

H E WAS a handsome son of a gun, I'll say that much for him. But the minute he came ankling into my office I knew he was worried about something. That's my business: putting a stop to other people's worries. And that's why plenty of citizens here in Hollywood are personally acquainted with the sign on my door that reads *Dan Turner, Private Detective.*

Anyhow, there stood Geoffrey Jackman looking upset. He was almost as tall as I am—six feet plus—and except for the scars on one side of his map and the black patch where his right glim used to be, he still looked pretty much like a movie hero. A property bomb had prematurely exploded on the set one day, wrecking his mush and his acting career simultaneously. Since then, though, he'd attained new fame as a director.

I opened the lower drawer of my desk, hauled forth two glasses and a fifth of Vat 69. "Have a snifter and tell me what's nibbling on you," I invited.

He poured himself a copious slug, downed it neat. It didn't seem to take the edge off his jitters,

however. His one good peeper had an uneasy gleam and he kept licking his scarred kisser as if he didn't like the taste of the words he wanted to spill.

I kept quiet. Letting the other guy do the warbling is one of my stocks in trade. And presently Jackman decided to unbutton his lip.

"It's about Leneta Leonard," he said.

I wasn't particularly surprised. The Leonard quail was Galatea to Jackman's Pygmalion. She'd been an

obscure and mediocre extra wren when he took her in hand; and he'd made a star of her—a big one. Her box office pull equaled anybody's in Hollywood, and Jackman's directing was responsible.

He helped himself to another shot of Highland tonic. "Leneta's in a jam. A bad jam. She wants your help."

I said: "Why didn't she come up and tell me about it personally?"

"She's afraid to. She doesn't want anybody to

know she's calling you in on the deal."

"Somebody already knows," I said casually.

He stiffened. "Wh-what—?"

I reached into my pocket, pulled out an envelope, handed it to him. He opened it and three nice crisp thousand dollar bills fluttered forth. Jackman's breath made a wheezing, startled noise in his gullet as he read the note that had accompanied the geetus.

I knew what it said, by heart. It had been shoved under my door, that morning, hand delivered; no stamp, no postmark to trace its origin:

"Dan Turner

It will be healthier for you if you lay off any case Leneta Leonard might ask you to handle. Here's three grand for being smart. Try a double cross and you'll wake up shaking hands with the angels.

—A friend."

Jackman gave me back the note. "Well, that outbids me," he muttered sourly.

"Meaning what?"

"Leneta's almost broke and so am I. Bad investments."

To me, this remark sounded like the old malarkey. He dragged down plenty of lettuce as a Paratone director; and the Leonard cupcake's weekly take was even fatter. I couldn't see how they could both be busted, this side of buying the Golden Gate

244

Bridge from some confidence expert.

All the same, Jackman stuck to his story. "Between us, Leneta and I couldn't rake up more than five hundred apiece," he made a bitter mouth. "And besides, your effectiveness would be reduced by this person's knowledge that you're on the case." He gestured toward the anonymous letter.

That scalded my tripes. Frankly, I'm out after the heavy sugar. Luck can't be with me forever; and some day there's going to be a lead slug all tagged with my name and telephone number. I crave to get my stack of chips and quit before the law of averages lays for me with a bellyful of bullets.

So under ordinary circumstances I'd have glommed onto the three grand in the envelope; told Jackman to take himself and Leneta Leonard's troubles elsewhere. But when he pulled this crack about my effectiveness being reduced, he made me bull-headed.

I REACHED for my phone, dialed the *Examiner's* want-ad department. "Take a personal ad," I said. Then I dictated it. "Friend. Send a messenger for your three G's. I'm running my own business to suit myself. Dan Turner."

Geoffrey Jackman hung the curious focus on me as I rang off. "Did you really mean that?"

I said: "Yeah. Now gargle your grief on my shoulder. You've just hired yourself a private snoop."

He hesitated. "Thanks. But look. In the first place, I don't want you to get me wrong. Leneta and I are just good friends—nothing more."

I let this slide. For all I knew, Jackman was leveling. Rumor had never linked him with the Leonard cutie.

So I nodded, kept my yap zippered.

"Leneta's in love with Victor Croft." Jackman stated it flatly, as if he were telling me something I didn't already know. As a matter of fact, I'd heard it from various sources. Victor Croft was a newcomer in the galloping snapshots; a tall, dark bozo with a smoothness that knocked the she-male customers in the aisles every time he pranced across the screen.

"So Leneta's in love with Croft," I said. "So what?"

"They're to be married next month. I'm in favor of it. I want her to be happy. But . . . she's being blackmailed. That's why she's broke. She's already paid out a hundred thousand dollars. Half of it was money I loaned her. And she's being bled for more."

I fished out a gasper, set fire to it, let the smoke cover my astonishment. I couldn't quite bring myself to imagine the Leonard lovely as the victim of a shakedown. In my game it pays to keep an ear to the ground for gossip, and I hadn't heard a single whisper of scandal in connection with her.

"What's the blackmail based on?" I asked.

Jackman's one optic got shifty with embarrassment. "She made a mistake when she came to Hollywood three years ago. She—well, she fell into the hands of a producer who made shorts of the burley-cue type. She appeared in one of his reels. Nothing terrible about that, of course, but it'd be embarrassing to have it turn up now that she's a star."

I nodded, poured him another drink.

HE tossed it off. "After she'd made it, I happened to meet her and see possibilities in her. I was willing to gamble on her future."

"It was a fair gamble," I said. "You hit the jackpot."

He nodded. "That's true. It's also true that I went to the creep who had produced the burleycue reel; bought it from him to protect Leneta. I destroyed the negative and, as I thought, all prints—"

"I can guess the rest," I said. "One print escaped you. It's still in existence; and now it has turned up. Whoever has it is threatening to make it public, eh?"

Jackman rasped: "Not public, exactly. Something just as bad, though. The blackmailer threatens to show it to Victor Croft. If that happens, Croft would ditch her—and she loves the guy. She'd go to pieces if he broke the engagement. That's why she's paid so much money to get the film—but this shakedown artist hasn't delivered."

"So you want me to locate the film, destroy it," I said.

"Yes."

"That ought to be easy. Who's the louse that

made the opus in the first place?"

Jackman's kisser twisted grimly. "He's dead. His organization is scattered. There's no angle in that direction."

"Then I'll find another direction," I stood up. "Leave it to me. And quit jittering."

He gave me a crooked smile and a handshake;

scrammed. As soon as he was gone I picked up my phone, called a friend of mine who works for the clearing house association; a mug that owed me some favors.

When I made connections I said: "Turner talking. I want you to trace three thousand dollar bills for

me." And I gave him the serial numbers of the dough that had been enclosed with the anonymous letter that morning.

"Okay, Sherlock. I'll call yon back."

I waited. In an hour I had the dope I wanted. The three G-notes had come from the Hollywood-Tenth National Bank; part of a ten grand withdrawal from Leneta Leonard's own account. She'd cashed the check herself just a week ago.

"Much obliged, pal," I said, and hung up. Then I barged down to my parked jalopy; headed for the Leonard cookie's wigwam in Beverly Hills. There were some things I craved to know.

In the first place I wanted to find out if Leneta's engagement to Victor Croft was on the level. A lot of that stuff is strictly out of some publicity agent's dream book; and if this particular love affair turned out to be phony, the case would be tougher than boarding house steak.

On the other hand, if it proved to be straight goods I figured I had a possible motivation to work on: jealousy. Some frail, in love with the Croft hambo, might have got hold of the blackmail reel for the purpose of busting up Leneta's romance with the guy—and, before doing this, decided to collect some shekels from the setup.

So I had to make sure Leneta was actually planning to marry Victor Croft. Then I'd know where to start.

WHEN I reached her sumptuous stash I hung around outside for damned near an hour before thumbing her doorbell. This was because I piped a sleek Cadillac convertible standing in the driveway. It was Croft's heap, and I didn't want to barge in on Leneta while he was on deck.

Presently I lamped him coming out. He didn't notice me lurking at the curb; and as soon as he wafted his swarthy good looks off the premises I made my play. Except for the maid who let me in, the Leonard chick was all alone in her wikiup. I ankled into the living room, fastened the fascinated glimpse on her.

She was a delishful little trick with more curves than the Burma Road. When she stood between me and the sunset streaming in through a window behind her, I got a swivel at the niftiest she-male silhouette I'd seen in a month of Mondays.

"I'm Dan Turner," I informed her. "Your friend Geoffrey Jackman was in to see me today."

She nodded listlessly. "He phoned, told me. He also mentioned the letter you received this morning."

"Nuts to the letter, hon. When was the last time you paid blackmail and how was it worked?"

"A w-week ago today. There was a note under my door. It said to leave t-ten one thousand dollar b-bills in an envelope, slipped between the pages of Baedecker's Guide to Vienna on the shelves of the

Hollywood Library at f-four in the afternoon. It promised the film would be delivered to me that night."

"You followed instructions?" I asked her.

"Y-yes. I got the bills from my bank; did exactly what the note demanded. But I didn't g-get the reel."

I nodded. Her story meshed with what I already knew. Which proved it was the blackmailer who had sent me the anonymous message and the three G-notes. That dough had been part of the Leonard doll's last payment.

The next problem was: how had the shakedown artist learned that Leneta was going to call on me for help?

I eliminated Geoffrey Jack man. He'd come to hire me, not to steer me off. Leneta must have tipped her mitt to somebody else. I asked her point blank: "Aside from Jackman, did you mention to anybody that you were going to engage my services?"

"Why, no," she seemed puzzled. "That's wh-why I can't understand the letter you got. It w-worries me. Geoffrey's the only one who knew—" her voice trailed away.

Apparently there was nothing more I could learn from her on that angle. So I switched my tactics, sat down alongside her on a big, deeply cushioned divan. I got confidential. "Look, sweet stuff. What would you do if I turned that reel over to you right now?"

I felt like a heel, raising her hopes that way. But I was after some pertinent information. She faced me, her peepers brimming with hope. "You—you mean you have it?"

"That depends," I said, and wormed my arm around her slender waist; hauled her close to me; her perfume drifted to my smeller, seeped into me like a shot of cocaine.

I breathed in her ear: "Would you give up this Croft slob for a sleuth that makes pretty good dough? We could . . ."

She wriggled free; slammed me across the mush with her closed fist. It stung. "You—you dirty creep!" she gritted. "Take your hands off me!"

"Still in love with Croft, eh?" I sneered.

She darted across the room, picked up an andiron from the fireplace. "Get out. Get out before I brain you."

"Calm down, Beautiful," I grinned and set fire to a gasper. "I was just testing you, is all."

"Testing—?"

"Yeah I wanted to know if you really love Croft."

She was still breathing hard. "You found out," she said grimly.

I admitted this, ruefully. I was almost sorry she hadn't fallen for my overtures. I liked her. But as long as she was another guy's private property there wasn't much I could do about it except wish I'd found her first.

I BLEW her a kiss; scrammed. The maid handed me my hat at the front door. I fixed the casual focus on this jane and she smiled back at me, not so casually. In fact, something told me she might be worth cultivating.

Right now was scarcely the time, though. So I tipped the quail a wink and hauled bunions.

Driving back to my office, I mulled things over. I knew now that Leneta Leonard and Victor Croft were leveling about their engagement; which gave me a hunch to play the jealousy possibility. One of Croft's discarded sweeties might be doing the blackmailing.

It was worth a toll call to New York. When I got to my quarters I dialed long distance; put through a connection to a columnist friend of mine in Manhattan who knew everything about everybody.

When I contacted him I said: "Hiya, chum. This is Turner talking from Hollywood, no less."

"Well, blow me down! What cooks, gumshoe?"

"I need some dope on a guy named Victor Croft. He's out here emoting in the yodeling snapshots; hasn't been on the coast long. I think he used to be on the stage, didn't he?"

"Sure. Played bits on Broadway. What about him?"

I said: "Who was his sweet patootie before he

came west!"

"Let's see. Oh, yeah, I remember. Some dame named Dorothy Manton. A chorine. Yellow hair, lots of yumph. Followed him to Hollywood, I think. I understand he ditched her for Leneta Leonard. True?"

"Right," I said. "You could make a paragraph of it if you want to. But maybe I'll be slipping you something even hotter in a day or so." And I rang off.

Whereupon a voice behind me said: "Freeze, louse."

I twitched as if I'd been rammed with a hot corkscrew. There was something venomous, deadly, in that rasped command; a quality of menace that gave me goose pimples big enough to hang your hat on. Like a guy in a slow-motion movie, I turned on my heel; piped Geoffrey Jackman standing inside my office doorway.

WITH the black patch over one glim and a roscoe in his duke he resembled a pirate hankering to make me walk the plank. The rod was trained on my brisket, unwavering, ugly.

I said: "You've got me, bub. What's the gag!"

"If you don't know, you're not as smart as I thought you were," he grated.

"Meaning what?"

"Meaning you're through. Washed up."

"With the Leneta Leonard case?"

"With any case."

I didn't like this. I thought fast; revised my entire conception of the whole mess. So it was Jackman, I thought, who was at the bottom of the deal. The pieces all fitted together like a completed jigsaw puzzle.

The Leonard cupcake had discussed hiring me with only one person: Jackman. Hence, he was the only guy in a position to send me the anonymous note I'd received that morning. The note had contained three one thousand dollar bills—which I'd traced back to Leneta as part of her last shakedown payoff. Then how else could Jackman have sent me those G-notes *unless he himself was the blackmailer?*

On the other hand, though, the one-eyed guy had come to me today, offered me a thousand fish to take the case. Why should he try to steer me off with an anonymous bribe, then attempt to hire me!

There was even an answer for this question when I put my grey matter to work. Jackman knew my rep; knew I'm in business for all the cash I can collect. He had probably figured that I'd take the three grand to lay off, rather than accept a third of that sum to work on the case. His original visit had been to make sure; to hear me refuse to handle the mess.

But he'd overplayed his hand when he intimated that my effectiveness would be minimized. That had riled me, and I'd agreed to thrust my probe into the Leonard jane's troubles. Thus Jackman's psychological shenanigans had snapped back at him, kicked him in the teeth.

So now he was scared. And he had a cannon pointed at me.

The reason for his fright was obvious. He knew I was getting on the right track. He'd stood there just now, eavesdropped as I phoned New York about Victor Croft's former sweetie. If this particular bit of information bothered Jackman, it could only mean that he and the ex-sweetie were in cahoots. They were working together in the blackmail scheme.

All of which I added up in a split instant. I also realized I was in a ticklish spot as long as his heater was aimed at my cafeteria. So I did something about it.

I pulled an ancient gag on the guy; a gag they use in the detective magazines. It was corny, but it worked. I stared past my visitor, toward the door. "Hi, Bill!" I said. "You're just in the nick of time."

Of course there was nobody there. Jackman turned, though; and I grabbed the inkwell off my desk, fired it at him. It maced him on the back of the conk and he dropped like a cut rope.

I CATAPULTED over to him, unfastened his suspenders and used them to truss his wrists and gams. Then I propped him in a corner, put his rodney in my pocket, went back to the phone on my desk. I dialed Central Casting.

When they answered, I said: "You got a dame registered by the name of Dorothy Manton? Blonde. Lots of curves. Just out here a little while from Broadway. Chorus cutie."

In a moment I got my answer. I'd scored a bull's-eye with my guesswork. Central Casting has a list of everybody who ever worked in pix or hopes to work in pix. "Yep," the clerk told me. "I can give you her address and phone number."

"Do that," I said, and wrote the information on my scratch pad. Then I dialed the apartment joint where this Manton chicken lived.

The apartment switchboard op said Miss Manton was out but would be home around eleven that night, and did I care to leave a message?

"Never mind, hon," I said, and broke the connection. Then I turned, took a gander at Jackman. He was conscious. His glims were open and so were his ears. He'd overheard my inquiries.

I barged over to him. "You know what happens to eavesdroppers, pal?"

"No. What?"

"This," I growled, and tapped him on the thatch with my .32 automatic. He went limp in a hurry. I felt his cranium to make sure I hadn't fractured it. I hadn't. There were just a couple of lumps, one from my inkwell, one from my gat. He'd have a headache in the morning, but that was all.

I tightened the suspenders around his ankles and

wrists, bestowed a curse on him and took a powder. Downstairs, I aimed my bucket back toward Leneta Leonard's igloo.

The blonde maid smiled at me when she opened up. "Miss Leonard has a visitor," she said.

I fished a five-spot out of my wallet, slipped it to the chick. "Stuff this in your sock and look the other way," I said. "Visitor or no visitor, I'm coming in." And I shoved past her; made my way to the living room.

The Leonard cutie got pale around the fringes when she piped me at the threshold. She was perched on the same davenport where I'd made that fake pass at her a few hours earlier. Aside from this, however, the scene had changed considerably. She now had a swarthy blister sitting beside her in a very chummy manner. He was Victor Croft.

Leneta flashed me the agonized swivel and I got hep to its meaning in short order. She was scared I'd open my trap, spill my adenoids about the blackmail setup. This would never do, with the Croft hambo present. He was the one guy in the world she didn't want in on the secret.

I PLAYED up to her. "Excuse me, Miss Leonard. I didn't know you were busy. I just came to see you about the plans for redecorating your studio dressing room."

"Oh," she gave me a grateful smile. "I'll leave it

entirely up to you, Mr. Smith," she improvised. Then she turned to Croft. "Victor, this is Mr. Smith, the interior decorator. Mr. Smith, of course you recognize Victor Croft. He's with Altamount."

I stuck out my mitt. The ham took it with the air of a king feeling the scales on a defunct fish. "How d'you do," he murmured in a bored tone.

I gushed all over him. "Mighty glad to meet you, Mr. Croft. I've seen you in pictures. You're swell." Then, to Leneta: "If everything's all right with you, Miss Leonard, I'll get right to work. I think I'll have the job finished by morning."

A pulse throbbed in her throat, "You m-mean it?"

I nodded, lammed. I was sure she'd understood my drift.

There was an opus I wanted to see at Grauman's Chinese. So I killed a couple of hours there, then moseyed to a groggery and inhaled a few snorts of Vat 69. Presently it was almost eleven o'clock—time for me to start rolling. I piled into my vee-eight, drove to the apartment stash where Dorothy Manton lived.

The automatic elevator whisked me up to her floor. I unholstered my gat, gumshoed to her portal, knocked.

The door opened. I shoved my roscoe forward and said: "Quite a trick, catching bullets with your kisser. You want to try it, maybe?"

The jane backed away. I barged in, kicked the

door shut and got a good hinge at her puss. For once in my misspent career I was too flabbergasted to say anything.

And no wonder. The wren before me was Leneta Leonard's yellow-haired maid!

She found her voice first. "Wh-what's the idea?"

I said: "Pardon my curly tonsils, sister, but I crave that reel of film."

"Wh-what reel of film?" she quavered. Fear slithered into her optics, told me I was on the home stretch. "I don't know anything about a reel—"

"The devil you don't," I snapped. "It's the pic Leneta Leonard made a long time ago I'm talking about. You know, the one you've been using to blackmail her."

The blonde quail's glance shifted involuntarily and briefly to a bookcase standing against the far wall. I'd been keeping tab on her optics, waiting for just such a break.

She said: "You m-must be off your chump, Handsome."

"Yeah," I lifted a lip. "I lost my marbles trying to dope out this screwy tangle." And I moved toward the bookcase.

She tried to block me. "You can't—"

"Look, kiddo," I made my voice ugly. "See this thing in my duke? It's known professionally as a heater, or hog-leg if you read western stories. And if you think it's loaded with blanks, just start something. I dare you."

She backed up to a chair, sank into it. She was trembling like a cat coughing beef-seeds.

I OPENED the bookcase, dumped all the volumes out on the floor. Back in the corner of one shelf I found what I was after: a flat, round can of cinema celluloid. I opened it, held up a length of the reel so light would shine through. You could recognize the delishful doll who appeared in miniature on each transparent frame. It was Leneta Leonard.

"Nice," I said. "Very nice indeed."

The blonde maid blinked at me. "Look, Hawkshaw. How would you like to make a deal'?"

"I hear you talking," I said.

"We could cut you in on the gravy if you'd play ball with us on this thing," she made a coquettish mouth at me.

I said: "No dice, babe. In the first place, the Leonard jane is broke. You've bled her for all the traffic will bear. And in the second place I don't play with rats."

"You think I'm a rat?"

"Yeah. Dorothy Manton, she-male rodent. That's you. You were in love with Victor Croft back in New York. You followed him here to Hollywood. He ditched you when he fell for Leneta. So you got sore; decided to do something about it. With Geoffrey Jackman's help, you located this reel of pix."

She said: "Smart, aren't you?"

"Smart enough. You and Jackman used the film for a shakedown. You probably figured to show the opus to Victor Croft when Leneta couldn't pay any more dough. That would wreck their wedding plans to hellangone. And just to keep an eye on your blackmail victim, you even wangled a job as her personal maid."

"All right," the blonde wren said sourly. "So now what happens to me?"

"You go to the cooler," I growled. "Jackman too. I've got him tied up in my office with his own suspenders. The two of you will serve a nice long stretch."

She stood up, swayed toward me. "Couldn't you give me a break, Handsome? If I paid back the blackmail money?"

I laughed at her, started to back toward the door. To my surprise she did nothing but step to the wall-switch and snap off the lights. I was still trying to figure her play when the front door of the stash swung open. You couldn't see it in the blackness, but you could hear the hinges creak.

Whereupon the blonde frail yeeped: *"I've got the dirty snoop! He almost glommed the film. Get him!"* And she clung to me, impeded my wild leap.

I swung the flat of my palm, bopped her on the chops. She let go, sagged back. I lunged toward the door just as a roscoe sneezed: *Ka-chow!* and spat a streak of orange flame in my general direction.

The slug missed me. I made a dig for my own shoulder-holstered gat—and found the holster empty. The yellow-haired Manton minx had glommed it when she had hung the grab on me.

Even as I discovered this, she started triggering. I ducked for a corner as the cannon belched its thunderous bellow. And then I heard a groan, a gurgle and the thump of somebody slumping to the floor.

The blonde chick quit firing. "Which—which one did I hit? Somebody *say* something!"

Instead of answering, I slithered across the room on all fours; ran into a prone figure I couldn't see. But I could find the guy's wrist; and I could feel that his pulse wasn't beating. He was deader than fried fishcakes.

Which was my cue to lam—fast. This defunct monkey had been creamed with my heater; and that would look plenty bad for me if the cops found it out. I straightened up, dived across the room by instinct, collided with the Manton dame.

She had my gat in one mitt, the can of film in the other. I punched her in the kisser, knocked her colder than January at the North Pole. I got the roscoe and the movie reel, pivoted, catapulted to the window. I raised the sash, went over the sill and down the fire escape to my jalopy.

It was midnight when I pulled up in front of Leneta Leonard's lavish igloo in Beverly. There was a light burning downstairs as I made for the porch, fingered the bell. She probably had Victor Croft in there with her, I figured. Not that it mattered. All I intended to do was hand her the can of film, then beat it without saying anything.

I rang again. Presently the door opened—and for the second time that night I got a shock. The guy standing before me was Geoffrey Jackman.

HE had a bandage around his noggin, and his one good peeper blazed like a four-alarm fire fueled with hate. He said: "You lousy son!" and lunged at me.

I sidestepped, glued the grab on him, pinioned him and gasped: "What gives?"

"Let go!" he choked. "Turn me loose so I can kill you!"

"Stew that kind of talk, bub. How did you get here? I thought you were—"

"Yeah. You thought you had me tied up in your office, you filthy heel. You thought you could come out here and make some more passes at Leneta!" he caterwauled.

I began to see daylight. "So that's it!" I said. Then I yelled into the house. "Hey, Miss Leonard. Come take this crazy jerk off me! I've got a present for you."

The cuddly cinema cupcake came to the door, her puss as white as fresh laundry. "Something . . .

for m-me . . .?"

I freed one hand, reached inside my coat, tossed the can of movie spool at her. "There's what you wanted, hon."

Droplets of brine started running out of her lamps, streaking her map with mascara. "You . . . you g-got . . .!"

"Yeah," I said, and shoved Geoffrey Jackman away from me. He had a stupid look on his mush. "Funny," I growled at him. "I had an idea *you* were behind this deal. You pulled a gun on me in my office—"

He blushed sheepishly. "That was because you'd tried to get fresh with Leneta. I was jealous."

"Then why did you try to mow me down in Dorothy Manton's wikiup?" I yelped.

"Me? I've been here since ten-thirty. When I got away from your office 1 came right to Leneta. Ask Victor Croft. He was just leaving as I arrived. He'll prove it."

But the swarthy Croft hambo would never prove anything. Inside the Leonard doll's stash a radio was already blotting: "Extra flash! Victor Croft, the new film star, was just found shot to death in the apartment of an extra girl named Dorothy Manton, who has disappeared—"

That's right. It was Croft who got cooled in the darkness of the blonde wren's joint. Croft was the blackmailer. He'd never intended to marry Leneta.

He merely made her fall for him so he could use that movie reel to shake her down for a stack of shekels.

His real sweetie was the Manton jane. He'd even planted her as Leneta's maid to keep in touch with things. She was the one that overheard Leneta and Jackman discussing the proposition of hiring me; which explained the anonymous note I'd received.

And now Croft was deceased; his own hot mama had browned him. Which was poetic justice.

The funny thing is, the cops never did nab that blonde bimbo. She simply dropped out of sight. And I'm not saying anything to anybody. Neither is Geoffrey Jackman. He's married now to Leneta Leonard, and they're perfectly willing to let sleeping dogs lie!

SING A SONG OF MURDER

This girl from South America was ready to kill the cowboy crooner who she said had married her, then stolen her money and deserted her. But Dan Turner could hardly believe that about a friend of his. He was in for the surprise of his life

OMEBODY put a nickel in the juke-box and that nickel brought me seventeen dollars' worth of trouble. I suddenly found an unconscious brunette on my hands and a burly bouncer barging at me, his eyes full of mayhem and a set of brass knuckles decorating his dukes.

It was late in the evening when this mess commenced. I had dropped into the place for a bedtime snort of Vat 69; settled my tonnage in a side booth. But I had barely tasted the first Scotch when I realized I had company.

The company was a gorgeous bundle of dynamite done up in a formal crimson satin gown that adhered to her curves as if it had been poured on while wet and then baked in the oven. She dished me a coquettish gander, smiled lazily and drawled: "Handsome senor look lonesome. You like Rosita Valdez to dreenk weeth you, maybe?"

I didn't answer until I looked her over. She seemed several notches above your ordinary B-girl or percentage wren; not the average type that cadges drinks from strangers. To begin with, she didn't use too much makeup and her olive complexion was clear, velvety. I also noticed she blushed a little as she braced me.

That spelled embarrassment—or good acting. I was curious to find out which. I patted the leather bench and said: "Sure, hon. Sit down and be sociable.

She started to obey but somebody teetered up behind her, glued the drunken grab on her arm. "Ix-nay, sweetheart," this staggering character hic-

cupped. "You're with me, remember? So no chiseling."

I FASTENED the focus on the guy; recognized him. His name was Lew Larchmont, he worked as a grip over on the General Service lot across the street, and

he was tanked to the adenoids.

"Scram, bub," I said.

He glowered at me. "Says who?"

"Me," I stood up. "Blow before I shoot a game of craps with your front teeth."

"Now, wait a minute," he rasped. "I saw the jane first, unnerstand? I bought her a snort. If you think you can—"

I looked at the quail in the crimson creation. "What about it, babe? Take your choice."

"I choose you, senor," she told me.

I said: "Okay, chum. You heard the lady. Now powder."

Larchmont scowled, hesitated. "All right. But you ain't saw the last of thish. I'll fix you. Jush wait." And he stumbled to the bar, mumbling in his gums.

"Thank you, senor," the brunette chick whispered as she sat down alongside me. "He was a veree onpleasant person. I am glad you sent heem away."

Her nearness filled me full of needles. "Forget it, sis. I don 't like the guy anyhow. How would you go for a slug of tequila to warm the veins and arteries?"

"Tequila, senor? But that ees a Mexican dreenk. I am not Mexican. I am from the Argentine. You buy Rosita some champagne, maybe? Ees good idea, no?"

Her voice was rich and sleek to match the smooth blackness of her hair; her peepers were dark and friendly, yet somehow remote, not too happy. I was on the brink of saying sure, I'd be glad to buy her some bubbly; after all, she probably drew a commission from the house and needed the dough or she wouldn't be in the racket.

Before I could beckon the waiter, though, hell erupted in copious quantities.

There was a coin-box music machine over by the bar opposite my booth; a new one. In fact, two workmen had just been installing the gaudy gadget when I'd first ankled into the drinkery. Now Lew Larchmont, the plastered studio grip, slipped a nickel in its slot.

When it lighted up like a rainbow I saw it was one of those recently perfected outfits where music comes off a celluloid sound track instead of a disc record. Earlier that same day a guy named Nick Spain had demonstrated one to me on a General Service sound stage. Nick was a microphone technician; owned a piece of the patent.

The machine had a small mirror-screen in front, where it projected a miniature movie synchronized with the song. You saw the vocalist in action while listening to his canned bleat, almost like being in a theater.

When Larchmont deposited his jitney the screen came to life and a guitar began strumming. I watched—and got quite a thump when I lamped an old friend of mine appearing in the thing. He was Chuck McConnell, the singing cowboy star; I tabbed him the instant he ambled his lanky length onto the halfpint scene, opened his yawp and warbled out the first strains of La Golondrina.

This was when my curvaceous brunette companion cut loose with a blistering screech that scraped scabs on my ear-drums. *"Arturo—!"* she shrilled; jumped up as if she'd been stuck with a red hot bodkin. *"Dios—Arturo!"*

HER sudden movement tilted the table. My Vat 69 and a bowl of salted popcorn hit the floor with a splattering smash; made my booth the center of everybody's attention. If you'd fired a cannon you couldn't have done a better job.

I gurgled: "What the devil—!" and grabbed the hysterical cupcake; tried to yank her down on the bench where I could muffle her yeeps. Then, as I fastened the clutch on her, she went into a swoon.

At the same instant I piped the joint's bouncer making for me with a load of brass knucks. He reached the booth, bestowed a professional snarl on me. "Slugging dames ain't permitted in here, Jack," he announced.

"The name isn't Jack; it's Turner," I told him. "Dan Turner, private dick. And I didn't bop this fluff. She nudged me a moment ago for a drink and then yelled, fainted when that juke box began to play."

Then the alcoholic Larchmont monkey staggered over; thrust his horn into the conversation. He was drunker than ever—and still sore because the doll had ditched him. He said: "Josh a female barfly. Tosh her out on her victoria."

"Toss me out on mine while you're at it," I stood up, supported the unconscious flossie with one arm around her slender waist.

The bouncer said it would be a pleasure, and made the serious mistake of reaching toward me. I punched him on the profile with my free fist and he went sailing across the barroom; took himself a swim in the cuspidor. He didn't know it, though. He was out before he landed.

Meantime Larchmont charged at me; swung a wild haymaker. I ducked and he missed me clean, hit the brunette chick's chin instead. If she'd been in a coma before, it was redoubled now. I could feel the poke's impact jarring through her inert figure like the kick of a shotgun.

I blew my top, lifted a knee and caught the saturated slob a neat foul that doubled him over, moaning. While his guard was down I hung a mouse under his left optic. "Want another dose of the same?" I asked him.

He whimpered, backed away. "I'll g-get you for thish. Jush see if I don't!"

I shrugged, hefted the Latin lassie and moseyed out of the dive with her; took her to my jalopy. Nobody tried to stop me—which was a good thing for all concerned. The way I was feeling, I'd have committed assault and bashery on the first bozo that got in my road.

BUT when I finally deposited the black-haired cookie in my bucket I was temporarily stymied; didn't know where to ferry her. I couldn't get an address from her purse because she wasn't carrying any; and she couldn't answer questions because she was still colder than raspberry sherbet. This worried me. What if Lew Larchmont had slammed her too hard? Suppose she never snapped out of it?

I drove home to my apartment stash in a yank; put her on my divan. Then I phoned a sawbones who lived in the building, got him to come in and examine her.

When he completed his inspection he said: "Minor concussion and shock, is all. She'll be okay presently, although you hadn't better move her for a while. That'll be five dollars."

He took his five skins and a powder; whereupon I sat down to await the jane's awakening. I craved to learn why the sight of my singing cowboy star friend, Chuck McConnell, had given this Rosita Valdez frill such a bad case of the screaming meemies when she lamped him on the miniature movie screen of that modernistic juke-box.

I chain-smoked a dozen gaspers and quaffed three or four jorums of highland tonic to kill time; and then, around half past ten, Rosita opened her dazed peepers.

"Wh-where am I?" she whispered.

I said: "Safe in port, sweet stuff. Take it easy."

She sat up. "Oh-h-h . . . now I remember! That voice . . . the song . . . Arturo . . .!" Her ivory puss went pale.

"Hey!" I yodeled and grabbed her, shook her. "No more swoons, please! Tell me what this is all about."

She faced me, her lips tremulous. "The man who sang from the coin machine . . ."

"Chuck McConnell," I nodded. "A pal of mine."

"Then you choose poor friends, senor. He ees a rat."

"Huh? What did McConnell ever do to you?"

"Hees name ees not McConnell. Eet ees Arturo Valdez. He ees my hosband. And I am going to cut hees throat!"

CHAPTER II

I HUNG the stupefied focus on her; wondered if I'd heard what 1 thought I heard. The wren's remark was screwier than hailstones at the Equator. "You must have some loose marbles, baby," I said. "If Chuck McConnell's got any Latin blood in his capillaries, I'm an almond eyed Mongolian. The guy comes from a long line of Micks."

"That ees not true! He was a vaudeville seenger in the Argentine. I would know hees peculiar voice

anywhere, no matter how mock he have changed hees face. I tell you I was married to heem. He stole my monee and abandoned me. I was forced to make a leeving the best way I c-could . . ."

My mouth tasted dry all of a sudden. She didn't look like a cutie with a past; she was too young, too sweet. But her tone told me she was leveling; and even in Hollywood a percentage jane's career is none too pleasant.

"You don't have to talk now if you don't want to,

hon," I said gently.

A catch came into her throat. "Bot I *do* want to. I have been alone so veree long . . . nobody to talk weeth . . . "

"Okay," I patted her shoulder. "Spill it if it'll help."

She said: "Arturo used the monee he stole from me to come to your countree. Eet was three years before I saved the fare and followed heem. I traced heem as far as Hollywood; then I lose hees trail. I am . . . how you say eet? . . . broke. I go back to selleeng dreenks in cocktail bars . . ."

"Not a very nice occupation, kitten."

She made a bitter mouth. "Eet ees the only theeng I can do. Bot now I have find Arturo. I hear heem seeng!"

"And you want to croak him."

"Yes!"

Whoever her husband was, I agreed he'd given her a rotten deal. "McConnell isn't your guy, though," I insisted.

"Hees voice I could not forget, senor. Hees face ees changed, yes. Movie makeup would feex that, or what you call thees plastic surgery. Bot when he seeng, I know heem!"

I said: "Tx-nay. Chuck McConnell has been in horse operas ever since silent days. Three or four years ago he was washed up. Even a world tour of personal appearances didn 't help—"

"A world tour, senor?" she tensed.

"Yeah."

"Eet eencluded South America?"

"Come to think of it, I suppose so."

"Then that was when he married me!"

"NO, hon," I argued. "You're wrong and I can prove it. You say his voice is the same but his face is different. Well, he's still wearing the map he always had. It hasn't changed a bit since the days when he was a silent star. Which kills your plastic surgery theory."

She faltered: "Explain thees, please, senor."

"Sure. You saw him in the jukebox pic. That's how he looked when he left on his tour; it's how he looked later when he got back. So he can't be the heel you married."

"Eet w-would seem so. And yet—"

"Forget the vocal resemblance," I said. "That's just an accident. As much a coincidence as his present starring status."

"How do you mean?"

"After he came home he made a western quickie out on Poverty Row; yodeled a cowboy ditty in it. The public fell for his crooning and he skyrocketed back to the top. He writes his own ticket now; owns a share of his producing company. He even has a one-third financial interest in the juke boxes he sings for. But he isn't your missing hubby."

"Can you prove thees? Weel you let me face

heem?"

"Darned right." I had a good reason for greeting. McConnell was a swell egg and I didn't want this misguided cookie waylaying him with a shiv for something he hadn't done. On a hunch, I pulled her toward me. "Come here, kitten."

"Yes, senor?"

She misunderstood my motives, though. "Oh-h. You want the kees because you are helpeeng me! I should have expected eet. Men are all alike." With a resigned sigh she snuggled against me; locked her arms around me and dished me a kiss.

For a second I responded automatically. Then I unfastened her from my wishbone; backed away. "I wasn't making passes, hon. I was frisking you for a blade."

"Blade—?"

"You threatened to do some throat-cutting. Re-member?"

"Oh!" she smiled ruefully. "I deed not really mean eet. I have no knife."

"So I discovered."

Her glims puddled. "Weel you forgeeve me for misjudging you, senor?'

I said: "That's okay. Let's go see McConnell." And we went down to my bucket; started for the General Service lot. That was where the cowboy star turned out his musical sagebrush offerings.

I happened to know his independent unit would

be working that night on some late takes, so I drove straight through the studio's main gates; parked and left Rosita in my coupe while I ankled into the sound stage building. Dead ahead there was a brightly lighted set. I made for it.

AS I approached, I tabbed somebody giving me the vindictive glimpse. It was Lew Larchmont, the drunken grip who'd tried to make trouble in the gin mill. Apparently he'd sobered up enough to be back on his job; but he was sporting a gorgeous shiner on his left lamp where my knuckles had dusted him. I wondered if he wanted to start another fracas; got myself all set to lower the boom on him in case of need.

He turned away, scrammed behind a pile of flats.

Then two other guys spotted me, waved a welcome. The tall one was Nick Spain, chief sound technician of the unit; the guy who had demonstrated a juke box to me earlier in the day. With him was an undersized shrimp named Sammy Kreech, director of all Chuck McConnell's pix. The pair of them were equal partners with McConnell on his movies and his musical slot-machines; their efforts had helped bring Chuck back to star caliber.

"Hi, Sherlock," Spain said. "What's cooking?"

"I'd like to see McConnell."

Sammy Kreech shook his head. "No dice. He's about to cut a song. You know what that means."

"Yeah," I nodded. The cowboy crooner was self-conscious regarding his vocalizing. He never warbled on an open set; preferred to use a private mike in a closed recording room where he couldn't be watched. The next day he would come on before the set's cameras and go through the labial motions in synchrony with a playback. It's standard cinema technique.

"Can you wait a while?" the Kreech shrimp asked me.

I said: "Okay. But look. When Chuck's through making with the musical moans, tell him I've got a South American cupcake in my crate. She calls herself Rosita Valdez and she heard his voice in a jukebox tonight; thinks he's somebody that pulled a snide trick on her in Argentina. I want him to meet her, disillusion her before she makes a stench."

Kreech narrowed his peepers. "Sure, I'll tell him." He and Spain gave me a chair, made me comfortable and scrammed toward the recording room.

Time snailed by; maybe five or ten minutes. Presently I fished in my pocket for a gasper; discovered my pack was empty. There was a fresh deck in my jalopy, though, I remembered; so I moseyed out to get it.

The Valdez quail was huddled down on the upholstery when I opened the door, and at first I figured she was snatching a nap. I reached past her. "Excuse me, sweet stuff. We'll see McConnell pretty soon, now. I want to get some cigarettes out of the glove compartment."

She didn't answer; and then my arm accidentally brushed her, tipped her over like a rag doll. She flopped grotesquely and I got a sudden swivel at her throat. it had been sliced open as deep as the Panama Canal.

She was deader than fried oysters.

As soon as I regained control of my fluttering elly-bay, I pivoted and pelted back across the parking lot. Then, suddenly, a guy catapulted at me from the shadows. He was the grip I had fought with in the groggery, Lew Larchmont; and he toted a hunk of lumber in his clutch.

"Got you, begahd!" he snarled. And he maced me on the conk with his improvised bludgeon; bashed me senseless.

CHAPTER III

WHEN I woke up I was inside the sound stage building, all stretched out in the middle of a western ranch-yard set. There was a bump on my noggin the size of Wyoming and I had a headache big enough to fit the entire population of Texas.

A tall, slabsided citizen was leaning over me, clad in a cowboy rig and funnelling rye down my gullet from a pint bottle. He was my pal Chuck McConnell, the sagebrush crooner, and his leathery pan was loaded with worry as he rendered me first aid in liquid form.

"Cripes, Hawkshaw!" he said as I opened my optics. "I was scared you mightn't make the grade!"

"Me too. Give me another shot of that snake-venom."

His bottle was empty but he took a replacement from little Sammy Kreech, who was standing nearby with the sound technician, Nick Spain. Then, as he held the flask to my kisser, he demanded: "What happened?"

"I got bopped."

"Sure. We know that. Nick and Sammy told me you wanted to see me about some dame; but when I started hunting for you, I found you outside in a trance. Who nailed you?"

I sat up woozily; tried to shake the bells out of my ears. "A louse named Larchmont," I mumbled. "Where is he?"

"Larchmont—? Why, he's gone. We dismissed the company as soon as we discovered you laid out. We were through shooting, anyhow. Are you sure—?"

I said: "Yes. But never mind Larchmont; he'll keep until I get around to putting the finger on him. I've got killery on my mind."

"Wh-what?"

I staggered to my pins. "You heard me. The chick I wanted to see you about has been beefed. Where's a phone? I want to call Dave Donaldson of the homicide squad."

The Kreech shrimp took my elbow, steered me to a telephone on the sidelines. I noticed he was shaking like a pup coughing lollipops, but I didn't pay much attention just then. I needed all my concentration to dial police headquarters without fumbling in the wrong holes.

Bye and bye I made my connection; heard Donaldson's voice rattling

the receiver. "Who is it and why?"

"Turner squawking. Flag your trousers over here to the General Service lot, and bring the meat

wagon. I've got a she-male cadaver for you."

I rang off before he could overload my aching cranium with unnecessary questions.

THEN the lanky McConnell ham glued the clutch on me. "For tripe's sake, gumshoe, what's it all about?"

"You know as much as I do, bub. This Rosita Valdez cookie claimed you married her and deserted her in Argentina. So now she's defunct."

He turned seven shades of pale under his sun-tan. "Great grief! You didn't believe her, I hope? You— you don't think I k-killed her?"

"I don't think anything. I'm too dizzy."

Nick Spain bought chips in the conversation. "Nobody can suspect Chuck. He's got an alibi. He was in the recording room until a few minutes ago, cutting a song. I'll back him up on that; I was handling the sound controls." Then he looked at the undersized Kreech bozo. "You were there too, weren't you, Sammy?"

"Y-yes. Certainly!"

I blinked at the three of them. If they were leveling, McConnell had a waterproof alibi.

Lew Larchmont!" I whispered.

They all stared at me. "What about Larchmont?"

I said: "He was sore at the wren. She'd given him the air in a cocktail joint across the street; then I pasted him when he tried to make like a tough guy."

"So that's how he got his shiner," McConnell breathed.

"Yeah. So maybe he bumped Rosita in my bucket for revenge; tried to do the same for me with a length of lumber."

Sammy Kreech clucked his tongue. "I can't imagine Larchmont doing a thing like that. He's worked for us ever since I don't know how long. A good man, too, except when he gets plastered."

"That's just the point," I rasped. "An alcoholic is liable to do anything when he's under the influence."

McConnell made a grim mouth. "What are you going to do, Philo? Send the cops after him?"

"Cops!" By this time I was feeling almost normal; anyhow my headache was fading and the knot on my noggin didn't seem to get any bigger. "I'm going to put the thumb on him personally!"

"But why? After all, the police—"

"Look," I said. "The guy tried to beat my brains out; so I owe him a jolt in return. Besides, I sort of liked that Valdez cupcake. She didn't deserve what she got. The least I can do for her is collar her killer." And I turned, headed toward the exit.

Sammy Kreech called after me. "What are you using for transportation, Hawkshaw?"

"I've got my jalopy."

"But didn't you say there was a corpse in it?"

THIS drew me up short. For a moment I'd forgotten my buggy was the same as useless because of its contents, probably because my think-tank was still a little foggy from being massaged with a scantling. I scowled, herded my grey cells into better order; came to a decision.

"Hey, Chuck," I said.

The lanky cowboy crooner said: "Yes, I)an?"

"How's for letting me borrow your heap?"

"Sure. Gladly. Maybe you'd better let me chauffeur you. It strikes me you might need somebody along, just in case. You're not in top condition if you ask my opinion."

I hesitated; concluded he had something there. "Okay, chum. I guess I can use you, at that. Nick and Sammy can stick around, explain matters to the cops when they get here. Come on, let's ramble."

We barged out to McConnell's modest sedan; piled in. "Where to?" he asked me. "Larchmont's house?"

I shook my head. "A murderer wouldn't risk going home. Not even a drunken murderer."

"You mean he'd find a hideout somewhere?"

"That would be my guess." Then I snapped my fingers. "I've got it!"

"What?"

I mentioned an apartment address on Normandie and the crooner gassed his cylinders. "A jessie by the name of Sue Meredith lives in this joint we're going to," I told him. "I used to be fairly thick with her; we went on a lot of parties together in the old days. Lately we've sort of lost contact, though."

"And—?"

"I've heard rumors she's been running around with the Larchmont blister. He might hole up in her igloo."

"Say, that's an angle! I hope it pans out." Then Chuck settled down to the job of driving.

Pretty soon we parked in front of the wikiup I wanted. I hit the sidewalk; but when McConnell started to follow I said: "Nix, pal. You stay here; keep a glim on the entrance in case our bozo ducks out behind my back. If he does, grab him quick and holler copper."

"Just as you say. You're running the show."

I left him, hotfooted inside the tepee and went upstairs; knocked on the door of Sue Meredith's second-floor dugout. The portal opened pronto and Sue herself hung the swivel on me.

AT FIRST she seemed disappointed; her crimson kisser took a downward droop. Then she brightened. "Well, dip me in wax if it isn't Dangerous Dan, the fenagling ferret! Long time no see, Sherlock."

"I've been kind of busy, babe."

"Yeah? Well, come in and make up for lost time. Let's kiss and get fried."

She was a nifty little parcel in spite of the fact that she used too much henna on her hair and paint on her face. At least her curves were plentiful—and alluring. But right now I had a lump on my sconce and a murder case in my thoughts. Kisses were

something I could do without, temporarily.

I accepted part of her invitation, though; ankled across her threshold as soon as she gave me the of-fice. "All by yourself, sweet stuff?"

"Not now I'm not," she wrinkled her tip-tilted

smeller in a funny grimace as she closed the door and undulated in my direction. "You're here."

I got a load of her breath and it smelled slightly brandied. Thinking back, I couldn't remember that she'd ever been addicted to thesolitary tippling habit. In the old days, her elbow bending had usually been confined to the sociability classification; which made me suspect maybe she was stalling me along about not having any visitors except myself.

The suspicion was intensified when she drifted close to me, flashed me a tempting smile. All this interest might be a means of occupying my attention while the Larchmont lug lammed from some other room in the wig-wam—although I could be wrong, of course.

I backed-pedaled before she had a chance to get a half nelson on me. "Build us a pair of highballs, baby," I suggested. "I'd like to inspect the plumbing system."

She got busy with the makings and I snooped on through her boudair into the bathroom, pausing to frisk the closets quietly en route. But I didn't see any trace of my quarry. I returned to the red-haired wren, took the drink she handed me, sipped it. She said: "Strong enough?"

"You must have milked a panther," I said. And I made a beeline for the kitchenette on the pretext of diluting the dollop with faucet water. Larchmont wasn't there, either. He wasn't in the joint at all; I'd covered the entire layout by now.

Back in the living room, the Meredith mouse settled herself on a davenport. "For heck's sake, Hawkshaw, light a spell! You act like you had termites crawling under your garter girdle."

I put my glass down. "I just remembered I've got an errand to do, kiddo. Will you please excuse me?"

"No. I won't. At least drink your drink."

I tossed it off obediently. "There. Now I'll be scramming." I made for the door, tried it; snake-eyes. "Hey, it's locked!"

"Sure." She grinned, constructed two more doses of ginger ale and lightning. "Come on, handsome. Down the hatch."

I humored her. Then I said: "Be nice, sis. Where's the key? I've really got to go."

"Key? Oh. The key. I hid it." She filled our tumblers again. "Stay a while and maybe I'll remember where I mislaid the darn' thing. Right now it's sort of slipped my mind."

I BEGAN to get riled. I knew I could drink her under the table nine nights a week. But I wanted to locate Larchmont and she was frittering my time away. All of a sudden I wondered if the whole thing could be deliberate—a prearranged plan to keep me out of action long enough for the studio grip to make tracks.

"Now look," I drained my third jorum. "Fun's fun,

sweetheart. But after all—"

"I wanna be kissed," she pouted.

I held my temper under wraps, sank down alongside her, gave her a quick one. Then I stood up again. "Goom-bye, please. The key, if you don't mind."

"But I *do* mind. Let's have 'nother li'l jolt." She giggled as she poured the fixings.

I hated to start a ruckus; and I realized she was just sufficiently blotto to throw a wing-ding if I got tough. I'd seen her do it before, many a time, when things didn't go to suit her. I decided to try strategy.

"We're not being fair, hon," I said as I gargled my fourth snifter.

She pinned the bleary glimpse on me, her peepers not quite crossed but almost. "Who aren't we being fair to?"

"Your boy friend."

"Haven't got one."

I said: "Sure you have. Lew Larchmont."

"Oh. That tosspot," she hiccuped. "Nuts to him." She reached for the bottle.

"Why nuts to him, babe?"

"He drinks too much." Coming from her in her present state of saturation, this would have been a laugh if I'd been in the mood for humor. I wasn't, though. She added: "I'm all finished with him. Washed up."

"Since when?"

"Since tonight. He had a date with me after he got through his late trick at the studio. He broke it."

"So that's who you were expecting when you opened the door so fast to my knock," I remarked.

She shook her head. "I wasn't expecting him at all. I knew he wasn't coming. Wanna know how I knew?"

"Tell me."

"I phoned him at his house."

Abruptly I stiffened. "You talked to him there?"

"Sure. He was corned to the scalp—Hey, what'samatter?"

I WAS already half-way across the room, catapulting to her telephone, cursing myself in a low tone of disgust. Here I had wasted nearly thirty minutes in a blind alley, while Larchmont had been in his own stash the whole time—the one place I never expected him to be.

Well, maybe there was still a chance for me to make up for my blundering guesswork. I could contact Dave Donaldson; steer him to the grip's tepee for a swift pinch. Most likely Dave was still at the General Service lot, sniffing for clues on the Valdez doll's bump-off; so I dialed the studio number.

A masculine voice answered. "Hello?"

I said: "Let me talk to Lieutenant Donaldson, please. In a hurry."

"Donaldson? Sorry. He's not here. He left some time ago."

"For headquarters?"

"I don't know. I suppose so. Who's calling?"

"Dan Turner."

"Jeest, gumshoe, are you in a jackpot! —This is Nick Spain. Kreech and I are just leaving for home." Then the sound technician added: "Better stay clear of the cops for a while. Donaldson is after your scalp."

"How come he is?"

"On account of that bum beef you slipped him."

I glared at the phone as if it had suddenly sprouted fangs and a forked tail. "What bum beef?"

"Why, the murder tip."

"What was bum about it?"

"You must have been off your chump from that

clout on the skull. Slap-happy. It's the only way I can figure it," he said wonderingly.

I screamed: "For the love of Whozit lay off the double-talk and tell me what the hell you're driving at!"

"Sure. Don't get excited. All I meant to say is, there wasn't any dead dame in your coupe. In fact, your coupe wasn't on the parking lot at all."

CHAPTER IV

I WINCED as if I'd been smacked across the features with a wet herring. "You mean my jalopy's gone? Donaldson didn't find the brunette wren's remainders?"

"He didn't find anything. He's sore. He thinks you were ribbing him," Spain said.

I rang off in his ear; twirled the dial so fast it smoked and gave sparks. Police headquarters came on the line and told me Dave hadn't got back yet. "He may have picked up a broadcast we sent out about fifteen minutes ago; a gunshot investigation," the desk sergeant volunteered.

I didn't bother to ask the details. My job was to collar Lew Larchmont, with or without police assistance. If he was the one who'd butched that Argentine cupcake he must likewise be responsible for glomming my bucket—probably with the drunken idea of secreting her remnants somewhere. Without a corpse delicti, no homicide rap could be pinned on him.

From across the room, Sue Meredith goggled at me. "What's going on around here?" she demanded plaintively. "What's all the shouting about?"

I barged over to her, fastened the grab on her shoulders, started shaking. "Cough up the door key before I wallop the everlasting custard out of you, sis."

"Don't be like that. Have a li'l drink."

I shook her some more. All of a sudden something metallic blipped out of her costume. It was the key. I snatched it off the floor.

She giggled owlishly. I unlatched the portal, sprinted from the flat, pelted hellity-blam downstairs to the street.

Whereupon, as I gained the side-walk, I lamped Chuck McConnell in the act of applying his brakes; bringing his sedan to a halt about five yards away.

He was humming off-key as I yanked the right hand door open. "Hi' Philo," he broke off the sour tune and took a squint at me. "What took you so long? Did you find the guy?"

I snapped: "No. Where've you been?"

"Me? Nowhere."

"You were just driving up," I said. "I thought I told you to stay anchored and watch this joint."

"That's what I did. —Oh, you mean the car being in motion. There's a yellow loading zone painted on the curb in front of the entrance where I was parked. A taxi wanted in, so I had to move and give it room."

"Yeah?"

He nodded. "It just left. I was rolling back to my original spot when you showed up."

I studied him. He sounded straightforward, plausible, a little puzzled. As a veteran actor, though, he could sham a lot of innocence and make it sound convincing. 1 wondered if he'd possibly had time to drive to the studio, roll my crate to a hideout and return before I came downstairs.

The more I thought about it, the less sense it made. No matter how fine he cut it, he still hadn't known exactly how long I might stay in the Meredith quail's flat. Moreover, the eye wasn't on him for cooling Rosita Valdez; therefore he wouldn't have any logical motive for stashing her corpse.

I dismissed my suspicions, got in alongside him. "Stoke this boiler, Chuck."

"Okay. Where to?" he meshed the gears.

"Larchmont's shanty. He's there. Or anyhow he was."

McCONNELL twisted his wheel in a U-turn and we headed toward the address on Fountain where the alcoholic grip lived. It wasn't more than six blocks away; I could have made it in five minutes on a pogo stick. Thanks to some expert driving, my lanky companion cut that time in half.

And then, as we pulled up before the Larchmont bozo's bungalow, we found ourselves spang in the middle of what looked like an unrehearsed riot. Neighbors in pajamas were all over the surroundings, trampling the lawn and chattering like monkeys. The cottage itself was full of lights and cops; two radio prowl buggies were parked at the curb and a meat wagon was just arriving, its red spotlight glaring.

I bounced to the pavement, an ugly hunch puckering my tripes. The crush impeded me but I slammed into it; shouldered my way forward and gained the porch. At the doorway stood Dave Donaldson looking as sour as a green persimmon.

"So this is the radio bleat you answered!" I greeted him.

"Yeah. Hello, slewfoot. I take it all back."

"You take what back?"

"Everything I said about you over at the General Service lot. You weren't ribbing me, after all."

"On that Rosita Valdez kill, you mean?"

He nodded grimly. "You were right and I was wrong. There actually was a murdered wren."

"Sure there was! But how did you check it? What's the score? Quit beating around the bush and say something sensible!"

"Well, for one thing, we just found your coupe."

"Where?"

"In the garage behind the house. With the dead

jane in it."

I said: "The devil you utter! So that's where Larchmont figured to hide the evidence. Have you made him spill?"

"He spilled, but I didn't make him."

"Meaning what?"

"Meaning he's defunct. He wrote a confession note that he'd butched the Valdez chick because she gave him the air. He toted her body here, hoping to dispose of it, but realized it wasn't possible. So then he browned himself."

CHAPTER V

INSIDE the stash I lamped a medical examiner probing Larchmont's lifeless husk with a scalpel, digging for the slug that had tunneled into the drunken grip's ticker. Presently he pried it out, wiped it on his pants and put it in an envelope.

"Thirty-eight," he remarked. "Made quite a hole." He looked around. "If I'm not needed any longer I thing I'll go out for a sandwich. I'm hungry."

I shivered and said: "Do post mortems give you an appetite?"

"Murder never bothers me" he grinned brightly.

Dave Donaldson overheard this and leaped five feet straight toward the ceiling. "Murder? What do you mean, murder? The gun was by the guy's hand, wasn't it? He left a note, didn't he? It was suicide."

"Oh. I forgot to tell you," the medico said. "The note must have been a plant. The gun, too."

Dave's puss went purple. "How do you figure?"

"Well, while you were out in the garage looking at that other corpse, I took paraffin tests of Larchmont's palms. Routine, you know."

"And—?" Dave yodeled.

"Negative. He couldn't have fired the slug at himself. Somebody else did." And the sawbones tinkled out.

For a minute I thought Donaldson was going to blow his top. He swayed on his dogs; made gurgling noises in his gullet. "Murder, he tells me! A planted gat and a phony confession note! And where does that put me? Up the stream without a paddle, that's where! Who could have—"

I waved him quiet; threw my grey matter into high gear and tried to dope out the puzzle's answer. Somewhere, somehow, I had a hunch I'd already found the one essential clue; but what was it? Where did it mesh?

Obviously, whoever had croaked Rosita Valdez was likewise the one who pulled this Larchmont kill, hoping to close up the case by pinning the guilt on Larchmont and leaving him too deceased to deny it. But who was the unknown murderer? And most important of all, why had the brunette Valdez cutie been chilled in the first place?

I tried to fit her into it. She's been searching for

an errant husband; a stinking swine who had swiped her dough and deserted her in South America. Okay; she had accused Chuck McConnell of being the bozo—because she thought she recognized his peculiar cowboy crooning in a gin mill juke-box.

"McConnell!" I yeeped suddenly. "McConnell, *who hums tunes off-key!*"

Dave hung the stupid swivel on me. "Hunh?"

I whipped my .32 automatic from the shoulder holster where I always carry it; pulled Donaldson toward the bungalow's front door. "Come on! We've got to find him!"

"Find who?"

"McConnell, you dope!" We wormed our way through the crowd, gained the lawn.

SOMEBODY called to me. "Did I hear my name mentioned, Sherlock?" It was Chuck himself, towering a full head above the mob around him.

I smashed a path to him, rubbed his ribs with the muzzle of my roscoe. "Into your sedan, chum. Fast."

"Why?" he blinked. "What's the b-big idea?"

"Get in the car. No questions." He obeyed; slid under the wheel.

"I don't get this. I'm not sure I like it."

"I don't care with what you like." I kept him covered, bounced in alongside him while Donaldson squatted in the tonneau. "Sing, Chuck," I said. "Sing!"

His glims bulged like squeezed oysters. "Sing wh-

what?"

"Anything," I snapped. "La Golondrina will do."

He opened his yawp; began bleating the Spanish senerade in a cracked and raspy croak like sandpaper an an infected carbuncle. It was so sour it made your ears sea-sick.

"Jeeze, that's terrible," Donaldson said from the rear seat. He made imploring gestures. "Lay off, will you?"

I growled: "Yeah. Okay, Chuck; choke it and get moving. Soup this heap."

"But I—you---"

"Drive," I prodded him with my rod.

"Wh-where to?"

"Sammy Kreech 's wikiup. Fast."

The lanky hambo kicked his starter and we whooshed forward. McConnell's shrimp sized producer and partner lived in a costly birdcage just this side of Westwood, about twenty minutes distant by ordinary standards. We made it hi twelve' give or take a few seconds.

En route, I said: "Want to know how I got my tip-off to the puzzle, Chuck?"

"What tip-off?"

"You were humming to yourself in front of Sue Meredith's apartment stash when I came back from checking on her, remember? You were singing off-key. I didn't realize it at the time, but later I knew it was the essential clue."

He gulped audibly. "Meaning wh-what?"

"Meaning you're tone deaf, pal. A cowboy crooner who actually couldn't carry a tune in a wash basin. You've got no more musical voice than a bullfrog."

"Listen, Hawkshaw. You mustn't—"

I SHUT him up with a wave of my heater as we came to Sammy Kreech's joint and parked under the porte-cochere. Then we all piled out, made for the front door. I took the lead, smacked the portal with my hundred and ninety pounds of heft, bashed it inward.

It didn't matter to me whether or not I found Kreech by himself; but the way it turned out, he had company. He was in his library with Nick Spain, the sound technician; and they surged from their chairs as I came slamming into the room. They piped the gat in my mitt, lamped Donaldson and McConnell at my heels. Kreech yeeped: "Wha—what—what's the—"

I faced the shivering shrimp. "Much obliged for the phone message, Sammy. Because of it, Chuck spilled his guts." I was lying, of course; the little guy hadn't sent me any telephone message and McConnell hadn't belched anything. My snare worked, though.

Nick Spain screamed: "So you two heels double-crossed me, eh? Sold me out!" And he hauled a snub-nosed .38 from his back pocket; started hosing a blurt of slugs around the room.

His first two maniac shots went wild; and then, before he could trigger a third time, Dave Donaldson's service revolver barked: *Ka-Chow!* across my shoulder. The report darned near deafened me and I felt the sting of powder burns scorching my ear.

Spain got a stupid look on his lineaments and slowly folded over, dropping his cannon and hugging his midriff. A spurt of blood came out between his fingers, and he fell down, moaning. "You got me . . ."

I stood over him. "The jig's up, Nick. *Or Arturo Valdez, to use your right name.*"

Dave Donaldson's jaw dropped. "What's that?"

"Yeah," I said. "This is the louse who croaked Lew Larchmont and that Rosita Valdez cupcake. He was her missing hubby, the one that married her and glommed her geetus and then deserted her down in South America."

CHAPTER VI

FROM the floor, the sound technician cursed me with his glassy glimmers. He did it with his mouth, too; except you couldn't hear him very well. He didn't have the strength to make a lot of sound. I could see a doc wouldn't even be able to save him for the state. I decided to talk fast and clear things up while he could still answer.

I said: "Valdez was your monicker in Argentina.

You were a vaudeville crooner there. But you craved a break in Hollywood movies; so you married Rosita and used her dough to pay your fare here."

He looked a lot of poison at me.

"Around the time you landed on the west coast,

Chuck McConnell had just returned from a world tour and was a washed-up star; a has-been. He was making one last western quickie on Poverty Row for Sammy Kreech. Sammy decided Chuck should warble a song in the opus; but there was just one hitch.

McConnell is tone deaf, can't sing worth a darn."

The sound man writhed. "You ... stinking snoop ..."

I said: "By chance, you were hired as a voice-double for Chuck in that one pic. It's common enough in the yelping snapshots; one guy bleats the musical number, while later the star goes through the lip movements in front of the grinding camera, synchronizing this fakery with a playback record. As a result, we think the actor himself is making with the croons; whereas in reality we're listening to an unseen vocal double whose map never appears."

"Oh ... my stomach ... on fire ..." the guy whispered.

"You'll burn worse than that, presently. In hell," I said. Then I went on: "Your voice coming out of Chuck McConnell's kisser made a terrific hit with the box office public. He became a singing star on the strength of it. From then on, he was a gold mine; turned out tons of musical horse operas. The deal was three cornered. McConnell, Sammy Kreech and yourself were equal partners; split the profits."

He pressed his middle. "Get ... an ambulance ... I don't want to ... die ..."

"What's the difference?" I asked him. "If you live now, the smokehouse will get you up at San Quentin. Besides, I haven't finished my spiel yet. To fool the public you even became a microphone technician. That way, you could go into the recording booth with Chuck and cut his songs with no questions asked. Everybody thought he was doing the crooning. That's why Chuck never yodeled on an open set. He couldn't!"

"Pretty . . . smart . . . aren't you?"

"Smart enough to reconstruct what happened tonight. Rosita tabbed your voice coming from a jukebox. Naturally she figured it was McConnell singing; because his yapper seemed to be giving vent to the tune from that short reel. Later I took her to the General Service lot for a showdown. I told you and Sammy Kreech the whole story—not guessing that you were the vocal double, the guy Rosita was looking for."

"I should . . . have croaked her . . . in Argentina . . . before I ever left there! She . . ." It was his confession of guilt, his acknowledgment that he knew the game was up.

I said: "When you realized your wife was after you, it made you panicky. You were coining lettuce hand over fist and she might wreck your setup or even kill you. So you butched her before she got the chance. You opened her gullet in my parked jalopy before you went into the recording room."

He made gurgling noises and his mush was turning an ominous grey color. He was slipping fast.

I TALKED quick to catch him while he could still listen to me. "Later, by giving Chuck McConnell an alibi, you also gave yourself one. Meantime, that drunken Lew Larchmont maced me with a scantling because he had a grudge. You saw a chance to fasten Rosita's murder on him, thereby clearing your own skirts. That's why you drove her corpse to Larchmont's igloo in my coupe. You browned Larchmont and planted a phony suicide note, then returned to the studio in time to make the cops think nothing had happened there. It was a clever stunt."

A tremor shook him. He started gasping.

I raised my voice a notch. "Sammy Kreech was hep to the real truth and so was Chuck, probably. But they were in a lousy spot. Your singing represented a fortune to them. Without you, Chuck couldn't pretend to croon his sagebrush ditties; couldn't act in any more musical westerns. So they kept quiet for financial reasons even though they must have known you were the killer."

He tried to focus his peepers on me. "I . . . I want . . ."

"It's all over now," I told him. "I forced your hand when I lied about getting a telephone tip from Kreech and a confession from McConnell. You started blasting and you wound up behind the undertaker's eight-ball."

Then the guy pulled a weird stunt. He opened his trap; started crooning La Golondrina. For the first few bars the song came out strong, rich. Then it faded to a whisper, stopped. For good.

Dave Donaldson turned to the two surviving partners of the enterprise. "Tough luck, boys. I'll have to run you down to the gow as accessories. By failing to put the finger on Valdez, you were the same as accomplices."

"Wait, Dave," I suggested. "After all, they're finished in Hollywood. Chuck's voice-ghost is defunct, which puts him on the permanent shelf. And Kreech with him. Moreover, they didn't know Spain—or Valdez—was guilty; they only suspected it. How's for giving them a break?"

He hesitated. "Well, I'll think about it." Then he narrowed his optics at me as I made for the door. "Where do you think you're going, Sherlock?"

I said: "I just remembered a jane named Sue Meredith. I had to leave her alone with a bottle of Scotch. Maybe she'd still like me to help her polish it off." And I hauled bunions.

TO THE READER

If you enjoyed this book, you will be glad to know that there are many others just as well written, just as interesting, to be had in the Fiction House Press Library.

You will find the Fiction House Press Library online at

www.FictionHousePress.com

www.ingramcontent.com/pod-product-compliance
Lightning Source LLC
Chambersburg PA
CBHW031158020726
47499CB00002B/418